SOMEWHERE IN WINE COUNTRY

A SOMEWHERE SERIES SECRET BILLIONAIRE ROMANCE, BOOK 1

TOBY JANE

Book Cover Design by: derangeddoctordesign.com
Formatting by Jamie Davis

For my niece Paige, who has been our family's MVP.
I've loved our growing friendship that could only have taken place
by moving to Wine Country. You have helped me fall in love with
the culture of the grape, and I'm forever changed by embracing a
life among the redwoods and vineyards.

This book is also dedicated to my dear mother-in-law, Shirley. You
were a classy lady all the way to the end, and you raised a
wonderful son who I've been privileged to love for all of my life.
You'll never be forgotten.
~Toby Jane

CHAPTER ONE

Meg

Gram had been gone a month now, and as much as I missed her, I was glad that she was in Heaven, and didn't have to sit with me on the back porch, look out across the dried-up grass to the vineyard, and watch the travesty of the foreclosure play out.

Tears prickled my eyes, and I smacked them away. "Stop it, Meg!"

Sir Henry Puddlejump, Grandpa's old Maine Coon, trotted up the back steps and yowled a greeting—just the distraction I needed. "Hey, handsome. Need something to eat?"

Sir Henry replied in the affirmative. An absolutely humongous cat, almost the size and fluffiness of a well-fed raccoon, Sir Henry didn't need to be fed twice a day, but I dared not resist his demands. He'd also earned his rewards—the cat had spent the last weeks of Grandpa's life on his bed with him and had fetched me when Gram had her heart attack and collapsed in the vineyard last month.

What a terrible month it had been. Yeah, I'd inherited Villier Vineyard, but I'd also been landed with the remains of Grandpa's cancer treatment medical bills, outstanding taxes, and a mortgage my grandparents had taken out to keep the vineyard going during the drought years in California. Operating a vineyard, even a small one that just grew grapes for other labels as ours did, wasn't a cheap operation.

Gram and I had got through Grandpa's illness, death and funeral leaning on each other. She hadn't said a word about how bad things were . . . and then *bam!* Heart attack. She was gone.

And I'd begun opening the bills.

I'd had no idea the vineyard had already been in foreclosure. I was reeling, with no time to do a thing about the upcoming auction at the Sonoma County Courthouse, already scheduled.

No wonder Gram had checked out for the afterlife.

I could sometimes feel her presence, a kind of sweet powdery rustle, as she watched me pack up the house, box her things to donate, and do what I could to get the fields and our generational family home ready for the gavel. "You know I tried, Gram," I said, petting Sir Henry as he rubbed his big furry body against my leg and purred like a chainsaw. "But I was too late to do anything."

I could almost hear her voice. "Don't blame yourself, Meg. Things were in motion long before you arrived."

But arrive I had, right after finishing a degree in teaching to prep for a career I wasn't sure was right for me. I'd been procrastinating on job hunting, hoping to reconnect with grandparents I remembered fondly from my childhood.

Gram, Grandpa and I fell in love on the steps of the big old farmhouse the day I arrived. There was no other word for the sense of homecoming and the rush of joy and endorphins I felt when they embraced me.

"You mean you fell in love," Gram had said. "I fell in love twenty-six years ago, when your mama brought you home from the hospital."

People said I looked like Gram, with my tall sturdy build,

wild reddish hair, freckly skin and hazel eyes. Certainly, I looked nothing like my pretty, petite, stylish mother. "Your mama took after Grandpa. He had many skills, for a skinny little Frenchman," Gram had said with a wink.

Great-Grandpa Villier had emigrated to California from France, with cuttings for our pinot noir grapes hidden inside a vest, along with enough money to buy the place during the wine desert years of Prohibition. Villier was a small operation at only eleven acres, but the vines, grafted onto acclimatized rootstock, were top quality.

Our farmhouse had been here much longer than the vineyard, and I loved every creaky board and sticky window jamb of its turn-of-the-century charm.

"No sense lollygagging," I told Sir Henry. "That won't hold off the inevitable. And I need every penny from the sale to get us out of debt."

I fed the old reprobate and left him muttering commentary into his Tender Vittles on the back stoop. I put on Gram's big straw hat, and headed out to mow the long, sloping lawn with its pools of shade cast by old-growth oak and walnut trees.

I was mowing the grass to make it pretty for the auction.

"Just push the damn mower, Meg." But every time I remembered what was happening tomorrow, I wanted to puke.

I couldn't do anything to change losing my family home. I could only mow the lawn and hope to have time to slap a coat of white paint on the porch before it got too dark.

Kane

I had a copy of the Santa Rosa Press Democrat open on my knees, an uncapped highlighter in my mouth, and the beginnings of a headache behind my eyes.

I hadn't planned to just plunge right into buying a vineyard. But I'd been driving around for days and applying for jobs all over Sonoma County, with no one even willing to give me a chance at pulling weeds in the fields, to start learning viniculture. "Harvard Business, huh? Don't need that here."

I was bummed. Seriously. Flea and I were sick of camping out of the back of the truck, pulling deep into the dirt roads of vineyards to crash at night.

The stupidity of my quest had begun to nag at me as I jotted notes in my logbook about the vineyards I'd approached: *La Crema. Hook and Ladder. Iron Horse.* Each time, nerving myself up, settling Flea in the truck with water, putting on my cleanest shirt.

Each time shot down.

But going home to Boston this soon, with my tail between my legs, wasn't going to happen.

The trouble with being the oldest son of billionaires was that you couldn't really talk about it to anyone. No one gave a shit about the perceived problems of someone who "had it all." My college buddy Dan had punched me when I'd tried to tell him about my existential angst. "STFO, bro. I'd say get a life, but you've already *got* the life."

As the oldest of the McCallum boys, I was supposed to set an example, which I'd done by anyone's measure. Mom and Dad had nothing to complain about: I'd been a star track athlete and class president at Andover, gone to my hometown Ivy League, and majored in business to take over McCallum Industries when Mom and Dad were ready to retire.

The issues had begun after graduation, when Dad gave me a small company to practice on: managing a strip mall just outside of Boston. *Ugh.* I hated it.

And then there was the breakup.

Hayley and I had met in college. She was smart, pretty and

sporty. Our parents knew each other from fancy fundraisers and whatnot. We dated, had mediocre sex, and I thought things would die a natural death—but near the end of senior year, Hayley told me it was time for an engagement announcement. "Everyone is hoping. They'll be so excited," she said. "Let's surprise our parents with a ring."

"Are you proposing to me?" My brows shot up. I liked Hayley, sure. But I wanted—something big. Something amazing. Something like the love my parents had—chemistry, passion, as well as teamwork.

I hated to say it about such a nice person, but Hayley bored me.

Hayley's cheeks got a little rosy. The girl never got flustered, though. "It would be a great partnership."

"Hayley, I think we've reached the end of the road. I'm not ready. Sorry if you thought that was where things were going."

I was wrong about her never getting flustered.

She turned bright red and balled her fists. "How dare you!" She spat. "You think you're the crown prince or something. Well, you're a lousy lay." She ripped off the silver bangle I'd given her for her birthday and threw it at my head. "You wasted my time."

She stomped off.

Lousy lay. Ouch. I could have sworn at least *she* had a good time—I believed in "ladies first."

I was done with women.

How could I trust that anyone wanted me, for myself, and not for the McCallum money?

And that had led me to the next big problem.

Our family were good people. We did good with our money. But the universe was skewed, and things weren't fair. I was the son of privilege, and I'd had every advantage available before I was even born. That said, it also felt like my future was already

5

mapped out, a dance with memorized steps, a part I'd been playing.

Looking down the line at what was ahead had made me claustrophobic to the point that I plotted my escape.

Dad was surprisingly cool about it when I nerved myself up to break the news that I was taking an extended road trip to figure out what was next for me. I'd already sold a bond and had seed money, my truck outfitted, and my camping gear. I was going all the way from Boston to California, and somewhere along the way, I'd find the perfect business to buy.

Dad's a big guy like me, six-three, with rough sailor's hands and the original dark blue eyes I inherited. "Pete, I get it. You know how I've always told the story about sailing around the world on the *Creamy Maid*, and meeting your mom on St. Thomas? Well, the part I never told you was that I left everything behind for three years while I was doing that. Your grandparents had just died, and I bailed on all the money and responsibilities of McCallum Industries. I sailed the world twice, and I lived on what I could earn with a skeleton crew to run the boat. I needed to know if I could even *make* it on my own. So, while I wish you didn't have to do this, I can't say I don't understand." Dad was the only one who called me Peter—I was named for both his and Mom's fathers, and even twenty-plus years after his parents' deaths in a plane accident, he seldom spoke their names.

"This won't work if it's not real." Mom's green eyes got a little watery as she put her hands on my shoulders. "I love you for being you, Kane. I'm just glad you finished college first. You may not want that MBA right now, but it's waiting for you anytime you might need it again."

My brother Colton told me I was nuts, and promptly took over managing the strip mall. Clearly someone had no problem with the family biz. David laughed his ass off and moved into my room because it had better light for his painting. Morgan just shook his head—our family inventor never talked much. Ben told his menagerie of strays and rescues what a nutjob I was. And Jesse? Jesse tried to stow away in my truck. He would have gotten away with it, too, if Flea hadn't sniffed him out.

I looked up as Flea woofed. We were camping in a grove of oaks at a county park, and he was wagging his tail in front of a gopher hole. "That rodent's not going to come out and play with you, buddy," I muttered.

I scanned the paper one last time. On the back page, I spotted an ad for a foreclosed vineyard up for auction at the Sonoma County Courthouse. The open house for the place was today. "Might as well check it out." I circled the address.

I whistled for Flea.

My boy was huge, and when he galloped at me, cheeks flapping, I could practically feel the earth shake. I named him Flea because (a) he's black, (b) he was the runt of a litter, and (c) he was supposed to be small. I'd adopted him as a rescue when he was a little fuzzy undernourished pup. They'd told me he was a terrier that wouldn't be more than fifteen pounds; a couple of years later, he was close to two hundred, and our best guess as to his breed was Great Pyrenees.

Flea hopped into the truck, I fired up the GPS on my phone, and we headed for Villier Vineyard.

CHAPTER TWO

Kane

The first clue that I was close to the auction property were all the cars, trucks and SUVs lining the road. There was going to be a lot of competition for this vineyard.

My stomach did a little roll. I didn't want to want it as much as I already did, but I'd fallen in love with the wine country of Sonoma County the minute I got to this area. I'd had a viniculture class in college, just an elective credit, but I'd never forgotten it, nor the way walking through the fields, dripping with grapes, had made me feel.

Villier Vineyard occupied a dip among gently rolling foothills, their curves defined by the even corduroylike lines of vines. I parked on a steep verge off the road, put Flea on his leash, and locked the truck. We walked down a meandering two-lane road, its sloping shoulders lined with sage, Queen Anne's lace, and little poufy blue flowers.

The vineyard's crop looked almost ripe: tidy bundles of small, dark purple, powdery grapes were visible beneath their canopy. Warm sun overhead brought my nose a whiff of the clusters someone had trimmed off and let fall below the orderly vines. The smell was insane—a rich fruitiness that made me a little dizzy. I was getting drunk just on the sight and scent of the gorgeous grapes, peeking out from under the leaves like an amethyst treasure trove.

Flea and I turned up a long gravel driveway and passed a weathered sign reading *Villier Vineyard*. Late afternoon sun lit a smooth but patchy golden-brown lawn rolling up to a big old white farmhouse. Flea and I walked on the grass because the driveway, lined with round river stones, was filled with cars.

The house looked to be crawling with people, so we cruised around outside, checking out a weathered silver-gray wood barn filled with rusting equipment, an old-fashioned well covered with plywood, and what must have been a wine cave in the past: a small stone building whose rotting roof admitted streaks and chinks of light.

The rich smell of the empty, used casks stacked inside went straight to my head. An open door with steep wooden stairs led down to a basementlike room lined with oaken barrels full of pinot noir wine, each vintage's year written on the lid in heavy pencil. There weren't that many of these; Villier was essentially a grape-growing farm, though someone had clearly made wine here in the past.

People roamed everywhere over the house and grounds. Older couples in golf shirts and chinos, young couples with kids running amok, a few serious-looking business types, some hipsters in skinny jeans and fedoras. Everyone was drinking red wine from clear plastic cups. Apparently, the vintage had been grown at Villier, and I listened to the comments: "Too young. Too sweet. A bit oaky for me. Got a lot of blackberry in it."

Funny how they bullshitted that stuff, and while the comments were mostly critical, everyone was finishing their wine.

I needed to get some.

I tied Flea to the rusty pump handle near the well and went up onto the porch. A woman was dispensing the wine from a spigot attached to a cask, filling the plastic cups. I stood and waited my turn, looking her over. *Was she an employee?*

A hand-lettered nametag that read "MEG" was stuck on the chest of the woman's baggy black dress. Meg was tall and leggy. Long, frizzy, reddish-brown hair tried to escape her ponytail. Her forehead was shiny. and freckles stood out on her tanned arms.

"You look like you could use a break, Meg," I said when I got to the head of the line and held out my plastic cup.

Meg turned the spigot without looking at me. Wine gushed to fill the clear plastic, a nice ruby color. I inhaled deeply, enjoying the waft of scent that came to my nose as I took the cup. "Merlot? Or pinot noir?"

Meg looked up at last. She was younger than I'd initially thought. She had brown eyes with a lot of green in them, or maybe green eyes with a lot of brown. Her mouth was pinched tight as a drawstring purse. "Pinot noir. And you're right, I need a break. Haven't had a chance to pee in hours."

I stepped forward and nudged her out of the way. "Go. I can cover for you."

She froze, but I reached for the next person's cup and filled it.

She turned and scuttled off. Poor girl didn't seem like she was enjoying her job at all.

This was my chance. I was sure as hell going to try to buy this place, but if I didn't get it, with all the competition there clearly was, I could at least finagle myself a job here so I could learn viniculture. Surely they'd hire me—I definitely had a better attitude than Meg did.

I grinned at each person as they stepped up for their complimentary beverage. "Welcome to the Villier Vineyard open house!

Got a sample of pinot noir here for you to try. Nope, we didn't bottle it, but we grew it."

I tried to answer the questions that came at me from what I remembered of the disclosures and from reading the sale brochure. "Yeah, I think the contents of the house are included. Was built turn of the century, and it's holding up great, don't you think? Eleven acres are in grapes, with an acre dedicated to the house and grounds. The Villiers brought over their own stock from France, and this vineyard has been in continuous production since 1922."

"I'm back, Mr. Hospitality." Meg finally elbowed me out of the way. "It took a while because I fetched that dog some water."

So, she'd noticed me and Flea walking around the property, and put Flea together with me. That shouldn't matter, but it did. "Thanks. Mind if I have a look around the house?" I cast a thumb toward the doorway.

Meg focused on the next glass of wine she was filling. Her tone was surly. "It's an open house. You don't need my permission."

I stared—at her unkempt hair, frumpy dress, at her bad freakin' attitude when I'd tried to give her a break. *This chick needed a different job, that's for sure.* "Okay. Well. Thanks for getting Flea some water."

I went inside.

The front room was one of those old-fashioned parlors. Stiff Victorian-era furniture draped in doilies faced a stone fireplace. The dining room table and chairs were good quality and shined up with beeswax, a familiar smell I remembered from Mrs. Knightly's energetic polishing of our Boston house's furniture. A crystal chandelier with some burned-out bulbs semi-lit the table. The kitchen was classic black and white tile, with appliances that didn't look like they'd been updated since the seventies. The one bath downstairs had a claw-foot tub and a pull chain toilet.

Upstairs, the bedrooms were decorated with clean but worn-out linens and vintage furniture that missed being antique quality. Only one room looked occupied, and I froze in the doorway at the sight of a needlepoint pillow propped up on the lacy white bedspread.

The embroidery on the pillow spelled out *MEG*.

Shit.

This was Meg's family place getting auctioned, and her grandmother that had recently died, according to the brochure I was holding.

No wonder the ugly black dress, the bad attitude. This had to be one of the worst days of Meg's life.

And she'd made time to fetch my dog some water.

Meg

The Sonoma County courthouse in Santa Rosa was a newer building of the "urban ugly" school of architecture, on the corner of a couple of busy streets. No pretty cupolas or Corinthian columns here—no gilt trim or dignified busts in the lobby. Strictly utilitarian, the place smelled like Mr. Clean, and my nostrils felt like they were getting scrubbed.

I didn't have to attend the auction, but I wanted to watch the carnage. Such a freakin' masochist. Like staying at the vineyard all day for the open house and dispensing wine—I shouldn't have had to be treated like a servant, while listening to all the comments, criticism and speculation as our quiet, peaceful vineyard was overrun with speculators, lookie-loos, dreamers and cash-rich dot-commers looking for a bargain.

But the alternative? Hiding at the library or my friend Gabriella's, while everything was being inspected, judged and pawed over behind my back—that would have been even worse.

One of the courtrooms had been turned over for the auction event, and a very dignified county clerk was in charge of the proceedings. I thought auctioneers did that patter sing-along thing as they tried to jack up the prices and rile everyone up, but this little man in a gray suit and red bow tie wasn't that kind. Instead, he invited the submission of a series of envelopes that were sealed bids. He'd open each bid, then turn to an assistant, tell her the amount, and she wrote it on the whiteboard.

The crowd that filled the room shifted and twittered below me like a murmur of starlings. Couples, singles, business-suited representatives.

Nobody interesting.

I didn't realize I was looking for him from my perch in the gallery until I spotted him, his arms folded, leaning against the wall—Stormy Sea Guy, the man with the dark blue eyes and the big black dog.

I was a dog person. Always had been. Sir Henry the cat was a recent development and the fact that I'd never had a dog was irrelevant to my passion. I'd noticed that gorgeous Great Pyrenees the moment he came lolloping onto Villier land with some young dude holding his leash. Even in my fugue state that day, I could tell that both of them were so excited they were practically vibrating.

I'd shut down by then, just enduring what must be endured, so it shocked me that I could still feel anything at all—but when the guy bumped me aside and made me go take a break, I felt something.

Resentful gratitude with a twist of *oh my God.*

Because the guy was even better-looking than his dog. Big, broad-shouldered, with a head of wayward dark brown hair, a swath of dark beard, and eyes that a romance novel would call "the color of a stormy sea."

Some girls like clubbing or shopping; I like swooning in imaginary strong, corded arms in my snuggly bed at home with a romance novel. My favorite escape is to dive under the covers with a nice fat fictional Regency, Pirate, or Scottish Highlander, preferably a first in series. Sometimes I'll go as far afield as a shifter or paranormal, but nothing modern. This day and age sucks in the romance department.

Stormy Sea Guy was over against the wall of the courtroom, and damn if he didn't have some nice muscular arms crossed on his chest. He looked around the room, straining up on his toes to see over the heads in front of the clerk. I ducked deeper into the shadows of the gallery above.

He couldn't be looking for me, could he?

He'd come down from upstairs onto the porch yesterday, after taking a look around at the house. "Meg," he said. "Meg Villier. You shouldn't be here, doing this."

Stormy Sea Guy had somehow figured out who I was.

I kept my eyes down; I couldn't look at him. The shame and grief of serving wine at my family's foreclosure was an over-whelming tar pit I'd sunk into.

"Where else would I be?" My hands shook as I held yet another plastic cup under the spigot.

He stood there for a long moment, his fists opening and closing—those hands were all I could see from under my lashes. And then he turned abruptly and left, clattering down the wooden steps. He strode over and untied his dog. He looked up and caught me staring. He stared back.

"It's overflowing," the woman in front of me said. Wine was spilling out of the plastic cup. I handed it to her.

"Sorry. I have to get a towel," I mumbled, and bolted.

I went upstairs and locked myself in my room. I pulled my tablet out from under my pillow, and opened it to my latest novel, *The Pirate's Lustful Treasure.*

I'd had enough of the open house.

Eventually, like a tide ebbing, the visitors all vanished and I spent another night alone, in the home I still owned. But time grinds on, and now Stormy Sea Guy was down there on the courtroom floor, trying to bid on Villier Vineyard.

There was a lot of competition. Not likely that a young dude like him would have the kind of cash necessary to win the auction.

When all of the amounts were on the wall and the debt ceiling had been met, the auctioneer picked up a cell phone and dialed a number. I was so busy watching I didn't realize he was calling me until my phone buzzed in the pocket of my jeans, making me jump.

"Yes?"

"Ms. Villier?" It was weird being up above the auctioneer and seeing him talk to me, hearing the room quiet down as the bidders tried to hear what was going on. "The minimum ceiling has been met and we are twenty-five thousand ahead. Do you want to continue to accept bids?"

The little man had explained how it worked—that once the minimum was met, I could keep taking bids like a regular auction for two more rounds. I'd pay the county a commission on the proceedings for holding it at the courthouse and their staff and so on.

It was a no-brainer—I needed every penny to pay off my grandparents' debt. "Yes, keep taking bids, please."

"As you wish." He ended the call and slid the phone into his pocket. "The seller has authorized me to continue to take bids on this property for another round. Please write your best offer on one of the notes provided, put it in an envelope, and pass it forward."

Stormy Sea Guy was staring up at the gallery; I could feel him looking for me. His searching gaze made my heart pound, but I was well back in the shadows and I'd locked the door to the gallery, where the clerk told me I could watch from in privacy. He couldn't get to me here.

He couldn't win. There was no way he had any money. I'd seen the state of his clothes, his shoes.

A flurry of murmuring. The scratching of pens, the stuffing of envelopes, the passing forward, the flash of the auctioneer's paper knife cutting them open, the recording and posting of the bids . . . all of it made me chew my nails, which were already down to nubs.

I'd know soon enough what the vineyard's fate was.

I opened the next in series on my phone, *The Pirate's Voluptuous Prize,* and disappeared into another world.

Another round of bids ended. I looked up to see the total. *Yay!* Enough to get rid of that damn hospital bill, as well as the mortgage!

I set aside my reading app and came all the way to the railing of the gallery as the clerk rang me again. "You see the winning bid, Ms. Villier. Want to go another round?"

"Yes," I said. "Yes, please."

The room had emptied more, but there were still some diehards: a few prosperous-looking couples and some business types. Stormy Sea Guy was on the phone, pacing back and forth at the back of the room. *Why hadn't he left? Was he just there to watch my humiliation all the way to the end?*

He got off the phone, wrote something on a paper, and stuffed it in an envelope.

Stormy Sea Guy was still bidding!

I couldn't understand it. "Shit. he must be one of those dot-com assholes who couch surfs but has millions."

And suddenly, I hated everyone in the room below.

HATED. THEM.

They were taking what was mine. *It wasn't fair.*

Yet, I couldn't stop watching what was happening—this time,

standing right out there in front against the gallery railing in my black grief dress.

Let them stare. I had nothing to be ashamed of, nothing, while they should be ashamed of being able to oust me from our family's home.

It was wrong for some people to have so much and others so little.

I could taste bile in my mouth.

The highest number in the last round of bids would leave me fifty thousand dollars that I would walk away with after all the debts were paid. Three rounds were as long as the process went, and the county clerk pointed to the winning bid on the board. "Sold!"

I'd walk away from Villier Vineyard with fifty grand.

Fifty thousand dollars.

Enough to have something, but not enough to buy anything, especially without a job or any sort of credit rating. I'd have enough to live on for a while, as I figured out the rest of my life.

But at least I wouldn't be walking away still owing money on my grandparents' debts. I had to be grateful for that.

I sat down because my legs wouldn't hold me up anymore.

I glanced down at the board again.

All of the bids were coded, so there was no way to tell who had won. Everyone trickled out of the courtroom.

Stormy Sea Guy was the last to go. Probably wanted me to come down from the gallery so he could say some sappy thing like, "I'm sorry for your loss."

I didn't want to hear it, especially not from him.

It was over. All but the packing and leaving.

CHAPTER THREE

Kane

I handed over the cashier's check to buy Villier Vineyard to the gray-suited clerk.

The man looked at the check, looked at me, looked at the check again.

I'd had an hour after the auction ended to go to the bank and get the money; after the second round when my best bid on the money I'd brought was getting beaten, I'd caved and called my parents to get more. It rankled to compromise on my plan to be independent so quickly, but I wanted that vineyard.

Wanted it so much.

I wanted that creaky old farmhouse, the falling down wine cave, the fields of fragrant dusty grapes, and the silvery wood barn full of old equipment.

And weirdly, I wanted to do something for prickly Meg Villier. I had a plan I'd hatched in a restless night tossing and turning in the bed of the truck. No idea why I gave a shit; Meg hadn't even been polite to me. I didn't owe her anything.

But if I won that vineyard . . . yeah, I did owe her something.

Not anything that anyone else would hold me to, but my winning it out from under her felt wrong in a fundamental way that bugged me, even though it was legal.

I'd spotted Meg hiding up above the courtroom in the gallery long before she finally came to the railing, wearing that baggy black dress, looking so sad and angry that she was disturbing, like she'd sprout wings and fly down breathing fire on everyone in the courtroom if she could. She was downright scary with her pale face and intense eyes, wild hair flowing down her back and over her shoulders like a witch's cape.

As usual, my parents were awesome and fronted the money I needed to put in a bid that would win—but being them, they weren't going to give it easy, either. "You said you wanted to be independent, Pete. This is a loan. And you're going to pay us back monthly, at fair market terms," Dad said.

"I think I need to learn the business before I can realistically pay you back," I argued. "I need a year." We'd negotiated down to a six-month grace period before I had to start repaying McCallum Industries, and they wired the money immediately.

I drove to Villier Vineyard later, when night had fallen. The farmhouse was dark but for a lamp shining in the window of one of the upstairs rooms.

Meg's room.

Where was she? I didn't see a car in the driveway. Hopefully she was out with friends, drowning her sorrows at a bar. Maybe throwing darts at a picture of the courthouse.

Technically I wasn't supposed to take possession of the place for a couple more days, but I had nowhere to go, nowhere I wanted to be more than on this particular bit of earth.

But I didn't want to piss Meg off, or be a creeper. Driving up to the house was not an option.

I kept going past the vineyard entrance until I found a dirt access road leading into the fields. I flicked out the headlights, turned onto it, and drove deep into the rows of vines.

The moon was high and full. Visibility was good, even without the headlights. I drove the truck slowly all the way to an oak tree on a rise in the middle of the field. Weird that they had left it there; the tree was taking up usable land. I pulled the truck up under the spreading branches where we'd be more out of sight from the house. Turning off the engine, I opened the door and let Flea out to do his business.

While Flea nosed around in the friendly dark, I put my hands on my hips and took stock, surveying the land around the rise. From the slight knoll, I could see the lines of the staked vines stretching away under moonlight, and the beacon of the house in the distance, set in its oasis of trees.

A huge boulder butted up against the oak tree—or likely, the tree grew up next to the boulder. That was probably why they'd left them alone—both were too big to move. I sat down on a wooden picnic table under the tree, and just looked out at the acreage rolling away into distance.

Flea came up and leaned on my leg. I petted his silky ears, soaking it in. Feeling overwhelmed, grateful, and pretty damn terrified.

This place had been so loved, so cared-for. Who was I to be trespassing under this hundred-year-old oak, presuming to own it because of a bank repo sale?

And yet, it had happened. Now I needed to be worthy of it.

I didn't know shit about farming or growing grapes. *Time to start studying.*

I said goodbye to the moonlight and climbed into the bed of the truck, closing me and Flea into our little cave on the comfy mattress in back. I turned on my flashlight and searched "viniculture" on my laptop.

Meg

I woke up at the first gray blush of dawn and just lay in my bed, holding that silly needlepoint pillow with my name on it that Gram had made for me after we moved to San Francisco.

"Making that pillow was a way to feel like you were still in my life." She'd stroked my hair as she told me that. Gram loved my wavy dark auburn hair; hers had been the same color when she was young.

Nathalie, my mother, was a wild child in high school. She'd told me that I had three possible fathers, and thus no one was listed on the birth certificate. Nathalie and Gram and Grandpa didn't get along. Eventually she met my stepfather, Raymond DeSylva, who'd promised to give her all she wanted. Ray was a businessman who'd met Maman at her waitressing job at the country club. I was five when they got married, took me away from the vineyard, and moved to San Francisco.

Even though I only visited the vineyard a few times after that, some part of me had known where I was born, and knew and loved Villier Vineyard. That part of me had always longed to return. I was born of this *terroir,* and I was happiest here.

"*Terroir* is the sum total of the influences of the land on a wine," Grandpa had held forth before he died. Propped up in his bed, he had still insisted on his nightly glass of Villier pinot noir, and he swirled the wine in the stemless goblet he preferred, his hand trembling badly, spilling drops of ruby liquid over the white bedsheets. "But *terroir* is so much more than just soil. It's the air quality, the type of grape, the water, and the effects of a particular season—whether it's hot that year, too dry or too wet. *Terroir* is chemistry, but it's heart, too. Nathalie never had a heart for this place. But you do."

I shut my eyes and pressed my face into the needlepoint pillow, wetting the precious stitchery with my tears.

Snotty-nosed and puffy-eyed, headachy from drinking an entire bottle of one of our precious reds put down when Grandpa still made his own garage wine, I finally got up.

Last night, I had called my one friend in the area to come assist in my debauch. Gabriella had been my student advisor for my teaching certificate, and was one of the only people from my college program who lived in nearby Santa Rosa. She hadn't been able to come drink with me, so I'd wandered the house alone, blasting Grandpa's Otis Redding vinyl and drinking, and then retired to bed with Book Three in the Pirate series. But this time, even the clash of blades and ripping of bodices had been unable to dull my misery.

I'd finished with most of my packing. I planned to do my usual field routine one more time this morning. Tomorrow I'd clear out. Diego, our farm hand, had helped me load my old Toyota Camry with the boxes of clothes, extra bathroom stuff, and few keepsakes I couldn't do without. Bigger furnishings were staying with the house.

I would pretend nothing was changing for just one more day. I was good at fantasies.

I dressed in my field clothes: heavy socks, a pair of denim overalls, and a long-sleeved thermal shirt. Downstairs, I grabbed a cup of coffee from the auto-timed pot.

I had a thumper of a hangover, and I sucked down that first cup of brew rapidly with a couple of aspirin as I went into the mudroom and tied on my heavy canvas gardening apron with its already loaded tool pockets. I refilled my mug with coffee, then opened the back door, sliding my stockinged feet into calf-high rubber boots.

Fog had rolled in, as it often did in this area, and wreathed the lines of the vines in mystery. Sun broke through over the hills to the east just a bit, gilding the top of the big oak on its hillock in the middle of the fields. The vines were magical looking at this time of day, timeless and eternal, draped in scarves of mist and light, the grapes gleaming here and there like jewels.

I felt my heart swell with love, and then burst with the pain of my losses.

I choked on tears, doubling over in pain from both my thumping head and aching heart.

Sir Henry Puddlejump walked toward me from the field, yowling his morning demand for breakfast, his long, poufy fur damp from dew. *What was I going to do with Sir Henry?*

I'd have to smuggle him into my car and take him wherever I ended up. Leaving him here with the unknown buyer was out of the question.

When the cat was contentedly munching on the back porch, I took my pruners out of my apron and headed for the fields.

The grapes were going to be ready in a month or so. Now was the time to watch for mold and do canopy management so that the sun could get to the fruit. Every morning I put in a couple of hours, trimming my way down the rows until I got to the oak tree. Cutting away the overgrowth that stole the energy from the grapes was meditative. I enjoyed binding up the shoots and nipping off individual leaves that shaded the plump black clusters with their natural protective powdery coating.

I liked to use Grandpa's old pruners and make the cuts just so. My fanciful brain imagined his hands where mine were as I dropped the cuttings in the row to pick up on the way back. Leaving them underfoot encouraged mold, the very thing we were fighting.

My favorite job felt like pure grief today.

But maybe I could take my experience elsewhere and get a job in a vineyard—at least I'd be in a familiar, lovely setting . . . I put my earbuds in, and let my favorite audiobook version of

Emily Brontë's *Wuthering Heights* talk me through the nipping, clipping, and tying up of the vines until I reached the oak tree.

I'd asked Grandpa why they hadn't removed the oak from its little knoll, and even the giant boulder it was snuggled against. The tree really cut into the field and took up possible cultivation space.

Grandpa had smiled, those sun-wrinkles from a lifetime spent squinting at grapevines bracketing keen dark eyes. "The oak tree is part of this vineyard's *terroir*, Meg. It would change the very chemistry of the soil, the nature of the land to remove it. Look around at any of the vineyards nearby. We all respect the oaks. They were here, a part of this California landscape, long before we came, and they will be here long after we're gone."

Damn, but I missed Grandpa sometimes. I hadn't had nearly enough time with him.

I headed for my favorite spot to take a break—sitting on the picnic table under the tree—but someone had pulled a black Tacoma truck with a camper shell on it up behind the boulder.

Someone was car-camping on my land.

I put my hands on my hips and checked the vehicle out. The windows of the camper were darkly mirrored, so I couldn't see in. The truck screamed "dude," with its surf racks and beefed-up tires with shiny chrome rims. Not the usual homeless vehicle we got around here, either—too expensive. Probably belonged to one of those "digital nomads," those guys who Instagrammed their way across the United States, posting arty pictures and microblogging on Tumblr, wearing clothes sponsored by Patagonia while they sold kitchen gadgets off a website or something.

Whoever this dude was, he needed to get off my land and get a job like the rest of us.

I walked up and banged a fist on the camper's back window hatch. "Hey!"

A "woof!" as loud as a cannon came from inside, and I

jumped back so hard that my hat flew off. I backed up several more feet as fierce barking ensued, a clamor like Cerberus the three-headed hound that guarded the underworld.

The rumble of a male voice hushing the dog reached my ears, and then the back hatch opened. A huge, black, silky-eared Great Pyrenees stuck his head out to bark, but his growl turned to a grin at the sight of me. This was the big gorgeous dog I'd given water to on the day of the open house. "Well, come on out, boy, and say hello," I crooned.

A muffled rebuke came from inside the truck, but the dog squeezed out through the hatch and jumped four feet to the ground, trotting over to thrust his nose into my crotch for a big sniff while lashing me with his thick, plumy tail.

I dropped to my knees to give him a hug. "You gorgeous thing, with your shiny black coat. What a lover you are."

"His name's Flea."

I looked up.

Stormy Sea Guy climbed out of the hatch. He was wearing a loose pair of sweatpants and nothing else.

We stared at each other, maybe a bit too long, because he cleared his throat and reached back inside for a sweater. He shrugged into it as I shut my mouth with an effort.

Stormy Sea Guy had just become my new mental picture for when the phrases "chiseled pecs" and "ripped abs" came up in one of my romances.

"I hope you don't mind us crashing here last night," he said.

"Uh, yeah. I mind." I pushed Flea's nose out of my lady bits, where he was still happily snuffling. "This is my family's property. Didn't you see the *No Trespassing* sign?"

Stormy Sea Guy froze, midway through tugging down his shirt, and glared at me.

His eyes flashed. Yes, *flashed*. Another phrase I wasn't used to seeing lived out. Those dark blues looked like trouble brewing. "This is *my* land now. I bought it at the auction."

I shot to my feet. *I was going to kill him.*

But I stood up too fast.

The blood drained out of my head, and my feet seemed a long way off. I swayed, my vision telescoping, and I grabbed onto the boulder so I wouldn't pass out. Squatting to pet the dog and then shooting up like a rocket to commit murder had been too much for my hangover. I gulped to keep from puking as black spots circled my brain.

"Aw, shit. I'm sorry. I didn't want . . . this isn't how I meant . . . damn it." Stormy Sea Guy reached for me, grabbing my elbow. "Put your head down between your knees. Breathe."

"Screw you. I don't want your help or your pity. Take your truck and your dog and hit the road," I snarled. "You can have my land tomorrow at noon, and not a minute before."

Stormy Sea Guy let go of my elbow. He stepped back.

Flea hadn't got the memo that I was pissed and didn't want anything to do with his master, the man who was taking my home. The dog herded me by pushing against my midsection until my legs hit the bench of the picnic table. I collapsed onto the wooden support and bent over to put my head between my knees, groaning.

"Are you sick?" Stormy Sea Guy asked. "Or just . . . deranged?"

"Hungover. And did you hear me tell you to go? *Go!*" I made a flappy hand gesture. "Get out of here before I call the sheriff!"

Stormy Sea Guy whistled for Flea, who had pressed himself between my legs and was now licking my face, administering wet, damp doggy kisses. "Leave Meg alone, Flea. Come on."

But the crazy pup apparently liked the taste of tears.

Flea refused to come. Stormy Sea Guy eventually had to grab him by the collar. He pulled Flea off of me, but then he just stood there while I kept my head down and focused on not puking or fainting or crying.

"Hey, listen," he said.

"No. I don't want to." I knew I sounded immature. I didn't care.

"I meant for this to go a lot different."

"What part of 'get off my land' and 'I don't want to listen' was not clear to you, sir?" I channeled my inner Emily Brontë, and very slowly pushed myself upright on the bench so I could glare at him properly.

He stared down at me as I scowled up at him.

My head was at, approximately, his belly button area. I had seen what that area looked like without the soft cashmere-looking sweater that covered it. My neck went hot because I couldn't forget what his abs looked like any more than I could his chest.

I glanced to the side, over at his truck, and the truck made me mad. "You think you can do anything you want. Well, you can't."

"Okay. I respect that you want me to leave. So, I'm just going to say this, and then get on the road and you can think it over." Stormy Sea Guy stepped back slightly, a relief to my feminine sensibilities. He blew out a breath as if gathering his thoughts, then spoke rapidly, spitting his words out in a hurry. "I don't know much about viniculture. I was hoping you could stay on and manage the vineyard and teach me what you know. You can stay in the house, in your old room. I'll pay you the going rate for a field manager."

I didn't answer. My brain had gone on hiatus. He continued.

"It's not a charity offer. I need the help and I'm willing to pay for it. If you don't want to work for me, I'll just find someone else. Think it over, and when I come at noon tomorrow, if you're still here, then you can have the job."

I stared down at the ground. I heard the words but couldn't take them in.

"Okay. I'll just be on my way, then." Stormy Sea Guy wrestled Flea over to the truck and forced the whimpering dog into the cab.

I studied the powdery soil, the round, golden acorns, and the poky-edged dried oak leaves around my dirty old boots as Villier Vineyard's new owner got in his truck, turned it on, and drove away.

I still didn't even know his name.

CHAPTER FOUR

Kane

I drove up the driveway to the farmhouse at Villier Vineyard the next day, feeling *weird*.

Weird as in: excited and apprehensive, with a side order of determined.

It didn't really matter whether or not Meg Villier had decided to stay or go; I was taking ownership of the place, and I was going to make this work.

But she had decided to stay.

The back of a gray Toyota Camry station wagon was open, and Meg and a Hispanic-looking guy were unloading boxes.

I felt a knot loosen in my chest.

And that was weird too.

I didn't even like Meg Villier. She was an emotional nutbag with a chip on her shoulder.

Flea spotted Meg and whined from the front seat—he'd decided that she belonged in his pack, though why he'd done so was beyond me. Maybe it was just the way she smelled; he'd certainly loved sticking his nose in her crotch.

I still felt sorry for Meg, though her attitude had made me second-guess my job offer to her ever since I impulsively made it. I needed Meg, or someone like her, if anything about this venture was going to work at all; but, if she continued to be so hostile, I'd have to kick her out, and keep looking for another manager.

I pulled up beside the house in an open area of grass, clearly not usually used for parking. I got out with Flea, and of course my dog bounded up to Meg and thrust his nose into her pelvic area, his favorite place to be right now. "Flea! Cut it out!"

"He's just saying hi. Aren't you, boy?"

I forced my mind away from a mental picture of "saying hi" to Meg by thrusting my face into the apex of her thighs like Flea had just done.

Meg was looking better today, not so blotchy and sick. She'd been wearing some farmer outfit yesterday; today she had on black jeans and a white T-shirt, and her long brownish-red hair was in a neat ponytail.

"I'm glad to see you decided to take me up on my offer." I put my hands in my pockets. "I really need the help. I wasn't kidding about that."

"Yes. I've prepared a contract for you to look over. But first, I'd like you to meet someone very important to the Villier operation—Diego Lopez." She gestured the guy over. He looked to be about mid-thirties with dark, soulful eyes, a deep tan, and a Giants ball cap. "Diego, this is the new owner."

"Kane McCallum." Stormy Sea Guy extended a hand.

"Good to meet you, McCallum." Lopez had a handshake like a weightlifter.

"Call me Kane, please. You been here long?"

"All my life," Lopez said.

"I hope you'll keep him on." Meg's eyes were pleading. "We need him. Trust me."

"Of course. Glad to have you, Diego."

Their relief was palpable. "I'll get back to work trimming," Lopez told Meg.

"Diego's shaping the canopy right now to optimize the sun getting to the grapes. Helps prevent mold," Meg explained. "It's slow work."

"Sounds good. I'd like to learn. I want to learn everything about everything."

Diego nodded. "Good. Because there's a lot to learn, Kane." He walked off.

Meg gestured to the front door of the house. "Shall we go in?"

"Yeah. You can . . . show me what room would be good. I don't have much stuff."

A flash of something showed on Meg's face—a twist of pain or anger—but she just nodded. "Sure. Follow me."

The whole situation was *weird*. Awkward. Awkwardly weird? Yeah. That was it.

I followed Meg up the bare wooden staircase, keeping my eyes off her nice round butt with an effort. Every tread squeaked as we stepped on it, and the aged, polished wood was slick under Flea's paws. His toenails clattered and he whined nervously, lunging up the stairs quickly to get to the top, nudging Meg aside. Getting him back down would take some doing. "I think I'll need to put some carpeting down for Flea."

"You're going to keep him inside?"

"Of course." I felt like I needed to say something more. "He's always been an indoor-outdoor dog. I keep him clean."

"It's your house. Do whatever," she said flatly.

Ugh. Maybe I had done the wrong thing asking her to stay . . . was I going to feel this guilty all the time? *Crap!*

Meg led me to the biggest bedroom at the front. A queen-size bed with an old-fashioned crochet cover faced a bank of windows. Sunlight streamed in through the square panes that took up the whole front of the wall, shining onto a gleaming wood floor covered in hand-hooked rugs. Two dressers faced each other against the walls. The room exuded worn, old-fashioned charm, and it felt haunted by the ghosts who'd lived and loved there.

I shook my head. "Nah. Too big for me." I walked down the hall past Meg's room to a small one that faced out the back, over the vineyards. A single sash window showed me the lines of the field, the grass of the backyard, the silvery leaves of an olive tree contrasting with those of a walnut. I dropped my duffle on the twin-size iron bedstead, and as if approving, Flea lay down on the coiled rag rug in front of the bed and tucked his nose into his tail. "This one is perfect."

Meg stood in the doorway. "This was my mother's room when she grew up. Gram and Grandpa finally took her stuff out and painted it about five years ago. When I came back, I took the guest room because it was bigger and shared access to Gram and Grandpa's bathroom. You'll have to use the one in the hall."

This was the most personal information she'd volunteered so far. "When did you come back to Villier?"

"About a year ago."

She hadn't been working at the vineyard as long as I'd hoped. "Do you have much experience with running the place?"

"Maybe you should have asked me that before you offered me the job." Meg had a long, full, mobile mouth with naturally pink lips, the kind of mouth that looked like it should be smiling or laughing or maybe singing. I'd only ever seen it turned down, trembling, or tight with tension like it was right now. "Let's go over that contract and you can decide if you still want me." She turned abruptly and clomped down the stairs.

Flea lifted his head off his paws, looking worried, and I made a hand gesture. "Nah, boy. Settle. You can stay. This is our spot." I gazed out at the sweep of the vines. The sun was bright on the leaves, burnishing the clusters of grapes, and my chest swelled with something *weird* again. Possessiveness? Happiness? Excitement?

Maybe a little of all three.

I was going to make this work no matter what it took.

CHAPTER FIVE

Meg

I seated myself at the big old dining room table to wait for the lord of the manor to get done inspecting his new domain. I wanted to hate him; I really did. But between Flea, who seemed to have taken a shine to me, and Stormy Sea Guy's niceness, it was hard to keep up a head of steam.

Still. The situation wasn't fair. I'd tossed and turned all night, struggling to make up my mind. Could I tolerate living in my family's home with this interloper who had no idea how to grow grapes, and who, by snapping his fingers, had been able to take my birthright?

But the truth was, I had no plan. Nowhere to go. The fifty thousand I would take away from the sale wasn't enough to do anything real with. If I'd had a career, any sort of clear vision for myself, I could have left. Hiked around the world until my money ran out. Enrolled in a college program. Gone to Paris and camped under the Eiffel Tower. *Something!*

But I'd come home a year ago to figure things out, and had immediately been sucked into Grandpa's illness and Gram's haphazard running of the vineyard. If it wasn't for Diego and our field manager Armand, who'd worked with Grandpa for twenty-five years, we'd have lost the land even sooner.

And now I'd have to tell Armand he was fired, and I was taking his job. *Ugh!*

But maybe I could get Stormy Sea Guy to tell him—he should do it. Part of the fun of being the boss.

Dread of that coming interview curdled my stomach and made my voice sharp as Stormy Sea Guy entered the dining room. "I didn't know your name." I tapped the contract I had cobbled together from internet resources. "Couldn't fill in the blanks."

"I'm Kane. Peter Kane Michaels McCallum." He smiled. *Why did he have to be gorgeous, too?*

But a fresh start seemed in order. God knows I needed one, on a number of levels. "Marguerite Villier." I extended a hand. "Thanks for offering me a job."

Kane shook my hand. "And thanks for being gracious about the situation we find ourselves in."

"It's a weird situation."

"That's just what I was thinking. It's up to us to make this work."

His hand was cool and smooth, not the hand of a man who spent his hours and days working outdoors—though I felt the strength in it. I flashed to my grandfather's hand, gnarled and hard as horn from using his cutters on the vines every day.

"Well. I appreciate the chance to continue to be on my family's land, no matter the circumstances." I said it firmly, because I meant it. "I can't promise I won't get triggered now and again. But this place means a lot to me, and I want to see it succeed, no matter who's in charge."

"About that." Kane drew the contract over, scanned it. "I see you have a three-month trial period outlined here. I think six months is fairer. We need time to get through the harvest and further into the season to know if this partnership is going to work."

A little bloom of something warm blossomed under my sternum. "I would think you'd want to know whether or not we can work together and be able to replace me sooner," I said.

Kane kept his eyes on the paper. "No. You deserve at least that long to figure out if you still want to be here. If you're not working out as an employee, I'll stop paying you, but you can still stay on until the six months are up in any case."

The warm fuzzy feeling disappeared.

Kane took a pen out of his pocket, a smooth silver thing that looked like an elongated bullet. He crossed out and made the change on the document.

"How will we know if I can do the job to your satisfaction?" I pointed to the clause about measurable objectives. "I put in this part about the tasks of each season."

"That's good." He scanned further. "I see you've given yourself a salary and a profit percentage." He squinted at me, his blue eyes sharp intelligent triangles. "Smart. But I think ten percent is a bit much. We'll go with five." The pen was poised.

"Seven," I said quickly.

"Seven it is." Kane scratched the new amount in and initialed it. "And I see you've added this sentence. Armand Graniere is working with us for another month?"

"We need him to facilitate the harvest." I explained how the longtime manager hired seasonal workers and had handled that for years. "He doesn't know about me replacing him. I'd like you to be the one to tell him, please. He has been here twenty-five years, and was my grandfather's friend." Armand's scowling face rose in my mind's eye. "He's not going to be happy about me replacing him."

"Well, too bad. I'm sure he's prepared for changes." Kane

signed the contract in a bold, slanting hand. "Let's go talk to him right after this."

I signed the contract beneath his name. My round, careful handwriting looked girlish, immature. I needed a more sophisticated signature to go with my new, professional status.

And, to make things worse, all I didn't know about viniculture pressed against the backs of my eyes, giving me the beginnings of a stress headache. Grandpa hadn't had long to teach me, and the vines had never been Gram's thing; she'd been the queen of hearth and home.

We stood up at the same time, our chairs scraping back on the wooden floor. Kane grinned. "Villier Vineyard is officially under new management. Let's go talk to this Armand character."

Hopefully Armand Graniere would be the bridge Kane and I both needed.

CHAPTER SIX

Kane

Meg and I headed for the barn. I already wanted to set up an area for my own projects in that cavernous, silvery wood building. As we walked through the grass, dewy with early morning, an enormous long-haired cat approached us from the vineyard. He was carrying a large rodent in his mouth, and he emitted rumbling meows around his furry prize.

From upstairs in the house, Flea barked loudly, spotting the interloper from the window.

The feline froze, one paw in the air, and glared accusingly at Meg.

"I'm sorry, Sir Henry, but we're going to be sharing the place," Meg said. "These are the new owners. This is Kane, and upstairs is Flea. Kane, meet Sir Henry Puddlejump, my grandfather's cat. He's a Maine Coon."

"You mean, *raccoon*. He's certainly big enough to be one." That this creature was even classified as a domestic animal seemed a stretch.

Flea barked jealously from the window. The prospect of

letting me make friends with a strange cat without him chaperoning was just too much, and that got him over his fear of the slippery stairs. Moments later, he was barking at the back door of the kitchen.

I sighed. "I need to put a dog door in that door. Don't worry, Flea's not mean to cats. He's afraid of them, actually. He just wants to say hi."

"Sir Henry doesn't like dogs and will kick his ass," Meg said. "You've been warned."

I walked to the back door and opened it. Flea roared out past me and screeched to a halt in front of Sir Henry, who'd dropped his breakfast and puffed up to be roughly the size of a lynx. The cat stared at Flea, his eyes slits and tail lashing.

"Flea! Mind your manners!" I yelled.

Flea whined and trotted over to Meg. He shivered and cowered against her legs, hiding from the evil glare emitted by the cat's yellow eyes.

Meg and I continued to the barn, leaving Sir Henry to his prize. This time, Flea was plastered to my side.

We stepped inside the vast, cool space of the barn. I looked around the dimly lit area with its bare bulbs dangling on cords from the faraway ceiling. I couldn't wait to explore all of the forgotten and abandoned crap in here.

Unknown equipment was stored neatly along one wall. Casks filled abandoned horse stalls. Another wall held tightly packed straw bales. My nose tickled with pleasant, musty smells.

"The field manager's office is down here," Meg said, her voice small. "Armand isn't going to like this."

"It can't be a surprise that the new owner would want to make changes," I repeated.

She glanced at me. Her greenish brown eyes seemed as hostile as the cat's. "He's old. He's worked with Grandpa his whole career. Please be kind."

I firmed my jaw. "Of course." We McCallums didn't shy away from hard things. We waded in and got shit done, but never cruelly.

The manager's office was built beneath a hayloft now lined with stacked empty casks.

"Villier used to make its own wine label back in the day. We just supply grapes to others now, but Grandpa always made some garage wine each year; those casks are extras." Meg gestured to the stored barrels above us.

"Garage wine" must be lingo for a small amount of the beverage created for personal use. The casks down in that old wine cave were filled with those private vintages; a tingle of excitement filled me that I owned this treasure trove now.

Meg led me to a closed door in the space beneath the loft, and knocked.

A short, neatly bearded older man opened the door. He ran an eyeball over us. "You kids must be here to talk about the new owners," he said. His voice sounded like he smoked a couple of packs a day, and the haze drafting out from the room confirmed it.

"I'm the new owner." I stepped forward with my hand out. "Kane McCallum. Pleased to meet you."

Graniere stared me up and down, snorted, and ignored my hand. "Not pleased to meet you, rich boy. Probably did a weekend seminar on viniculture and want to gamble with the place I've worked at most of my life."

This was too close to the truth not to make me squirm—but I was sick of feeling guilty, and angered by Graniere's rudeness. "Well, we might as well cut to the chase, then, since you appear to have made up your mind about me. I will not be needing your services any further, sir. I have a new field manager."

Graniere blanched as if struck. Clearly, the idea of being fired had not occurred to him. "Who would work for *you*? You're hardly wet behind the ears, and one look at those hands tells me you've never touched a vine before."

Meg stepped forward, white-faced. "I'm sorry, Armand. I'm the new field manager."

Graniere took another step back. He swore ripely. "Like you could run this vineyard, missy! Run it into the ground, more like!"

Two red spots appeared on Meg's high cheekbones. "I was hoping you would stay on awhile and show me the ropes, but clearly that's not how you want it." *Good, she wasn't intimidated.* "Perhaps we should just give you some time to clear out your things."

"You'll regret this!" Graniere ranted, raising a fist toward Meg. "Your grandfather is rolling in his grave right now. Thank God he's not here to see what's happening to this place!"

No way was this nasty old codger going to hit Meg! I inserted myself between them, pushing Meg behind me, and Flea stepped up to show his teeth with a growl. "Do I need to call the sheriff to have you removed, sir? Or can you go quietly?"

Graniere slowly lowered his fist. "You'll regret this," he ground out, and this time the words were for me.

He withdrew into the office, and slammed the door so hard that dust sprinkled down on us from the loft above.

"We'll expect you to have cleared out your things by the end of the day, or the offer to call the sheriff stands," I said loudly to the closed door. A heavy thump, as if something was lobbed at the portal, was the only reply. Flea barked again, and I quieted him with a hand on his head.

I turned to Meg. She was shaking, her hands over her mouth, her eyes huge.

"That was a lot rougher than expected." I put a hand under her elbow and physically turned her toward the bright open square of sunlight that marked the barn's distant exterior door.

"Why don't you take me on a tour of the fields? Show me a typical day in the vineyard."

"Okay." Meg walked like a robot toward the exit, her body trembling. I kept hold of her elbow, hoping like hell old Graniere wasn't around when we returned.

CHAPTER SEVEN

Meg

I felt like a coward as Kane escorted me out of the barn with a hand at my elbow. I shouldn't be so relieved that he was there, but . . . *I hated confrontation.* Really hated it. I'd known Armand wasn't going to be happy about the changes, but I had no idea he'd take one look at Kane and go apeshit.

"Armand must still be grieving Gram and Grandpa's passing. I've never seen him like that." We could hear cursing and the thump of objects being slammed around as Armand presumably packed his things.

"The vineyard was being auctioned. If it wasn't me, it would have been someone else, replacing him." Kane seemed to be saying it as much to himself as to me.

For the first time, it occurred to me that Kane was more than a little brave, jumping in like he had—dealing with the stiff competition of the auction. Dealing with me. Dealing with Armand. And all of that was just the beginning of the kind of iron constitution it would take to run a vineyard. "How old are you?" I asked as we exited the barn.

"Twenty-six."

"Holy crap. We're the same age!" I stepped around to the side of the barn and leaned against it, covering my face with my hands. "We're doomed."

Kane laughed. *Laughed!* Not just a little chuckle either, but a great big belly laugh with his head tipped back. "Doomed! Because I'm twenty-six? What are you, a withered old crone?"

Why did he have to be good-looking and likeable, as well as all the other things he was? *Unfair!*

I lowered my hands from my face and glared at him. "Our age speaks to our collective lack of life experience. I don't know a single vineyard owner under forty."

"Maybe that's why this industry is struggling. Why your grandparents lost this place." Kane had gone serious. "Times are changing. I'm not trying to be offensive."

"No. That's not it." *But he might have a point.* Grandpa and Gram, and Armand too, had been very traditional—but that didn't mean their methods weren't sound. "Any kind of farming is a high-risk business. You want to know how to make a small fortune in the wine industry?"

"By spending a large fortune on it." Kane was ridiculously handsome smiling: a Ralph Lauren ad in his button-down, rasp of dark beard and *those eyes.* "I've heard that old joke."

"Yep. A large fortune, Kane. Buying this place was just the beginning, and now we've lost Armand." I pushed away from the barn wall and walked toward the house. "Armand has a 'little black book' of contacts to call to work the harvest, and our most reliable grape buyers are in it, too. I'm sure he won't give us those names and numbers. I have no idea how we'll get the grapes in now." I rubbed my chest to loosen the panicky feeling. "Armand has told me that his worker contacts are a valuable asset, one of the things he controls and will never share. Not to mention all the buyers who are our regulars."

"I'll do an online search on how to get it done." Kane took out his phone.

"Seriously? You're Googling how to do a harvest." I bit back another exclamation of, *"We're doomed!"*

The pirate romances were wearing off on me, and not in a good way.

I was the new field manager. I was supposed to have the answers. Imposter syndrome reared its ugly head—because, honestly, I hadn't counted on losing Armand like this.

I headed to the back porch for my apron and shears. "I'm going out to the field. Catch up with me when you're done with your internet research."

I didn't want to say anything more that showed my lack of confidence until I'd calmed down and sorted out next steps. Kane would fire me the minute he realized I didn't have much more of an idea of what to do than he did.

Flea followed me, his warm bulk a comforting presence. "You're a good boy. My personal Cerberus. I liked how you stuck up for me." I patted Flea's head. He leaned against me, making me stagger, as I tied on my apron. I slipped on my gloves, and marched down the grape aisle to the place where I'd left off yesterday.

As always, being in the field calmed me. The slightly nutty smell of the late-season vines was perfume. Birds twittered, and the occasional caw of a crow and the sound of the breeze in the leaves were all I could hear besides the *snick* of my pruners.

The dusty dark purple of the grapes looked good.

I took out the tool I used to measure sugar content and tested some samples. *Right on track.* We'd be ready for harvest soon. We had to figure out what to do by then.

I worked quietly, trimming and tying up the vines, feeling the sun on the top of my head. My heart rate came down, and as it did, the truth of my feelings about Armand began to bubble up.

I had never liked the man.

I felt guilty admitting it, because Grandpa and Gram had loved and trusted Armand—but I'd felt the manager's negativity towards me the whole time I'd been at the vineyard. Subtle digs and put-downs about my mother and her lifestyle. Attempts to exclude me from conversations about the vineyard, even as Grandpa tried to teach me. Eyerolls and interruptions.

Armand had been jealous. He'd resented my return, and the place I held in my grandparents' hearts.

Kane or no Kane, Armand would never have helped me run this place. And in light of that, would he actively sabotage us now? There were many ways he could do that, besides withholding his little black contact book.

I heard the rumble of a truck in the distance, and lifted my head to look back toward the house and grounds. Armand's white Ford was moving down the driveway.

What destruction could he have wrought on his way out?

I dropped my pruners into my apron pocket, and, spurred by a fear I couldn't put a name to, I ran toward the barn.

CHAPTER EIGHT

Kane

I sat at the dining room table, hunched over my laptop and simultaneously working my phone. It felt good to be rolling up my sleeves, metaphorically speaking, and moving on all the massive amount of shit I needed to get done.

I needed a better office; perhaps the old parlor with its stiff Victorian furniture would work. The phone signal was terrible in the house; I'd just finished calling the local cable company to put in a work order for Wi-Fi. I was checking off more items on my to-do list when I saw a flash of color passing the window.

Meg, running by, with Flea at her side.

Flea'd attached himself to her like a burr. Faithless hound.

But why was she running?

I stood up so I could see where they were going—and they disappeared into the barn.

I'd heard the sound of Armand's truck pulling out and felt nothing but relief. She wouldn't have gone back in there while that jerk was still around.

Harvesting the grapes, a task that Meg thought was going to

be insurmountable, was actually no problem. Several companies listed services; I'd already called for estimates, and now I was waiting on bids for professional, seasonal crews to come bring in our grapes when they were ready.

Meg was probably just working off a little steam from the freak-out about Graniere by checking out what he'd done in his office. That dude had been intense, and it wouldn't surprise me if he was up to something . . . *Maybe Meg thought so too.*

I shot to my feet, slid my phone into my pocket, and ran out of the house, the front door banging shut behind me as I clattered down the steps of the front porch.

Flea was barking his *danger* warning inside the barn.

That lent my feet further speed. I smelled the tang of smoke the minute I got inside the dim, cavernous structure. "Meg!"

"In the office!" *She was coughing.*

I looked around frantically for a fire extinguisher. I spotted a huge old red one beside the door, heavily frosted with dust. I picked it up and ran for the office at the other end of the barn.

Inside the small room, Meg was beating out a lick of flame on the floor with a broom. It had apparently escaped from a nearby burning wastebasket.

"I got it," she rasped, as I fumbled the pin out of the extinguisher, aimed the nozzle at the wastebasket, and pressed the trigger on the head.

Nothing happened.

I pressed it again. Still nothing. "Shit!"

Meg grabbed a fleece cushion off the rolling office chair and stuffed it into the wastebasket, snuffing the fire. The room filled with foul-smelling smoke and the stench of burning sheepskin. "There. It's out."

We both stared at the smoking metal wastebasket for a moment. Flea whined worriedly.

I dropped the useless extinguisher and went over to the

window, unlatching and shoving open the sash. Fresh air gushed in.

Meg came over and wedged in beside me. We both hung our heads out and gulped clean air.

"I started a list of things we need—gotta add new fire extinguishers to the list. God knows how old that one was." Meg coughed between words. "Thank God you got here before the fire spread."

Her face was pale, but her cheeks were red. Wisps of hair had escaped from her ponytail and curled around her face. They caught the light like flames. She wiped her open mouth with the back of her hand, leaving a streak of soot on her cheek. Her long, strong body felt great squeezed in tight beside me in the window frame.

"I was thinking about Armand and realized that he was never a friend of anyone but my grandparents. I was just suddenly . . . worried that he might sabotage us."

Us.

I liked the sound of that. She said *us.*

I reached out and used the ball of my thumb to wipe the soot off her cheek. "Thanks for coming to check."

Her skin felt like warm silk.

I wanted to touch a whole lot more of it.

My mouth went dry. I forgot to blink as I gazed into her eyes.

Meg shied back suddenly, ducking her head as she turned away. "I dread finding out what Armand burned in that trashcan, but we should air this room out and see."

She marched off to open the office door wider, and grabbed a fan from one of the shelves. She plugged in the fan to blow out the smoke and stench. Then she wrapped the hot, still-smoldering metal can in a small rug, and jogged out through the barn, carrying it toward the vineyard's disposal pile back behind the wine cave.

This girl was brave, capable and dedicated. She cared about the place. That was why I'd hired her. But I was *not* attracted to Meg Villier.

Hell, I hardly liked her! She wasn't my type at all.

I broke out of my paralysis at last, and hustled out of the office. I scouted around the barn for a trash bag. Finally locating a box of them, I returned just as Meg arrived.

The black smudge was still there on her flushed cheek.

I squinted, trying to decide if she was pretty.

Meg's mouth was pink, wide, and full, curling at the ends. There were little brackets around it, like she smiled a lot, but I'd hardly seen her smile at all. Her nose had a high bridge that gave her an unusual profile. Her eyebrows were bold, untamed arcs over eyes filled with green and brown. She wore no makeup.

No, she wasn't pretty, she was something better. *Striking.* Her mouth was a magnet I couldn't stop looking at.

"What?" Meg snapped. "You got something to say? Say it."

"You still have . . . soot on your face." I reached out slowly, prepared for her to bolt, but she glared at me defiantly.

There were definitely flecks of yellow in her eyes, along with the green and brown. Reminded me of a summer I'd spent in the Rockies with my dad and brothers, fishing and panning for gold in a mountain stream.

My fingers touched her cheek gently, and I rubbed the smudge away. "There."

We didn't move. My thumb drifted down across her parted lips. Their supple feel and her warm breath seemed to ripple across my hand, up my arm, and straight down to my groin, igniting a painful throb.

I stepped back and turned away, staring at the wall with its framed, vintage photos of the vineyard in various stages. I did mental times tables, my favorite activity to kill an unwanted boner. *Six times seven was what now?* "Where do we begin with all this mess?"

I heard Meg draw a shaky breath, but her voice sounded as irritable and bossy as ever when she spoke. "Since this is the manager's office, why don't you start setting up your work area in the house and adding to that list of stuff we need—I'll text what I started to you. Meanwhile, I'll clean up out here and get a handle on what Armand was up to."

"Sounds like a plan." I kept my back to her and hotfooted it out of there, still trying to remember what six times seven was.

CHAPTER NINE

Meg

Holy smokes! I could have stared into Kane's eyes all day. They were not just one shade of blue. The iris had an indigo ring around it, while the main part was more of a smoky cobalt with little bits of white, like foam on a wind-whipped ocean. And why had God wasted such long, thick lashes on a guy?

Thank heavens he'd left when he had; I was downright weak in the knees and warm in the lady closet just from his touch on my cheek.

I dropped into Armand's creaky old office chair abruptly.

I was a wreck! Clearly, way too celibate for way too long. I needed an hour alone with my battery-operated boyfriend and the latest chapter of *The Pirate's Lusty Prize.*

Instead, I had a smoke-filled shambles to clean up, and no idea how bad the discoveries would be when I did. "Perfect. This project will dry my panties," I muttered, reaching for a pair of Gram's old leather gardening gloves, hanging from a peg on the wall.

Pulling the gloves on gave me a twinge of grief.

I was literally putting my hands where Gram's had once been; I could almost feel the warmth of her touch through the sturdy leather. "Thanks, Gram. I know you're here, giving me strength."

Flea whined at the sound of my voice, and I frowned at him. "Go, boy! Go see your man." The huge dog hunkered down instead, making like a big black throw rug. "Fine. But stay out of my way."

I pulled a trash bag off the roll Kane had located and sat down. I pulled open the file drawer where copies of invoices, billing, and other business impedimenta had been stored.

Those files were gone, along with the big green ledger Grandpa had shown me where the business income and outgo had been logged.

"Can't lose data this way, and you can't teach an old dog new tricks," Grandpa had said, showing me the ledger with its neat rows of figures in black and red—mostly red.

"Turns out you *can* lose data this way, Grandpa," I muttered. I'd spotted a shred of the green canvas cover of his ledger in the ashes I dumped from the trash can. "That bastard!"

Now that I knew what Armand had burned, I felt panicky again. How could I recreate Grandpa's careful lists of buyers and suppliers without that ledger?

Maybe there would be some clues stashed away somewhere in the messy desk.

I sorted the entire huge, battered old desk, throwing away dried-up old pens, ancient receipts, and copies of invoices sent to buyers going back to the nineteen-fifties.

The good part about discovering those invoices was that I now had a list of winemakers who had bought Villier grapes going all the way back. The bad news was, I had nothing but the old addresses printed on the bills as a way to contact them. All of this information would have to be computerized and updated—

every company tracked down and contacted. But, at least it was a place to start.

Once the desk was cleared, I felt like I'd made a little island of sanity in a sea of chaos. I was ready to tackle the ancient computer and see what was on it.

And of course, the awful old relic was password-protected. Kane seemed handy in the tech area; maybe he could get it open —but in any event, "new company computers" had to go on his buy list.

A knock at the door brought me around, startled out of my reverie.

Kane stood in the doorway, holding a plate crowned by a pair of towering sandwiches. "I hope you don't mind that I raided the fridge for lunch."

"Great!" I stood up, stretched my arms over my head, and shook them out. "Perfect timing. I was just making you a note that the computer might be past saving."

"I expected that."

"Good. Let's go outside to eat, I need a little fresh air." I took the plate and walked through the barn carrying it, filling Kane in on what I'd discovered. "I'm worried about the harvest, but even more worried about locating our usual buyers since Armand destroyed the contact info. But, on the plus side, I've collected a list of all the winemakers who bought from us since the fifties . . . just the old invoices, though. It all needs to be updated and organized—phone numbers tracked down. And someone to contact all of them and see if they're interested in buying from us."

We reached my favorite spot, and sat down on the late summer grass under the oldest of the olive trees, a gnarled old friend who looked out over the fields at the edge of the yard. Its silvery bark felt good on my back as I set down the plate between us. "I'll go grab us something to drink."

Kane frowned. "I should have thought of that."

"No problem. You made sandwiches, which is more than Grandpa did for Gram in his eighty years on the planet."

I trotted back into the house and grabbed a couple of root beers out of the fridge. I returned to Kane just in time to see Flea roll, kicking his legs in the air on the sun-scorched grass and making me laugh.

"It's a dog's life," Kane said, as he handed me a sandwich.

In exchange, I handed him a root beer and sat down, leaning back against the tree.

I eyeballed the huge sandwich, opened wide, and took a hearty bite. My cheeks bulged as I chewed, and I rolled my eyes back in ecstasy, moaning. When I could finally speak, I said, "You found that stone-ground mustard Gram loved. So good with ham." I hadn't bothered to empty the fridge the day before my supposed move, and now I was glad that the essentials were still edible.

Kane stared out across the fields, eating meditatively; the house was on a slight rise, so we had a bit of a view. "Don't worry about the harvest. I've got several bids coming from professional crews. This destruction of the records is a marketing opportunity —for us to start over. Rebrand, and reach out to a whole new batch of buyers. I need to build a website for the vineyard; once I do, we can develop a sales campaign and send out a notification to all the buyers we can find who make wine with pinot noir grapes."

I glanced at Kane over my sandwich. "That's a lot of work."

Kane shrugged. "We're here to work. We could end up doing better than your grandparents and Armand did, selling to the same customers. We already know that didn't pay the bills."

"That's not entirely true. From what Gram said after Grandpa died, the vineyard would have at least been breaking even if Grandpa's medical bills hadn't sucked everything out of it."

"Well, that's good to know." Kane fed Flea a bit of ham. "Gives us a baseline of sorts."

I took time to finish my sandwich after my initial attack on it. I wasn't in a hurry to finish my lunch—I liked how companionable things felt, enjoying a bit of a break with Kane and Flea.

I also liked how Kane said "we" and "us" all the time.

I cleared my throat. "I need a new computer, and unless you're going to do all that on your laptop, you need one too. I'll keep cleaning out Armand's old room, and it can be my office. I want his tobacco smoke and his bad juju out too. Seems like a trip to town is in order for you."

Kane's eyes flashed good humor. "You bossing me around again?"

"Maybe. A little." I shrugged. "Just an idea."

"Well, it turns out I was planning on that after we ate. I cleared out the parlor to make it my office." He turned to point at a pile of ugly old Victorian furniture out on the porch, that had populated the seldom-used room. "While you were doing what you were doing, I was working too."

I felt a pang looking at that pile, but just a minor one. Truth was, other than weekly vacuuming and fluffing the doilies, we hadn't used that room either. "Maybe someone will love that hideous old crap. I'll call Goodwill to pick it up."

"Whew." Kane grinned. "Glad you weren't mad that I hauled your priceless heirlooms outside."

"Oh, you'll know when I'm mad." I smiled back.

"Of that I have no doubt." Kane reached out a finger and swiped a bit of mustard from near my lip, holding up a yellow-smudged fingertip. "You missed a spot."

"I'm a messy eater." Possessed of an impulse I couldn't name,

I leaned forward and sucked his fingertip clean. "There. All gone."

His eyes widened and darkened. His nostrils flared.

"Inappropriate. Sorry!" I jumped up. "Back to work! Thanks for the sandwich!"

I fled like my pants were on fire . . . because in a way, they were.

CHAPTER TEN

Kane

I took the truck to Santa Rosa that afternoon after lunch. I needed to get away, to clear my head and cool my jets—*and Meg was right*. We had a shit-ton of stuff for me to buy.

I was getting used to Flea opting to stay with Meg.

In town, I met with a CPA I'd found who had the best reviews in an online social media site. I filed papers with her to set up a corporation in the name of McCallum, Inc.

I didn't want to steal Meg's family name—the vineyard was going to remain Villier. It was the least I could do to honor the family who'd given their lives to that land. But my corporation would own Villier as one of its growing assets—or so I hoped.

With my newly drafted Articles of Incorporation, I went to a nearby bank and opened a business account. I had the remainder of the money Dad had loaned me transferred into the account, and then applied for a business credit card on the spot.

A little headachy from all the form filling and paperwork pushing, I grabbed a coffee and went to a big hardware store and bought tools to replace the rusted and falling apart ones on the property.

Buying the tools restored me. Nothing like picking out your own chainsaw, shovel, axe, pruners, rake, and gloves, just for starters. I had my eye on a lot more than that, when my credit card came through.

I stopped in at an office supply store and browsed computers next.

I called Meg as I stood in front of a long row of choices. "What would you like to work on? PC or Mac?"

"Oh gosh." I could almost see her squinting, biting her full lower lip. "I don't know. I'm not much of a computer person."

"Mac it is, then. I work on a Mac so that'll be easier for us to coordinate calendars and such. Do you want a laptop or a desktop?"

"Hmm. I think I'd like to keep my computer work out in the barn and not be tempted to work on it at all hours. So, a desktop?"

I put the iMac computer in a wheeled cart, the phone wedged between my ear and shoulder, but I grabbed a laptop for her, too. She'd soon be a convert. "How about some headphones? I like to listen to music when I work. Tune out the rest of the world."

"Sounds *great*, Kane." Meg's voice went breathy. She sighed in my ear, and the soft sound raised the hair on my arms and took me right back to watching her take that enormous bite of her sandwich and just about have a foodgasm. None of the girls I'd gone out with in the past would just chomp into a big sandwich like that, no shame, and watching Meg had been sexy as hell. "This is going to be *so* nice. Makes me look forward to learning all the computer stuff I'm going to need to know," Meg went on. "You seem pretty comfortable with all of that."

"I get by." I forced myself to focus as I hunted for the various tech elements needed for each of our workspaces. I wasn't about to say how buying these things for the business felt like I was buying them for *her*, and that I liked that feeling. "You'll catch on fast. I'm picking up a copy of some accounting software so we can just connect to the business bank accounts and have our info right there."

"You'll have to show me everything. How you like to do it."

"Sure. No problem." *You're a dog, Kane! She didn't mean to sound like she was talking about sex!*

"Can you pick up some food at the market? The fridge is almost empty. Unless you want me to make a run and restock," she offered quickly.

"Got it covered. Anything special you need?" I pushed the cart loaded with office stuff toward the checkout. "Got any diet needs, or anything like that?"

She laughed. "No. In case you can't tell by looking at me, I'm a steak and potatoes, anything goes kind of gal."

"Steak and potatoes, anything goes here too. And you look great. I mean, you aren't fat. Just kind of curvy and . . . just right. Not that I was looking or anything . . . *crap*." I smacked my forehead. "I'm mucking this up."

Meg laughed. "I appreciate the compliment. There's something wrong with the world when a guy is afraid to tell a girl she looks great, even when they work together. See you later." She ended the call.

I felt a warm tingly feeling.

She liked steak and potatoes. Didn't mind a compliment. And "anything goes" had a lot of possibilities.

My first week at Villier Vineyard passed in a blur, but every day we made progress.

I spent several hours in the early morning following Meg as she worked her way down the rows, doing "canopy management."

I called it "optimizing the grapes," and that made her laugh. I liked making her laugh.

Every day I reveled in the cool, misty early morning air, the intensifying smell of the fruit as the fields warmed—the sight, sounds and smells of it all. Every day, I knew a little more that I'd made the right choice in buying Villier.

We took our time to set up our offices. I loaded all the software onto our computers and began building a basic website for the vineyard, using photos Meg had taken. She'd been using her phone camera for the last year to document the vineyard in all its moods and seasons, and many of her photos were well-composed and beautiful. I used one of her shots of the fields at sunset with the oak tree in the background as a header, and built out a clean, spare, modern-looking site around that theme.

Meg began inventorying the harvest supplies we had on hand. She and Diego developed a calendar, counting down toward the harvest, though the exact time we brought in the grapes depended on their ripeness—and we had to have buyers lined up before that, because the grapes could not be stored on the property. They needed to be processed right away by buyers, or they'd spoil.

"We need to find those buyers within the next month," she told me. "You've got a lot to do."

But so did she, and I was beginning to enjoy that it was "we" getting it all done.

CHAPTER ELEVEN

Meg

I woke early one morning. The night air had made my room chilly, and I shivered in the dawn just a bit. I took my favorite sweater off the hook on the door and put it on, heading down to make some coffee—but as I hit the stairs, I smelled fresh brew from the expensive ground beans Kane had bought.

I was getting spoiled—not only by the quality of the coffee, but having him make it for us.

Kane stood in the kitchen facing the window, watching dawn inching up to illuminate a spectacular sunrise, one hand using a spatula to stir a frying pan yellow with eggs. He was wearing a tight black waffle weave shirt and a pair of jeans that showcased his excellent ass. Flea sat just outside of what Kane called the "cooking zone" and thumped his tail to greet me with a happy grin.

Kane turned, holding up the spatula in a wave. "Cheesy eggs?"

"It's too early for me to eat. My tummy takes a while to wake up." His shoulders sagged a little in disappointment, so I rallied.

"But it smells good. I'll have some of whatever you're having." I fetched my chipped Villier Vineyard mug and filled it with coffee. "And you know I love your designer coffee."

"You'll never want to go back." Kane plated the eggs and sprinkled cheese over them. Four slices of sourdough toast popped up on Gram's old toaster. *Eek, what a lot of food!* I was going to get even more curvy in the hips if I ate a full breakfast like this. But that toast, fresh from our local bakery in town, smelled great too. I spread a little butter across the slices and put them on a plate on the table.

Kane set down a plate of cheesy eggs in front of me, and doused his in hot sauce. "I learned cheesy eggs from our housekeeper, Mrs. Knightly. I think she taught my mother as well, to be honest."

"Well, thank you, Mrs. Knightly." I sat down and took that first sip of coffee. Even though my rational mind told me it didn't work that fast, that first sip always seemed to lift a fog from my brain.

I piled some eggs onto a piece of toast and took a bite. "Do you have things you need to work on today? On the website or anything?"

Kane passed Flea a scrap of toast. "A little. Some final touches to put on the website. Mainly we need to get started contacting wineries to partner with, but nothing that can't wait a bit. What're you thinking?"

"I'd like to show you a few things with the grapes. With harvest approaching, we're both going to have to put in some time in the fields and I'd like to be sure you know what you're doing." I finished my food and stood up, clearing my plate from the table and taking it to the sink. I glanced out the window. The sight of the first morning rays hitting the lines of vine never failed to lift my spirits. "Time to get out there."

"Right on your tail. Can't have you thinking I don't know

what I'm doing." Kane ran water over his dishes. He winked at me. "Let me get the website finished up and some contacts organized. After that I'll join you for a little alone time?"

Was he flirting? I felt a hot blush on my neck as I washed my hands. We were almost touching. Should he be radiating that much heat? Or was I the one? "Yep, sounds great!"

I headed upstairs, taking the steps two at a time.

Meg, you are NOT crushing on him. He's out of your league —and he's your BOSS. "Damn you, Stormy Sea Guy, and your tasty eggs and good coffee."

In my room, I quickly pulled on some wool socks and jeans, switched out the sweater and my nightgown for a long-sleeved shirt, and headed back down. I allowed myself the briefest of glances in his direction as I pulled my boots on at the bottom of the stairs.

Kane was already in the parlor-turned-office, sitting at the desk with his computer. He looked up with a grin. He was so freakin' handsome, like one of my Highlander heroes wearing a Henley and a little morning scruff. "I'll be out soon."

"Don't wait long. It's going to be hot later." *I shouldn't have sounded so grumpy and bossy!* Why was I so agitated? I turned away and stomped into the laundry room off the back porch, and tied on my work apron. I gathered my tools and emotions together. "Stop this, Meg!"

I fed Sir Henry on my way down the steps, and at last I was in the rows.

Calm settled over me as I walked down the aisles of vines, checking each trunk, cane, leaf and stem. Mentally, I tracked every area that might need some more TLC, nipping off leaves that showed the slightest indication of mold and stowing them in a bag at my waist.

I wasn't sure, yet, what Kane's real motivation was with buying the vineyard.

It seemed like he might be trying to prove something, but I didn't know if that was to himself or to someone else. Despite how everything had come about, he could be good for Villier. Where Kane lacked experience with hands-on agriculture, he more than made up for it with his tech and business skill set. He'd made a website that most places would pay big bucks for in less than a week, and his plan to reach out to buyers was solid. That he'd chosen to take on a demanding personal business instead of sitting in a comfortable corporate setting somewhere told me a lot.

Kane wasn't what I'd expected.

He was kind, and patient, and seemed to have a budding affection for Villier. He had kept the Villier name when he started his corporation, and that meant a lot to me. Maybe keeping the name that everyone knew instead of trying to rebrand was just smart marketing, but it seemed like more than that.

I wanted it to be more than that.

A twig snapped down the row and I turned my head to look.

Kane was walking toward me, a thermos in one hand and pruners in another, Flea at his side. He'd changed into his work clothes, rubber boots, and even a denim work apron. Man, he looked good.

Stop it, Meg!

"Hey, take a look at these." I moved a cluster of grapes to reveal the leaves underneath. "See that white, powdery-looking stuff?" I pointed.

Kane stepped closer, his arm brushing my shoulder. "Yeah, I think so."

"This is why we check each row every day; it's called odium—mildew, basically."

"How do we treat it?"

"There are a few different options. Gram and Grandpa used sulfur, but we can use something else if you want. There are fungicides, oils, other dilute solutions, and potassium salts. All of them work to different degrees and have different price points."

Kane moved back, looking down the row and frowning. "How bad is it?"

I shrugged. "It's common. We don't have much at the moment if we keep on top of it." *At least he wasn't freaking out.* When Grandpa Villier had first shown me the common mildew on the leaves, I'd thought it would cost us the whole harvest.

"We can figure out something different later, after I have time to research it. For now, let's stick with the sulfur, since that's what you know and, I assume, have on hand." Kane reached past me toward a cluster of grapes, and his arm brushed my breast. His touch zapped through my body and pebbled my nipples, and I jumped at the intimate contact.

"Whoa. Sorry." Kane turned away. "I was just trying to see . . ."

"No worries." I cleared my throat "So, once we finish checking the rows for mildew, we'll mark the spots we find with a plastic tie, and later we can come back and treat with the sulfur. Afterward, I want to show you how to taste the grapes, so that you can tell when they're ready."

"Sounds like a plan." Kane turned to the vine across from me. We worked our way down the last of the rows together, the sun rising against our backs. Flea wandered with us, sometimes going off to sniff a rabbit trail or something, but always returning. Finished with the final row, Kane unscrewed the thermos and poured water into the lid as I drank from my canteen.

"Did you train Flea to be off leash?" I twisted the lid back onto the canteen. It'd been Grandpa's, and I loved the battered old metal thing with its green canvas covering and strap.

"Yeah." Kane set his thermos down and snapped his fingers at the dog. "Although I would never take him anywhere off leash publicly." Flea returned to Kane, his tail wagging as Kane stroked the top of his head.

We stood there for a moment, amidst the leafy vines, birds chirping around us and a soft breeze blowing over the slopes.

We were, maybe by the skin of our teeth, on our way to harvest. The grapes were looking good so far. I was beginning to feel hopeful that we could get them in with the professional pickers, and sell them, too, with the contacts I'd scraped together.

It felt good. I smiled at him for the first time that day. "I want to show you a few different things, but first, and probably the most accurate measure of a grape's readiness, is the refractometer." I pulled the small tubular device out of my apron pocket and presented it to him. "It measures the brix, or sugar content, of the grapes."

Kane took the refractometer from me and turned it over. "How exactly does this work?"

I dug in my apron until I found the small bottle of distilled water with the eyedropper lid. I showed Kane how to calibrate the refractometer using the distilled water against the daylight plate, and then to look through the lens to where the sample juice would be displayed. "Now we have to actually test one of the grapes." I pulled a ripe-looking grape from one of the clusters.

Kane tried to pass me back the refractometer, but I shook my head. "I already know how to do this." I offered him the grape, and pulled another from the vine. "Break the grape open, like this." I demonstrated, pinching the fruit between my index finger and thumb, pushing the nail of my thumb into the center.

Kane did the same with the grape I had given him.

"Now squeeze some of the juice onto the cover plate." I leaned over to check that the cover plate was clear of solids, explaining to him that if it weren't, it could break. "When there's only liquid, you close the cover plate." Kane snapped it closed. "Good. Now tell me what you see."

Kane lifted the refractometer and gazed through the eyepiece. "The bottom half is white, the top part bluish-gray."

"What does the line in-between read?"

"I think it's seventeen, just above fifteen?" Kane lowered the refractometer, his gaze shifting to mine.

Those stormy sea eyes!

And his eyelashes were just ridiculous. His mouth was gorgeous too, chiseled at the edges but plump in the middle, the better to kiss . . .

Focus, Meg.

I took the device from him and checked the visual. "Yeah, I see seventeen too." I opened the cover plate and cleaned it with a bit of soft cloth I kept in my apron. "For winemaking, we want the number higher than that, twenty-two or above." I put the refractometer back in the basket. "Senses test next. Look, feel, taste, and to some extent, smell."

I inspected a bunch of grapes, cupping the cluster in my hand, as Kane moved in to examine them. "The darker ones are the ones that are closest to ready. Notice that deep sort of purplish hue?"

He studied the grapes. "Like this one?" He touched one with the tip of his finger, his hand resting on mine.

I could feel his heartbeat through his skin.

Get a grip, Meg!

"Yeah, that's a ripe one." I moved away. "Show me one on another vine."

He went to another bunch. *Distance, that's what we needed.*

Kane showed me a few different clusters, holding up grapes that had ripened to almost black for my feedback.

Growing grapes for wine was like math: you could get by without learning the basics and move to the more advanced stuff, but eventually, you would come across something that required knowledge of the entry-level steps.

"Here." I picked a fresh grape for Kane, and one for myself. "Don't eat it, just explore it by touch in your hand." I dropped the specimen into his open palm. "How does it feel?"

I rolled my grape around in my palm. Kane imitated me, passing his from hand to hand. "It feels different than a grape you would buy at the store, like it's tougher. More durable, maybe."

"Good. What else?" We had nearly reached the rise with the oak tree on it, so I walked to its shade and sat on the bench of the picnic table.

"Getting out of the sun. Good idea." Kane sat next to me, still rolling his grape around in his palm. "I'm not sure how to describe it."

"The words don't matter. You're talking to me, not impressing someone at a wine tasting." I tried a flirty wink, and he smiled back.

He shut his eyes, and squeezed the grape between his thumb and forefinger. "It feels bouncy and plump. There's a support to the softness . . . it's firm underneath."

He was getting it!

"Yes! Okay, now open the grape, like we did for the refractometer." The edges of our cupped hands touched as Kane exposed the translucent flesh hidden behind the protective skin. "Notice the seeds?" I sifted through the insides of my grape with the tip of a finger, hunting for the small hard hearts of the fruit. "The seeds start out white, and as the grape ages they turn a darker brown."

"I didn't know that." He tipped his palm towards mine. "These don't seem that dark."

I peered at his seeds. "They aren't. Those are a bit too light still. Now, the taste test." I tipped my palm and let half of my grape roll into his. "Tell me what you taste."

He put the grape into his mouth and shut his eyes, concentrating. "It's tangy, but almost plumlike in fruitiness. There are

74

some layers to the flavor." He put another half into his mouth, chewing, focusing. "This one isn't the same. Too sour."

I smiled. "Exactly! Good! Once they're ready for harvesting, you'll taste the difference even more. Let's deal with some netting that needs repair, a few rows from the back." I took some folded swatches of netting from my apron, along with some ties. We ambled back to the vines, and I showed Kane where I had seen tears in the covering. Grandpa Villier had netted the vineyard a couple years ago, but after he died Gram and I hadn't been able to keep up.

"Why only cover the outer parts of the field?" Kane held the mesh while I tied the patch in place.

"Honestly, it's expensive and a lot of upkeep." I pulled two ends together and applied the ties. "We're close enough to forest that we do lose some grapes to animals and birds." I finished the repair and led him to where the other tear was. "This will help keep the bulk of wildlife away from the ripe grapes."

This one was bigger than the last. "Let me do it." He extended his hand for the ties and the piece of netting I held. I watched as he repaired the tear.

As we moved on, I showed Kane how to check for pests and where I had placed rat traps earlier in the year; thankfully they remained empty.

We reached the picnic table under the oak again, and stopped for a drink of water. Kane leaned back against the tabletop and I steered my eyes away from the way his shirt stretched over his arms, chest and abs. "We might actually be able to pull this off."

"I sure hope so." I gazed out over the fields. Even in the difficult years leading up to Grandpa's death and then Gram's, Villier had been producing quality grapes. This place was all I had left of them, besides memories, and thanks to Kane hiring me, I could still be a part of it—but not if the harvest failed.

"You don't choose a vineyard, it chooses you. If you try to do anything else, it will call out and haunt you," Grandpa had told me one evening.

Kane could have picked any vineyard or business, but he had chosen Villier. *Maybe it had chosen him, too.* Did the history of the place come alive for him like it did for me? Did he see the beauty in the vines and the old but well-maintained farmhouse?

We headed back. "Have you seen the wine cellar?" I asked.

"Just stuck my head inside."

"I'll give you the grand tour, such as it is. It's just been a place to store our garage wine for years now."

We neared the wine cave and I stopped. "I forgot my keys." I hadn't been in there since the day before Kane had bought the place, thinking it would be the last time I would see it.

Kane drew his copy of the keys out of his pocket, unlocked and opened the door.

I stepped into the dimly lit stairwell after him. He reached up and pulled a cord marked by a cork dangling from a lightbulb. The smell of oak and earth wrapped around us, luring us down the rickety stairs and into the actual cellar.

"Grandpa wanted to update all this." I ran my hand over the rough stone walls. "Gram convinced him not to, though, said they didn't need any of that since we weren't making wine professionally at Villier."

Rows of wooden barrels stacked five by five lined the walls beside us, leaving a narrow path to the back wall, where, behind the last barrel on the bottom left-hand side, Gram and Grandpa's names and wedding date were carved into the soft stone, along with those of my great-grandparents.

"I'm glad they kept it this way." Kane patted the front of the barrel beside him. He tilted his head thoughtfully. "What was it like, being here as a kid?"

"I wish I could have come here more, actually. I was born here and lived here until I was five with my mother. I visited during summers when I was little, but Maman and my grandparents fought all the time, so after elementary school, Maman stopped letting me come. I graduated from college with a teaching degree, and then went on for my certificate, but I just wasn't sure that was what I really wanted." I sighed. "So I came back to visit my grandparents. And the rest is history."

"Sounds like it was in your blood." Kane swiveled slowly, his gaze moving over the casks, his expression thoughtful. "I always wanted . . . I don't know. Something I never had. I kept waiting for it. Trying things, hoping to find it." Kane turned his attention back to the barrel his hand rested on. "I did everything I thought I was supposed to, you know?"

No, I wanted to say, *I have no idea.* "Nothing was ever expected of me other than I would do well, somehow, with whatever it was I chose to do. I ended up in teaching because I wanted a solid career, and thought I should 'do something' with my reading and writing abilities. But I didn't actually enjoy my student teaching."

"Not me. I had a lot of expectations to carry. I've got five younger brothers, four of whom look to me as a role model—Colton, who's next down in age, thinks it's his job to take me down, so I'll leave him out of that—and yet, all my life, I feel like I've just been going through the motions." Kane tipped his head and looked up at the dim, cobwebby ceiling. "I did the right things, and the world told me I did well, but at the same time I knew that I hadn't lived up to my potential—even as I acknowledged that I didn't know what it was." He turned to focus on me. "Don't get me wrong, Meg. I wasn't neglected in any way. I had a loving family, every kind of lesson and enrichment. I ran track all four years of high school and continued throughout college. I did well there, too. But when it was time to join the family business, I just . . ." Kane shook his head. "Suddenly I felt like I was suffocating. That's why I left and got on the road with Flea. I wanted to find that thing I'm supposed to do. This vineyard was the first time I felt a glimmer that I might know."

"I think everyone feels that way sometimes, no matter who they are or where they come from." I felt his gaze on me, heavy as a touch, as I rested my back against the barrels next to him.

I couldn't imagine having his life. I had no siblings, no family but Maman and a stepfather I barely liked. I had finally found a place to belong, here at Villier with my grandparents, and among the vines—only to have it snatched away.

"First world problems, right?" Kane's hand slid away from the barrel.

I finally glanced at him. He was staring at me, and I remembered why I'd nicknamed him *Stormy Sea Guy*. Those blue eyes were a crime, and they lit me on fire.

A flush heated my chest and went north, then south. *What would happen if I touched him?*

Kane slid his hand down my arm. Sparks flew up in its wake. He squeezed my hand. "You're so easy to talk to."

He was leaning closer . . . *was he going to kiss me?*

Surely not! I had to be imagining the intense look on his face. I couldn't let him know how much I wanted him; I'd never survive the rejection if I'd misunderstood.

And he was my boss!

I yanked my hand away, spun and headed for the steps. "Maybe we should go back up to the house, work on those contacts for the harvest."

Kane didn't answer.

I hurried up the stairs ahead of him. I could feel his gaze on my behind as he followed slowly, and that sense of him being there burned as I opened the door and blinked against bright sunlight outside.

"I have to stop in at the barn. I'll meet you back at the house."

I probably looked like a frizzy tomato right now, with my cheeks and chest on fire. *Show some dignity, Meg!*

"See you later." Kane said coolly. He shut the door firmly behind us and I heard him locking it as I walked away as fast as I could without breaking into a run.

CHAPTER TWELVE

Kane

A week later, I was still thinking about that almost-kiss. I even returned to the wine cave, poking around down there, hoping like an idiot she'd read my mind and join me. I replayed the scene in my head again and again.

I'd really enjoyed learning more about the grapes and working with her. I couldn't believe I'd told her all that I had, but it had seemed so natural to talk to her, and she really seemed to get it.

We were standing so close, down in that shadowy cool. I wished I could have captured the way the light from the open doorway had filtered through her hair; I'd wanted to reach out and tuck those rebellious reddish curls behind her ear.

Freakin' hell, I'd wanted to do more than that.

I'd wanted to kiss her, to taste that lush mouth of hers and make it mine. I'd wanted to touch her, everywhere, to explore that warm silk skin. Wrap her crazy hair in my fist, feel those beautiful lips under mine, hear her moan . . .

And Meg could tell, because a flush had bloomed on her

chest, spread along her neck and across her face, all the way up to her hairline. She'd made some excuse, ran up the stairs and took off.

What was I doing?

Meg was my employee! I had taken a gamble on Villier Vineyard, and maybe even a bigger gamble in hiring Meg. I couldn't endanger the delicate working relationship we had.

I went back up and locked the wine cave's door. I headed for the house, hardly noticing my surroundings as I neared the back steps.

Meg was not my type. She was bossy and emotional; she had a chip on her shoulder the size of Texas. *No.* Getting involved with her was a bad idea. The couples I'd known who dated and worked together got bitter when things didn't work out, and their businesses suffered when their relationships dissolved. I'd never been in one of those situations myself, and I never wanted to be.

Mom and Dad were the only couple I'd ever known who made business and personal work.

I looked around, finally noticing the long shadows on the dry grass, the approach of evening as the sun hit the golden Sonoma hills; the colors got brighter as gentle rays lit the corduroy lines of the fields and the changing leaves on the vines.

Where was Flea?

"Flea!" I hollered across the grounds. "Here, boy!" I gave my special whistle.

I was nearing the house and still didn't see him. "Flea!"

I heard the familiar jingle of his tags and turned to where they were coming from—*the barn*. He lolloped towards me, jaws agape, tongue hanging out in a happy grin. Of course, he was with Meg! The big hairy dude was totally in love with her.

He bumped up against my leg, then turned and ran back toward the barn.

"Flea!" He wasn't usually so disobedient. One of the barn's

double doors was open a bit, and Flea ran inside. "What the hell?"

The cool dim building smelled pleasantly musty, of machine oil and hay. There was still so much to do in here; we'd hardly got started clearing and organizing it. "Flea? Where are you, buddy?"

Flea barked again. He was standing over by the lawnmower, his thick, plumy black tail waving. "You want to show me something, don't you, pal?" Flea whined, as if agreeing.

Meg came out of what had been an old tack room. "I was putting away the tools. What's he doing?"

"I don't know, but he seems agitated about something."

Flea whined, lowered his head, sniffing behind the mower and still wagging his tail, then looking back at me.

"What is it, boy?" As I approached him, I heard the faintest sound—a soft mew. I squatted down and peered over the edge of the mower. "Oh, man. Look, Meg!" I pointed.

Three tiny kittens were curled in an old T-shirt lying beside the mower: a tabby, a black with white mittens, and a multicolored calico.

Meg leaned in next to me, her round hip pressing my side. "Oh my gosh! Sir Henry is fixed, so these babies must be from a feral cat. They're so cute! I wonder how old they are."

Our voices had woken the kittens. They began wiggling and crawling over each other, mewing in their squeaky little voices. "Their eyes are open. I think they've got to be at least ten days old for that to happen."

"Oh, I so want to hold them." Meg was squeezed in alongside me in the best way. I was in no hurry for the situation to end. I eased down to sit on the mower, and pulled Meg over against my legs. She leaned on me, her whole attention on the kittens. "I wonder if we can tame them."

"We shouldn't touch them. We don't know how scared of people the mama cat is. Be awful if she abandoned them."

"I know. That's just what I was thinking." Meg wrapped her arms around herself, as if to keep from reaching for them. "I can't stand how cute they are."

I couldn't stand how cute *she* was, hugging herself with a big smile on her face. Flea was still trying to get a sniff, and I grabbed him by the collar. "We don't want to scare their mama away with your doggy smells, either, Flea."

"I guess we should just leave them here, then." Meg sounded regretful. "Maybe when they're a little older we can bring out some food and begin making friends with them. A few more cats roaming around catching mice and rats wouldn't be a bad thing. Those pests can really do a number on the grapes."

"We can't keep all of these cats, Meg." I hauled Flea toward the door. "C'mon. We still have work to do."

"Why can't we keep them?" Meg sounded as surly as a teenager as she followed me. "I'm sure they won't be in the way."

I rolled my eyes skyward, still holding Flea by the collar so he wouldn't try to get back into the barn. "We'll cross that bridge when we get to it."

"Just a couple of the kittens?" Meg wheedled. "You'll never even notice they're here. But how can we decide? That calico, the tabby . . . and *oh my God* . . . that teeny black one with the little white socks . . ." She trailed me into the house. "I *so* want to see what their mama looks like. I'm surprised Sir Henry let her move into the barn. Cats can be really territorial, you know."

"Yep. Mama cat must be friends with Sir Henry." I closed the door, trapping Flea inside the house with us. "Now, are you ready to work on that list of sales contacts? I've already got started but we really need to make some progress."

"I'd rather hold kittens," she said morosely.

"Can't say you're alone in that." I laughed and tugged her ponytail. I couldn't seem to keep from touching her. "It's getting late in the day already; how about we just go through all those old invoices, pull together the most recent websites and phone numbers. And if we get done with that, I'll take us to dinner in town as a reward. We can start our cold calls tomorrow."

Meg looked up at me through her bronzy-brown lashes, a dimple beside that long, sweet mouth. "I definitely earned a reward after bestowing all my extensive grape knowledge upon such a city slicker."

"Not even going to argue with you there. Where are those invoices? Let's divide them up. You can use the laptop and the dining room table, and I'll be in my office." I didn't want her going all the way back out to the barn to work alone—I wanted her one room away, where I could talk to her. "I'll get your laptop booted up."

"I've got some late season lemons from the tree out back. Let me make us some lemonade, then I'll be good to go." Meg headed for the kitchen.

I watched her walk away.

I really liked Meg's tall, sturdy shape. I liked that she was going to squeeze us homemade lemonade; then we'd be working together on our business, practically in the same room. We'd also just found a batch of super cute kittens in the barn.

A weird, unfamiliar feeling tightened my chest and made my extremities tingle. *Holy shit!* It might just be happiness. "Freakin' Hallmark moment, right here," I muttered.

Flea grinned, and sat on my foot. We both waited for Meg to reappear.

CHAPTER THIRTEEN

Meg

"Some of these invoices are barely holding together." Kane held up a crumbling sheet of yellowed paper, foxed with age. "I wonder if it's even worth it to try to see if they're still in business. Maybe we should cut off even checking them at the nineteen-nineties."

I glanced at him from my station at the dining room table. "Lots of the vineyards have gone through multiple ownerships and rebrandings. That's the problem. I think you're right—but that's still more than twenty years ago."

"Let's go with the last ten years, then," Kane agreed. We'd been working steadily for a couple of hours, and I'd been able to amass twelve or so active winery labels that had bought from Villier in the past.

I sneezed as I sorted the invoices, pulling the oldest ones out and setting them aside.

"Bless you." Kane said, his gaze on his pile of papers. He looked so yummy sitting at the secondhand desk he'd found at a junk shop in Santa Rosa. Evening light fell through the panes of the window onto his rumpled dark hair. I loved that rich dark chocolate color, such a nice contrast with his eyes . . .

He looked up and caught me staring. "What? Do I have something on my face?" He swiped at his cheek, stuck his tongue out comically. "I know I need to shave."

"I like you scruffy." My stomach gave a loud rumble. "No, I was just starting to wonder how long until this reward dinner you promised me."

"Let's just finish sorting out the old invoices, and then we'll go." Kane rustled through the papers in front of him, and I did the same, quickly sorting them by date.

Kane was decisive, and he always seemed to like to come to a logical stopping point in his work before he moved to something else. He had good organizational skills. I liked that about him; even though he was inexperienced, it made me feel like I could trust his judgement about the vineyard, and that was starting to feel really good.

He stood up. "How fancy do you want to get?"

"Let's just go someplace casual so we don't have to change. I'm starving." But I felt a little warm curl of happiness in my tummy as I went to get my purse from its hook on the back of the door—*he was willing to take me somewhere nice!* What did that mean, exactly? I could have sworn he'd almost kissed me last week, but now we seemed to be back on familiar ground, working side by side companionably.

I shouldn't read something into it that wasn't there—it could ruin everything.

I directed Kane as he drove us in his truck to my favorite little Mexican food hole-in-the-wall only half an hour away. "*Hola,*

Jaime," I greeted the man behind the counter. He was a cousin of Diego's. "*Como esta?*"

"*Muy bien*, Meg." Jaime, a weathered older man who owned the place with his wife, led me to my favorite table in the corner, right under the *pinata* lamp. "Who's this?"

"Jaime, *esta es* Kane McCallum. The new owner at Villier." I was proud of how steady my voice was, of how I could hold my head high as I made the intro.

"*Hola.*" Kane shook the man's hand with his easy smile. "*Tengo mucho hambre esta noche!*"

"You've come to the right place for that," Jaime responded in English. "Ask Meg."

"That's why we're here," I said. "We're both hungry." We unrolled our burritos of silverware wrapped in a paper napkin. Jaime brought us each water and a Mexican beer.

I pointed to the *Specials* board near the front door. "I always just order off of there. Jaime's wife Maria does the cooking, and it's terrific."

Pretty soon we were digging into the special of the day, *chile rellenos* made with huge chiles Maria had grown herself. I was just mopping up the last dregs of delicious sauce when the front door opened with a *ding*, making both of us look up.

A couple came in dressed in the wine country equivalent of business casual—chinos and polo shirts. Neighbors on the same road as ours to the south, this couple owned a glitzy vineyard and winery, and had probably pulled up in one of the fleet of antique Mercedes they liked to park ostentatiously around their place. Grandpa had complained about their snooty attitudes on more than one occasion.

"Ugh," I said into my glass of ice water. "Frank and Betsy Gumbaugh."

Kane raised his brows. "Neighbors?"

"Don't look. I don't want to talk to them," I hissed. "They were at the auction."

Too late. Frank made a beeline for us. "Meg Villier! Nice to see you out and about." His voice was overhearty.

I forced a smile but didn't get up. "Hello, Frank. Betsy."

They stared openly at Kane. "Who's this?"

Kane stood up, setting his napkin aside. "Great to meet you folks." He smiled with easy charm and good manners, offering a hand. "I'm Kane McCallum. Do you live in the area?"

I gestured. "This is the new owner at Villier."

"Surprised to see you breaking bread with the enemy," Frank told me, as he shook Kane's hand.

"Kane took pity on me and kept me on as vineyard manager," I said with a fake smile.

"How charitable," Betsy purred.

"Nothing charitable about it. Meg's a great manager and I needed the help," Kane said.

"We own Peerless Wines, down the road from you a few miles." Frank jingled the change in his pockets. "Congratulations on winning the auction for Villier. I hope you don't have too much trouble with the old place."

"Oh, no trouble at all since I was smart enough to hire Meg." Kane's smile was dazzling. "Maybe you're aware of the quality of our grapes? We're close to harvest and still looking for a few select buyers."

I blinked. We didn't have *any* lined up yet! "Select buyers" was definitely a stretch—we were *desperate* for buyers, at this point.

Frank frowned. "I heard your grapes had a serious mold issue and there were problems with your harvest workers."

Kane laughed, and if I hadn't known him so well, I would have thought it completely genuine—but I *did* know him, and I heard the tension in it. "You've been seriously misinformed, sir! Who've you been talking to?"

"Armand Graniere, Villier's former manager. He said he quit when you came on." Betsy leaned toward Kane confidentially, diamonds flashing in her leathery cleavage. "Graniere said the current crop was rotten. He had been with Villier donkey's years —he ought to know."

I shot to my feet, throwing my napkin down in agitation. "Armand was fired! He's literally spouting sour grapes. Don't listen to a word that man says. He even tried to burn down the office when Kane . . ."

"It's okay, Meg." Kane put a restraining hand on my arm, still smiling at the Gumbaughs. He squeezed gently but firmly. "We handled it."

I was making a scene. I got the message, and subsided into my chair.

Kane moved his hand to my shoulder, his touch firm. He went on. "I'm sure Frank and Betsy understand how tricky it can be when there's a major change in leadership. Being let go can bring out the worst in people. Graniere's sour grapes notwithstanding, this year's crop is gorgeous and mostly spoken for, but we'll hold back a few tons for you if you'd like."

Kane ended up getting Frank Gumbaugh's personal card, and a promise from Peerless that they'd take as many grapes "as we could spare."

"I even bid on the place myself because we've bought from Villier for years," Frank said with a flash of his big white veneers. "I'm glad to hear that your crop is good again this year. You might want to have a word with Graniere. He's not doing you any favors in the community."

"We certainly will," I growled. "Maybe we'll even slap him with a defamation lawsuit!"

"Well, we'd love to visit but there's still more to do back at the vineyard." Kane peeled off a hundred-dollar bill and casually tossed it on the table, way too much money for our modest dinner. Jaime and Maria would be happy, and they more than deserved it, but I gritted my teeth at the display for the Gumbaughs. "Glad we'll be doing business together, Betsy. Frank."

The couple exclaimed and waved as Kane hustled me out with a hand at my elbow.

"I can't believe you threw down a C-note like that. Did you think you were impressing someone?" I fumed, the minute we got outside. I wasn't sure who I was most mad at—Armand, for his sabotage, or Kane, for being so good at dealing with upscale folks like the Gumbaughs.

Kane had turned a stumbling block into a stepping-stone—so why was I so angry? He'd reined me in before I lost my shit in public, and he'd done it in such a way it didn't even seem like he was doing it.

I should be grateful.

But I wasn't.

I had been managed. I yanked my elbow out of Kane's hand, and strode past the truck to head down the darkening country road.

CHAPTER FOURTEEN

Kane

I stood outside the little Mexican place watching Meg storm off into the dark—her long legs striding, her tangled ponytail bouncing, emotion radiating off her like heat shimmer on a summer road.

Damn, but I thought I'd done good with that potentially awkward situation. "Turned milk into cream," as Mrs. Knightly, our housekeeper, used to say. And I'd helped handle Meg's emotional outburst pretty tactfully, too.

Had I done the right thing in hiring her? Let alone starting to really like her. Meg was supposed to be my vineyard manager, nothing more, and how she was acting right now wasn't professional. I got it that she was outraged about Graniere's betrayal, but airing our personal business in front of people like the Gumbaughs wasn't good business.

No sense standing out here. Might as well head for home, see if she'd walked it off enough to get in the truck.

I got into my vehicle and fired it up, glancing at the lit windows of the little restaurant. The Gumbaughs were sitting in a far corner, away from the view, so hopefully they hadn't seen our little scene.

Irritation tightened my chest—*Meg needed to get a grip, and pronto.*

Night had fallen, dropping like a soft warm Indian summer blanket over the fields. With my windows rolled down, the air was filled with the soft twitter of birds going to sleep, and abuzz with crickets. The sky was just beginning to glimmer with the first stars; the road was a quiet black ribbon whose center stripe glowed yellow in my headlights.

As I drew abreast of Meg, I smelled dust and ripening grapes.

"Get in the truck." I didn't bother to temper my tone. I was pissed with her, and I didn't care if she knew it.

Meg opened the door. Got in beside me. Buckled her belt. Stared straight ahead.

"What was that little scene about?" I hit the gas, maybe a little harder than I needed to.

"I just needed a minute." Meg turned toward the open window. "I'm okay now."

"I don't appreciate the drama."

Meg finally looked at me. Tears had left shiny trails on her cheeks and her hair frizzed around her head in a messy halo. Her eyes were deep green in the light from the dashboard, and that sweet mouth of hers was trembling. "I'm sorry for that. I'm really so embarrassed." She heaved a giant sigh, shut her eyes, and hell if some more tears didn't slip down her wet face.

"Aw, Meg, dammit." I looked around for a spot to pull over, and did so in front of the giant, golden, metal scrollwork gate of one of the wineries, thankfully closed and locked at the moment. "I'm sorry I snapped at you."

Meg put her hands over her face and spoke through her fingers. "I know I shouldn't have talked to them like that. But I can't help it—Armand doing that to us felt like a total stab in the back! And I can't stand people like the Gumbaughs—pretentious country club one-percenters! They think they're so superior!"

I dug in the side pocket of my door and found a crumpled but clean fast-food napkin.

A sinking sensation filled my chest. I came from a family with enough money to buy a whole empire of country clubs, if that's what we wanted. *What would Meg think of me when she found that out?* Being rich didn't mean you couldn't do good in the world—in fact, being rich meant you could do more for others, and that's what we McCallums were all about.

"Here." I handed her the napkin. "It must have been really hard to hear from the Gumbaughs what Graniere said, when he was with your family for so long."

"Yeah. That mean, vicious old man." Meg opened the napkin and spread the whole thing over her face. She patted it carefully, then removed the wet paper. She folded the napkin up, and honked her nose with it hugely.

I felt a smile tug my mouth—*she was so unselfconscious*. She was completely authentic, and that was a rare thing. I'd never known a girl like her: someone who never seemed to notice how she looked and yet was so honestly, naturally beautiful—inside, and out.

"I'm sorry." Meg disposed of the abused napkin in the trash can behind my seat. "That outburst wasn't professional, and I know we need to present a united front when we interact with the public." She raised her eyes to meet mine. "You can count on me, Kane. I won't embarrass you again."

She was trying so damn hard—and she'd lost so much: her grandparents, her home, and the support of Graniere, who'd been a mainstay in her life. "You've been through a lot. You're still grieving. Don't be hard on yourself."

Meg turned fully toward me. Her gaze was resolute. Yep, those changeable eyes were definitely green, her lashes spiky with tears, and her mouth was so, so tender and pink and vulnerable. "You deserve better. We're a team."

I just couldn't help myself—I leaned over, and planted my mouth on hers.

God, she tasted good—a little bit salty, a little bit sweet, warm and slick and juicy as the ripe grapes I'd been sampling in the field.

She made a little noise that reminded me of the kittens we'd just found. She wound her arms around my shoulders, pulled me closer, and her tongue touched mine.

Now I made a sound—no idea what it was—and I was all over her, my hands sliding over her recklessly, my mouth greedy, starved for the taste and texture of her.

She wrapped around me as much as the awkward seats would allow, giving back as good as she got. Soon I had a hand on one round breast, and another on that firm ass. "You feel so good."

She slid a hand underneath my shirt and across my chest, stroking my abs and down past my belt buckle. "So do you, Kane . . ."

I took her mouth again, swallowing her moan, molding her body to mine.

Everything was in the way. The gearshift. Our clothes. The steering wheel. But I was relentless when I knew what I wanted.

And I wanted Meg. So much.

Heat and weight pooled in my groin in a way that told me that—however we did this, I wasn't going to last long. But I had to have her—it felt as necessary as my next breath.

Meg broke away with a gasp. "Kane!" Her hands were on my shoulders, pushing back. "You don't want to do this!"

But I did want to.

Couldn't think of when I'd ever wanted anything more.

My head and my erection seemed to be throbbing out the same message—*now, now, now, I need her now.*

My hands were on her thighs, pushing them apart so I could reach her center, still annoyingly hidden by clothing. Her eyes were half-lidded, swollen from crying. Her mouth was shiny and plump from kissing.

She'd be slick and plump below, too.

I wanted to touch her there. Couldn't wait to, in fact. I wanted to taste all of her. Feel her satiny skin with every inch of my own. Bury myself to the hilt in her and feel her waves rippling around me.

But she deserved better than a quick bang in the front of my truck.

"You're right." I flung myself back into my own seat. "What the hell was I doing? I'm sorry."

I turned on the truck with a roar. I rolled down the window so I could put my hot face into the wind as I drove, but there was no cooling off the rock-hard boner straining at my zipper.

The twenty-minute drive felt like an hour, but finally we turned into the Villier driveway. I parked beside the house. A lamp shining upstairs in her room looked warm and welcoming. Inside, Flea barked.

We were home.

Meg put her hand on my arm as I turned the truck off. "Don't feel bad. I wanted it, too." Her voice was low, husky.

I couldn't look at her or I was going to grab her, and this time I'd embarrass myself for sure. I got out, slammed the door, and fled.

CHAPTER FIFTEEN

Meg

I sat in the truck as Kane practically ran up the stairs onto the porch and unlocked the front door. I stayed there as he greeted Flea; I heard the big dog's happy bark. Kane put Flea on his leash, and they vanished out into the dark yard.

Of course, he needed to take Flea out for a pee before bed.

But it felt like Kane was running away from me, both of them were, as fast as they could go. *It felt like I'd never see them again.*

My stomach clenched around the *chile relleno* that wasn't sitting particularly well anyway. Why was I so upset?

I was the one who had stopped us from going any further.

I hadn't wanted to. Oh no. I'd wanted to keep going.

And so had he.

Stormy Sea Guy had kissed me like a dying man finding water in the desert. His hands on me had lit me up like a neon sign. I'd loved every minute of our kiss and, in fact, my only real regret was that I hadn't been able to kiss him with both of us naked and no gear shifter in the way. Hell, it wasn't just a kiss if I was honest. It had been a full-blown make out session, and headed for a lot more.

But a tiny, rational voice in my head had known the whole thing was a bad idea.

He shouldn't get involved with me, his employee. Too much could go wrong; and we both needed this 'partnership' to work more than we needed to get laid, though it hadn't felt like that in the moment.

And then he'd pulled back so completely . . .

Kane had withdrawn so totally from me that I couldn't even sense him in the dark as he drove. A peek at his face had shown it to be drawn in harsh lines. His mouth—oh, that pillowy but well-cut mouth—was a stern line. His jaw was tight, his eyes on the road, and his hand on the steering wheel was white with strain as wind blew through the window and tossed his hair. He reminded me of the pirate captain of my novels, gazing on a far horizon.

Clearly, Kane regretted kissing me and was being hard on himself. He was so honorable.

But when I'd tried to make him feel a little better—it was both of us making a mistake—his rejection felt total, devastating. An echo of how I'd felt when Maman had dropped me off at child care or left me with a sitter.

Every day Maman left me with whatever warm body she could find that would take care of me. After she started dating my stepdad, the excuse that she had to work wasn't the reason—she had just never wanted to be a mother. But her high school mistake had followed her into the new life she built in the city as she reinvented herself into the chatelaine of Raymond DeSylva's fancy art galleries.

I'd never been a part of that world. I was the secret shame she kept at home, out of sight and out of mind. I never even had a consistent nanny that I could have attached to. I was good at entertaining myself with my books. But my favorite activity was playing with the doll set my Gram and Grandpa had given me, inventing a loving family with that set of old-fashioned wooden dolls in clothes that Gram had sewn for me, and the simple plywood house Grandpa had built for them to live in. That imaginary family had lots of brothers and sisters, a loving mama and papa, and even a grandma and grandpa, all living together in one place.

That's why, before I settled into a career I was lukewarm about—at least Ray had paid for my education and I wasn't burdened with debt—I'd gone to find Gram and Grandpa Villier, and reconnect with a place where I'd felt loved. Where I felt like I belonged.

And look how that had turned out.

I got out of the truck and went into the house. I climbed the stairs, deliberately pressing on the one that creaked—*I was here.*

I knew every board and joist in this house. I belonged here. Kane was the one who didn't belong.

I paused on the landing, and looked into Gram and Grandpa's room. Fresh grief tightened my chest, bringing another rush of tears.

I'd had so little of them before they were gone.

And now I was only here in the family home by the grace of Stormy Sea Guy, and I better not ruin it with some messy relationship drama.

I went into my room and shut the door, leaning on it. The bedside lamp illuminated Sir Henry Puddlejump, draped decoratively across my pillows.

"Hey buddy! What are you doing here?"

Sir Henry stood up and stretched, complaining in his raspy voice. He was an outdoor cat for the most part, and this was the first time he'd come in and found my bed—but we did have a cat door for him that led into the kitchen, which must be how he'd got in.

"I bet I know what happened. Between that mama cat moving into the barn and Flea, you're feeling in need of some TLC."

Sir Henry padded over to me as I stripped out of my jeans and sweatshirt and wound his huge, fluffy self around my legs. "Yeah, you can stay with me. God knows I need a big, hairy boyfriend right about now."

I got in the shower, rinsing away the stress of the day. And yeah, the handheld shower wand spent a bit more time than usual pummeling the doorknob of my lady closet.

I desperately needed the release after what Stormy Sea Guy had stirred up in me, and afterward, I cried a bit with my forehead resting on the tiled wall—because nothing would ever come of rousing that sleeping tiger.

CHAPTER SIXTEEN

Kane

I sat down at my desk in the former parlor the next morning, feeling hungover—but I hadn't had a single freakin' drink yesterday, more's the pity.

My second cup of coffee still didn't seem to be doing the trick, even with a teaspoon of sugar, a rare concession to my low mood. If I could've stayed in bed all day, staring at the ceiling and jacking off to thoughts of Meg, I would've. Instead, I'd gone for another run, then done my usual workout with my travel weight set—normally that was enough to get rid of the cobwebs.

Not today.

Flea thumped his tail on the floor beside me as I arranged the list of names and numbers I'd gleaned from the invoices. Today's chore was the cold calls to arrange sale of the grapes. I glanced over at the empty dining room table.

I missed Meg.

I hadn't seen her at all after I got home last night and took Flea for a vigorous run through the moonlit rows. I'd jogged back, feeling slightly better, until I heard the rush of water in her shower. Damn, but she was taking a long shower!

And I couldn't help picturing her in it.

I'd had to take my own shower in cold water because the hot was gone by the time I got in. Which was just as well.

And then I hadn't seen her this morning either, though somehow she'd gotten up earlier than me, made coffee, and left a note next to the nearly full pot:

"I'm doing mildew patrol on the grapes, then I'll be working on my phone call list to get buyers out at my office. Text if you need anything. Have a great day! ~Meg."

She was doing her best to put us back on the friendly teammate track today, and I appreciated that.

Did I?

I probably did.

I should.

But looking over at the empty dining room table and not seeing her there left a hollow feeling in my stomach.

"Maybe I just need some breakfast, Flea," I said. "And thank God I have you there to talk to or I'd be talking to myself, and that's a slippery slope."

I went into the kitchen and whipped up some eggs. Having breakfast together had been nice. *Should I text her?*

"No. Get a grip, Kane. Eat your damn breakfast and get to work." I tugged my own hair, needing the punishment.

Flea whined, apparently thinking I was talking to him. I patted his head in reassurance.

Then I ate my eggs. And I got back to work.

But it wasn't fun. The phone calling was grim. Meg had taken half the list and left me half, and I ended up leaving a lot of messages on a lot of voicemails. I got my message patter down: "Hey, there. This is Kane McCallum calling. I'm the new owner at Villier Vineyard, and I understand you've been a customer of ours in the past. I wanted to let you know that we're about to harvest a crop of top-grade pinot noir grapes, and we're looking for just a couple more buyers who'd be interested in premium fruit. If you call me right back, we might be able to save you some. We're harvesting in the next week, so don't wait!" And my cell phone number.

I only spoke to one live person, a vineyard manager who told me "they were covered" for their winemaking needs this year. Hopefully, though, some would return my call, or the tentative sale to the Gumbaughs might be our only outlet.

I couldn't think of that. I couldn't let that worry take root—couldn't imagine all those beautiful grapes rotting in their harvest boxes . . . no. *No!*

First things first. I needed to firm up the harvesting team, because indications were good that the grapes would be ready in the next few days, especially if it stayed warm.

I called the teams I'd collected bids from, arranged for a crew with the most competitive bid, and lined it up to move forward when Meg and I determined the grapes were ready.

I finally stood, arching up to stretch, then bending down to put my palms on the floor. Then, needing to get my circulation going, I dropped to do a hundred push-ups, my go-to energy pickup.

I was closing in on the last ten, pumping as fast as I could, when I heard a delicate throat clearing. "Excuse me."

I paused and looked up, arms extended.

Meg stood in the doorway.

Had she been watching me do push-ups? Maybe she had, and maybe she liked what she saw, because Meg was pink in the cheeks and biting her lip. Her guilty expression made me want to cross the room and kiss that naughty mouth.

"What's up?" I jumped to my feet and put my hands on my

hips, elbows wide, the better to show off my guns. *Yep, I'd use any dirty trick I could to keep her looking at me.*

"I got an account!" Meg broke into a grin and clapped her hands like a kid at Christmas. "In fact, I think I might have sold all of our grapes! Except what you want to hold back for Peerless."

I grinned right back. "What? How'd you do that?"

Meg stepped into the parlor and walked around me, telling the story with much hand gesturing. She'd reached out to a couple on her list, people she'd met at dinner that were friends of her grandparents. "They confirmed that they usually buy from us; they were really shocked that Armand was going around badmouthing the crop. I gave them an estimate of the size of the harvest, and they promised to take all we wanted to give them— said they knew our grapes were the best and they were so glad I called." She gave a little skip, and twirled around for good measure.

Meg was wearing her field apron over work pants, but her frolicking made it seem like a big belled skirt circled her waist instead of that canvas work tote.

"Meg, that's awesome. A huge relief."

"Yeah, it really is." Meg stopped her spinning right in front of me, rose on her tiptoes and kissed me, a big smack right on the lips.

She jumped back and clapped a hand over her mouth. "Oh, dammit. I swore I wasn't going to do that, but there you were, looking so yummy. It won't happen again."

"But what if we both want it to?" I kept my hands where they were, tucked in my pockets to keep from reaching for her. "Can't say that you're the worst kisser I've ever had."

Meg's smile quirked up at one corner. This morning her eyes were brown, the color of a good lager with a few green bits here and there. "You damn me with faint praise, sir. Well, I haven't had a ton of experience."

"You haven't?" One of my brows quirked up too. "I'd think there were guys lining up to have a taste of that mouth."

The pink spread from her cheeks to her neck. *How far south did that blush go?*

"I've only had one boyfriend. In college. And I have to say, the whole thing was pretty lacking." Now the blush had risen to her hairline. "Maybe I *do* need a little more practice. To get it right."

"Oh ho. Are you flirting with me, trollop?"

Meg widened her eyes. "Trollop? You used the word *trollop* in a sentence, and you called *me* one. Now *that's* funny!" She threw her head back and laughed the big laugh I'd always thought she might have, but had never heard.

I couldn't keep my hands in my pockets anymore. Two strides, and I had them around her waist, cinched tight by the apron. I pulled her in, sliding a hand into her hair to angle her head, drawing her up against my chest—and she felt just right in my arms.

Not too tall, not too short, not too thin, not too fat. *Just right.*

But as soon as my mouth touched hers, I stopped thinking entirely.

CHAPTER SEVENTEEN

Meg

We were kissing again.

Standing up this time.

And *ohhhhhh*, Kane's mouth. His tongue. His hungry lips, his wicked teeth. And his arms, so pumped with muscle, holding me up against him since my knees were sagging. His big hands, one at the back of my neck, stroking my skin with his fingers, the other kneading my ass, rubbing me against him in a way that let me know I affected him.

Tingling pulses of feeling seemed to shoot out from every place he was touching me, and all of those pulses came together to make my center ache in the best possible way.

I lifted a leg and wrapped it around his, slid my hands under his shirt—one palm sliding up the column of muscle that was his back, the other caressing those abs I'd never forgotten the sight of. Everything I touched was firm and supple and silky, his chest hair just a little rough under my palm, his nipples hard pebbles.

So much better than my best imaginings from *The Pirate's Lusty Treasure*.

But it was hard to isolate each sensation, because taken together, what was going on between us felt overwhelming. I was falling headfirst into an unknown pleasure palace where *everything* felt good.

Yeah, I was a trollop all right, and if his kissing was anything to go by, the lackluster lovemaking of my last boyfriend was about to become a distant memory.

And then his phone rang.

"Ignore that," he muttered, his lips against my neck. "You sold the crop. We don't need any more buyers."

I nipped at his delicious lower lip, catching it between my teeth. "Not professional. You should get that."

"But I want you. Now." He lifted me by my butt, and my legs wrapped his waist automatically. He staggered across the room with me in his arms until we hit the wall.

I giggled.

Flea barked.

The phone rang again.

My legs slid down. I kissed him one last time, between the collar bones, in that sweet little dent at the base of his throat. "You should get that. Really, truly. This is game time for the vineyard."

"Argh," he groaned, and tore himself away from me.

That's what it felt like. Tearing something apart that was meant to be stuck together.

Like Velcro.

That was me, now. I was ruined. I'd become one side of a strip of Velcro, every little hook on it screaming "*Kane!*"

This was a disaster.

Kane grabbed the phone off the desk. "Villier Vineyard. Kane McCallum speaking." He spun to face me as he held the phone to his ear. His eyes were so, so blue. Not stormy this time. Just the bluest blue, a summer sky at noon, the color of the bluebird of happiness. I ran out of analogies as his eyes gazed at me—and even as they made me feel hollow, hungry, throbbing with need, I was also a feast begging to be consumed.

His feast.

Oh boy.

Kane turned away, and it was like a searchlight lifting off of my body.

"Yes? Thanks for calling back. Well, our grapes went fast. We're spoken for at the moment, but we're beginning a backup list. Can I get your best contact number?" He scrabbled around for a pad and pen.

I slowly straightened up from the wall. *Had I really just been thinking of having sex with my boss in the middle of a workday?*

With nothing but "what if we both want it" between us, in the way of an agreement?

Kane didn't have anything to lose.

But I sure did—and my heart was the least of it.

A draft of cool air blew in through the window, dousing my hot cheeks. I covered them with my palms, then caught his eye. I pushed away from the wall and gave a little wave as I headed for the door.

"Wait! Meg! Don't go!" He covered the phone with a hand, but I kept going.

I needed to stop thinking with my nether regions.

I was already wearing my apron, so I jogged to the barn, grabbed a barrow for the cuttings, and headed for the fields. The grapes were going to be ready in the next couple of days, and I needed to stay far, far away from Kane.

CHAPTER EIGHTEEN

Kane

Other than an acute case of blue balls, I was feeling a lot better about the harvest two days later when Meg pronounced the grapes ready for picking. She had studiously avoided any physical contact with me since that over-the-top kiss in my office, and as I got over the sting of her withdrawal, I couldn't blame her —much as it pained me to admit.

We were better off not getting any further involved, what with a business to run and living in the same house.

I'd spent the two days building the list of backup buyers, inputting all the contact info we'd collected into an email list builder to create a newsletter for advertising, and finalizing arrangements for the harvest team of pickers. Meg called in the main buyer she'd secured, Fred DiVine from DiVine Wines, to get a second opinion on our harvest date, and so he could get a look at the crop.

Fred was a short man with a girth that showed he liked living well. His full red beard put me in mind of one of the dwarves from the Lord of the Rings.

"So, you're the new owner, eh?" DiVine wrung my hand in a fist with the hardness of an oaken wine cask. "Meg tells me you're all right."

I glanced at her, but she had her eyes firmly on the vintner. "Fred DiVine. I thought your name had to be made up, it's so perfect for a winemaker."

DiVine made a loud noise I'd categorize as a guffaw. "Caught me! Or my daddy, rather. He thought it was clever, and legally changed our name. A man who's addicted to the grape will do anything for the business."

"I get it. I took one look at this place and fell in love," I said. Meg shot me a quick glance but this time I was the one to avoid her eye. "So. You're here for a second opinion on the ripeness of our crop?"

"Wanted to see what I'd bought, sight unseen." DiVine clapped Meg on the shoulder. "You've got a treasure here in this little lady. I hope you know that."

"Fred, gadzooks!" Meg squawked, but I spoke over her.

"I sure do know that, Mr. DiVine. The best first decision I made after purchasing this place was to hire Meg as my field manager."

Meg waved her refractometer, rolling her eyes. "Let's just go take a look at the grapes, shall we?"

I trailed the two of them, Flea at my side, as they tramped into the fields. DiVine certainly knew his stuff, and there was no shortage of opinions on the state of the grapes, the mildew we'd beaten back, the influx of birds and bugs attracted to the grapes now that they were at their peak, the dryness of the soil . . . nothing appeared to be off-limits.

A couple of times I bit my tongue, wanting to defend myself, Meg, or even her grandparents, but I hung back and kept quiet, waiting to see how Meg handled him.

And handle him she did. "Well, Fred, thanks for the input.

You can be sure Kane and I will talk over your recommendations. But for now, you agree we're ready for harvest? And still on board for taking as much as we can give you?"

"Sure am. These look to be in great shape." DiVine handled a cluster of dusty, almost-black grapes like a handful of quail eggs. "Let me know when they're in, and I'll be here to pick them up and cut you a check."

Meg

Harsh portable lights lit the field with a strobelike effect, and two generators rumbled as loudly as lawnmowers, providing power for the lights and the moveable trolleys that the pickers carefully loaded the fruit into. The rich, ripe smell of grapes filled the night air, so tangy-sweet that just breathing it was like eating the fruit.

I was here, there and everywhere around the field, my hair under a kerchief to keep the dirt out of it, wearing long sleeves, pants, boots, and my usual apron. I was nervous, I admit it, and when I'm nervous, I tend to get a little "fratchetty," as Gram would call it.

"Watch the rows. Make sure you get all of them," I barked at Diego, as he walked off carrying a tray of coffees. I was in charge of the all-night beverage and refreshment station, and making sure everyone had everything they needed.

We were going to try to bring in all of the grapes tonight, and that was no small feat, even with a big crew like Kane had hired. Fred DiVine was slated to pick up most of the grapes in the morning, the Gumbaughs would get the rest—and then we'd be letting the fields lie fallow before going into winter pruning.

I filled paper cups with coffee and water, set the beverages on a bamboo tray, and headed down the row where Kane was picking behind an expert grape handler who'd agreed to shepherd him through the process.

Kane wore a long-sleeved denim work shirt, tan dungarees, and a dark blue canvas work apron, same as mine, cinched around his waist. He wielded a pair of cutters in one of his gloved hands, clipped a bunch of grapes and swung to set them into the large plastic bin set on wheels behind him. He was closely imitating the man in front of him, who'd left every other bunch of grapes for him to remove.

"I brought coffee," I held out the tray in offering. "Or water. You two should stay hydrated—and you know the porta-potties are at the end of the rows by the house."

The picker, a Latino man in similar garb to Kane, whisked a cup of coffee off the tray and downed it in three quick sips. A nametag on his chest read *Enrique*. "*Gracias.*"

Kane kept his head down and kept going, but he was falling behind his mentor. He didn't take anything from my tray.

I frowned. "You guys need anything?"

"Nope. Just faster hands," Kane said.

"You're not doing too badly."

Enrique snorted. *"Any slower and he'd be a turtle,"* he said in Spanish.

I pressed my lips together to keep from smiling. *"I'm sure he's trying,"* I replied in that language. *"But he's from the East Coast."*

"Ah, city boy."

"Thanks a lot," Kane said stiffly.

"Just complimenting your quick learning," I said.

Enrique snorted again.

"See you later. I'll bring more in an hour or two." I walked off with my tray, and that time, I definitely heard Kane groan—and I couldn't help smiling. He'd never forget how hard the work was after tonight.

CHAPTER NINETEEN

Meg

Morning was lifting the last dew off the leaves of the grapes, gilding their edges with gold, when our team brought the last of the harvest in. I handed out hundred-dollar bills to each picker as a tip and, talking desultorily, they ambled off to the fleet of cars parked willy-nilly all over the lawn of the house. Engines roared as the team pulled out and away, one by one. Finally, Kane and I were left alone with a huge row of stacked yellow bins, each filled with grapes.

"Fred is bringing his own forklift for these." I checked off the tasks we'd completed on the clipboard I'd been toting around all night. I was wired from nonstop coffee. "I think it went well, don't you?"

Kane had sat down on an upturned, empty harvest box, leaning against one of the ones that held the ripe fruit. I glanced at him when he didn't answer—and grinned at the sight of his slack jaw and closed eyes. *He'd fallen asleep!*

I put down the clipboard and walked over to Kane, lifting one of his arms to loop it over my shoulder. "C'mon. Up you go. Just a little way into the house."

"I can do it," Kane muttered, but clearly, he couldn't. I helped him across the lawn, up the steps of the porch, and inside.

Flea trailed us as we navigated the steep wooden staircase, creaking and bumping, and finally down the hall and into Maman's old room. Dawn seeped through the lace curtains and filled the small, white-painted room with faint light, making the walls seem to glow.

I steered Kane across the room. He tripped over the coiled rag rug on the floor and collapsed onto the bed with its old-fashioned iron headboard and immaculate white *matelassé* cover. Dust and dirt rose from Kane's clothing in a pouf as he flopped onto his back.

"Oh no! You're a mess. Let me help you get your clothes off."

"Let's do it." Kane plucked ineffectually at his buttons.

"Just lie there. I'll get your boots, pants and shirt off so you don't get the comforter dirty. Or at least, no dirtier than you've already got it."

Kane shut his eyes. I heard a soft snore as I undid the laces of his boots—expensive Columbia hikers now caked with dust from the fields.

I peeled Kane's socks off, and moved up to his shirt.

Oh boy.

My hands were trembling as I undid the plain white plastic buttons on the denim work shirt. I flicked my gaze to his face—he was out. Jaw slack, eyes fluttering under his closed lids, long lashes a fan on his high cheekbones. *Why did he have to be so gorgeous?*

And yeah, the guy was dirty right now, but I was one of those girls who didn't mind a man's sweat if it came from honest hard work.

I undid the shirt's buttons all the way to his waist before parting the material.

"Oh, boy." I said it aloud this time as I gazed my fill on his upper torso—the man could be an underwear model if he decided not to work in a vineyard anymore. His chest was cut in elegant lines, his nipples tidy copper-brown disks, his abs . . . Oh, I could write a poem about his abs, all by themselves. Even softened in sleep, they were an anatomy lesson.

I tugged the shirt out of his pants and eased the cloth down off of one shoulder, then the other, threading his limp arms through the sleeves.

Amazing he could sleep through all of this, but who was I to argue? I had my hands on his sculped biceps, triceps, deltoids and pure yumminess—never mind where dirt had darkened his skin at the neck.

I followed a dark line of happy trail along his belly to his waistband. His pants were cinched by a supple leather belt, the kind that looks plain but costs a fortune.

I frowned at it. "Where did you get this?" I undid the hammered brass buckle, eyeing a tiny Gucci stamp on the metal. "Someone probably gave this to you. It has that 'I'm an impersonal gift' look about it." I tugged the belt out through the loops of his pants and set it aside.

I faced Kane's fly, and frowned—he was definitely bulging there, and though another quick glance up at his face assured me he was still sleeping, something *else* definitely wasn't asleep. "Maybe I should stop. What do you think, Flea? Probably a bad idea to go any further." Flea thumped his tail on the rag rug and whined encouragingly. "You're no help, big boy."

My fingers were itching to get those dirty pants off and see what was under Kane's boxer briefs. *Was that bad?*

"Probably very bad," I muttered. "I'm taking advantage of an innocent sleeping man so I can ogle him."

Flea thumped his tail again, and I glanced at Kane's face. Was his mouth twitching?

No. Just my imagination. Poor guy was sleeping like the dead.

I couldn't let this nice white bedcover get all ruined . . . I'd just get the pants off, put the coverlet over him, and sneak right on out.

I touched the button at his waist.

He twitched.

And *moaned*.

I yanked my hand away. Had that bulge at his crotch increased in size? *Maybe it had!*

But I couldn't stop now—I had to see what was under there. "Yep, I'm a bad girl. I really am." I undid Kane's pants button and tugged the zipper down—and his giant erection pushed both sides of the fly open all by itself. The smooth, dusky head of his shaft protruded from the waistband of a pair of black cotton briefs.

"Oh my," I breathed, feeling an answering surge of heat between my thighs. "Wow. That's . . . impressive."

I eased the fabric open, sliding the pants gently down his hips. He moaned again, and one of his hands fisted in the white material of the coverlet.

I had to work fast, before he woke up—never mind that my mouth was dry, my heart pounding, my girlie bits slick and pulsing, begging for action. Just looking at Kane was making me hornier than Esmeralda when Captain Bone ripped her bodice open and made her his cabinmate.

I eased Kane's pants down. *Was he lifting his hips?*

Had to be my imagination—or wishful thinking.

I worked the pants down his legs and slid them off. "There." I took a step back to observe my handiwork. "You really are something, Kane."

Heavens, but this man was perfect! Everything about him

was ideally proportioned—except for that piece of male equipment trying to fight its way out of his briefs.

Kane seemed to be having some kind of dream. He writhed, and now he was definitely thrusting his hips. Both hands fisted in the covers as he arched up, every line of his body taut with entreaty, his face drawn, his jaw tight. "Meg," he breathed. "Meg."

He was dreaming of me! My eyes bulged as I clapped a hand over my mouth, just like Gram when she was surprised.

Would it be so terrible if I—went down on him? Would he remember it? Was I taking advantage? Was this sexual harassment of my boss?

Because damn, but I wanted to feel that silky shaft in my mouth. Taste him, have him fill me—any orifice would do, at this point. I was a throbbing sex-crazed nympho, and passing the point of no return.

"Please," Kane moaned. "Meg, I need you." He tossed his head, clenching his fists so hard on the cloth that his pecs and abs rippled.

"Okay, I'll take that as consent," I whispered. "I'll just rub along and get mine too." I dropped my pants and undies quickly, then slid his briefs down. "Oh, my gracious, that's a wonder right there." But I was done looking. "I'm no expert at this. I'll just have to fake it 'til we make it." I stifled a nervous giggle by putting my mouth on him.

Kane's hands clenched the covers beside me. His hips thrust urgently. He filled my mouth, hard and hot and needy, so deep I almost choked.

"Meg!" a hoarse, haunting cry. I throbbed and ached in response, my whole body lit up with a matching longing.

I got onto the bed, straddled his thigh, and rode it with my hot, hungry core as I sucked and licked and teased. He tasted so good, salt and musk and delicious man. I couldn't get enough, taking him as deep as I could handle as he bucked and tossed beneath me.

I was shocked by how I was acting, and yet it was like discovering something I'd always known—I was a sex fiend, and it was awesome.

I bore down on Kane's thigh, rubbing my hungry lady bits against him in rhythm with my mouth on his shaft.

Suddenly I felt him beneath me—stroking, penetrating. His fingers, his palm, the heel of his hand—he touched me right where I needed it, hard and fast and confident.

I redoubled my efforts to bring him pleasure—dragging my tongue from base to crown, swirling as I sucked, then pulling him in as deep as I could. He was racked by shudders, thrusting blindly, and in only a few moments he came deep in my throat, finding his release with a shuddering groan. I shut my eyes and swallowed, taking all of him, delighting in a feeling of sexy, womanly power.

My own release came as he pinned my trembling clit with his thumb: a fluttering, clenching arc of white-hot bliss zoomed up my spine and threatened to blow off the top of my head. I heaved up and arched over Kane, throwing my head back in a gasping cry, and rode his hand until I collapsed.

I must have slept after that, because I woke with my cheek on Kane's abdomen, his heartbeat a slow, deep rhythm under my ear.

A ray of sunshine struck me directly in the eyes. I unsealed them reluctantly.

How long had we been lying there passed out? Had to be a couple of hours at least, from the height of the sun.

I was right where I'd fallen, splayed over Kane's naked leg, still wearing my shirt—and he was definitely not wearing anything.

I gently extracted myself and tugged Kane's briefs up. I covered him with half of the coverlet as I'd meant to do before I got distracted. I sneaked out and shut the door, leaving both him and his dog deeply asleep.

What the hell had we just done?

Was he really sleeping, or were we both fooling ourselves?

Probably the latter.

But because of the way it had gone down, I could pretend it had never happened. A girl was allowed one stupid mistake per lifetime, wasn't she?

I had to check my phone. Fred DiVine was supposed to be picking up the grapes this morning.

I went straight to the shower and washed myself from stem to stern.

Had I really just done what I'd done? Had he?

I giggled under the fall of water. Maybe I had a few of my French grandfather's "skills" after all.

CHAPTER TWENTY

Kane:

I'd had the best dream ever.

Meg was going down on me, all eager hands and talented tongue, just incredible. I was getting her off with my hand. She was so responsive, mewing and tossing, not even aware of the sounds she made because she was so intent on pleasuring me. She was insatiable, a little clumsy and rough, but so enthusiastic it didn't matter.

I came so hard I saw the back of my eyeballs. *Holy crap! So freakin' good.*

Meg was everything I'd always wanted and never knew I needed. A true partner in work, a lioness in bed, and what a laugh that girl had.

I could fall in love with her . . .

I woke as suddenly as if someone had hit me with a bucket of water, and I sat up so quickly my head swam.

I was naked, lying on top of my bed with half of the cover tossed over me. My shirt and pants lay on the floor, along with my belt, and my boots were set neatly beside the wall with the socks tucked in. The constant sense of need that had coiled in my groin, the ongoing half-boner of wanting her—that tension had eased.

It hadn't been a dream.

The sun slanted in at a late afternoon angle—I'd slept half the day away.

Flea raised his head off his paws and whined. "Where is she, buddy?"

He thumped his tail on the rag rug in answer.

I lay back and threw an arm over my eyes, not yet ready to get up and get on with whatever came next—things had shifted too deeply for me.

I "needed a moment" as my mom used to say, when she wanted to particularly savor something. She'd shut her eyes and smile a secret smile, clearly remembering something she didn't want to tell us boys about—and it likely involved Dad. We'd long ago learned never to barge into their bedroom.

Weird to be remembering Mom at a time like this—but maybe it was because sometimes the red glints in Meg's hair reminded me of Mom's dark red locks—because the feeling I had in my chest right now was something to be savored, the way Mom had savored her "moments" with Dad.

I got up eventually and dragged my sore body down the hall to the bathroom for a shower. I scrubbed at the evidence of the hard work of the harvest. It had gone remarkably well, and I was eager to see how things were progressing—*and to see Meg.*

How would she act? I bet she'd pretend nothing happened. I wasn't going to let her get away with that, because I wanted more of what we'd just done. A lot more.

I went downstairs, freshly dressed, with Flea at my heels. "Meg?"

No answer.

In the kitchen, a note was held down by one of her endless

pots of coffee. *"Fred DiVine picked up his grapes and I went with him to help with the sorting. I called Peerless to tell them that the grapes were ready; they should be by at four p.m. to pick them up. See you soon! ~Meg"*

I glanced up at the red enamel, old-fashioned clock over the door. Three forty-five p.m.

"Just in time." I splashed some of the (*still hot, thank you Meg!*) coffee into one of the new Villier Vineyard mugs we'd ordered as giveaways for the harvesters, and headed out onto the front porch.

The fields looked battered and bare, as if a stiff wind had torn through them and ripped away all of the fruit and a good deal of the leaves. Debris littered the once-tidy rows in ragged piles. Diego was already out there with a rake and a barrow. He tipped his straw hat to me from halfway down one of the rows.

Diego had been terrific; the only one of us besides the professional team we'd hired to have actually gone through a harvest, he'd been everywhere, lending a hand or a cup of coffee wherever it was needed. He'd been the foreman of the operation; I made a mental note to add a bonus to his paycheck this month.

I went to the remaining four bins that held the grapes for Peerless, lifting a cluster to my nose to smell them. "Perfect." Purple so dark it was almost black, the grapes were firm and round and bursting with juice—perfect for wine, but too tart for eating.

Flea barked as a shiny red Mack truck turned into the driveway, followed by a tan Range Rover emblazoned on the doors with the Peerless logo. The truck pulled alongside the bins, and I was relieved to see a forklift hitched to the back—loading the grapes should be one of the things we helped provide, but Meg must have let the Gumbaughs know our forklift was out of commission.

I advanced to shake Gumbaugh's hand as he got out of his

SUV. The truck driver was already unhitching the forklift. "Hey, Frank. Glad you could make it."

"I wanted to see what you were doing with the place, but then I heard the radio on the way over. There's a fire about ten miles north of us—and the emergency services are warning us to keep our eyes open, monitor its progress." Gumbaugh's highly colored face had hectic patches of red at the cheeks. "We've been through several fires in the last few years here in Sonoma, and we take them seriously. I thought I'd pass on the info since you're new here, and with this news, I'm sorry but I don't have time to chat. I told Hannibal just to load up the grapes and get back to our operation as quickly as he could."

Hannibal appeared to be doing just that, already driving the forklift toward the first of the huge yellow tubs.

"Thanks so much for the heads-up." I scanned the clear horizon to the north—I could just see a smudge of heavy gray gathering over the nearby hills. "Hope the wind backs off or it changes direction." As if in answer, a gust blew in, and rattled the house's windows.

Gumbaugh gave the grapes a cursory inspection. "These look fine. Here's your check." He handed a cashier's check for a nice round figure to me. "Now I better get back to Peerless and make sure we dust off the evacuation plan." His brows drew together as he frowned at me. "You have one, don't you?"

"Of course! Thanks again for the info," I said, with no intention of doing any such thing. *A wildfire threatening wine country?* The fire looked miles away. Gumbaugh'd had one too many martinis with his lunch.

The Range Rover pulled out, and shortly after, so did the Mack, its flatbed loaded with four harvest bins of Villier grapes. I savored the sight of it trundling down the driveway, then looked back at the check in my hand. "An even better sight. At this rate, I'll be able to start paying Dad back soon."

Flea sniffed the air and whined nervously, and I turned to look at the smoke off in the distance. *Had that gray cloud gotten bigger?*

Maybe it had . . . I felt a little hollow grind of anxiety beneath my breastbone.

Where was Meg? She should be home by now.

CHAPTER TWENTY-ONE

Meg

"I'm a coward." I sipped my margarita, careful to press my lips against the crusty salt on the rim—I loved the sweet and salty, together. "I'm afraid to face him after taking advantage of him."

Gabriella snorted. "You told me you had consent. I'm guessing he was no more asleep than you were."

"But you see why I needed an emergency drink." I glanced around our favorite little taqueria. Unlike the night when I'd eaten there with Kane, Jaime and Maria's place was packed. "You can tell the harvest's over." I gestured around the room. "Everyone's blowing off steam."

"And you certainly did, too." Gabriella's full, scarlet lips curved in a knowing smile. "It's about time you got some action with someone besides a paperback hero."

"I'll never give up my romances," I swore, laying a hand over my chest and rolling my eyes heavenward. "Captain Bone and highland Chieftain McFierce are my book boyfriends forever."

"Whatever rubs your hot spot, girl. So how do you plan to play it?"

"I was thinking complete denial." Imagining talking with Kane about what I'd done made my face heat, and I gulped the margarita too fast. "Ow! Ice cream headache!" I clutched my temples.

"And that's why I order mine on the rocks." Gabriella sipped her drink with dignity. "I recommend playing it cool, *chica*."

"Since when have I ever been cool?" My *chile con carne* had begun to congeal. I dug into it with a fork. "And what does 'play it cool' mean, exactly?"

"It means you act casual. No blushing, no acting guilty, no loaded glances. Business as usual. Maybe even a little distant." Gabriella forked up a bite of enchilada. "Mmm. I never get tired of the food here."

"Me either." We paid homage to Jaime and Maria's cooking for a few moments of lip-smacking silence.

The door banged open and all heads in the busy restaurant turned to look. A yellow-jacketed firefighter, complete with axe in hand, stood in the doorway. "Attention! There's a fire on the way, and this area is officially evacuated!"

Kane

I was running from a fire.

Smoke swirled after me with giant, reaching, clawed hands. I pumped my arms and stretched my legs, exerting all the strength I had to leave the monster behind; but there was no getting away —the fire chased me like a flaming demon from hell, and engulfed me in a black, terrible wall that brought me to the ground, choking and coughing.

Barking.

Right in my ear. I shoved Flea away as the dog woke me up. "Stop it, buddy!"

Flea vanished, and I coughed on the remains of the night-mare—only it was real.

Smoke. *I smelled smoke!*

I remembered Gumbaugh's warning. I flung the covers off and leaped out of bed.

The lace curtains blew in the ashy wind to cover Flea, who stood at the open window that looked out over the vineyard. He barked his alarm bark and turned to me, his eyes wide, his ruff risen huge on his shoulders. I'd gone back to bed for a nap, still tired from the harvest—and woken to the smell of danger.

I peered out. The hot wind lifting the curtain reeked of burning, and off in the distance an ominous orange lit the edge of darkness at the tree line of the hills.

I expected to hear sirens or something, but I heard nothing but the rattle of the branches of one of the old walnuts against the house. Still, something was seriously wrong. I yanked open the dresser, fumbling quickly into clean clothes.

I opened the door. The reek of smoke was stronger, filling the house.

"Meg?" I clattered down the stairs, Flea pasted to my side, and ran into the kitchen. "Meg!" She wasn't here. "Shit!" I grabbed my phone off the charger. Sure enough, *FIRE EVACUA-TION ALERT* scrolled across the screen.

I stood there paralyzed—I couldn't just walk away from all of this! And where the hell was Meg? I couldn't leave without communicating with her. Just then, I heard her Toyota revving as it pulled in behind the house. A minute later, Meg ran into the kitchen from the back porch.

"Kane!" Meg's eyes were huge and terrified, her hair wild over her shoulders. She waved a square transistor WeatherRadio at me. "The hills are on fire, and the Sonoma Fire Department has called for evacuation. We have to wet down the house and barn!"

"Are you serious?" It seemed crazy that the fire department wasn't going to take care of us. "Should we take the time to do that?"

"Yes!" Meg hurried back out and down off the porch to the side of the house, turning on the water at the hose there as I followed her. "We're too far out here to get any help with the house or vineyard. The fire department won't be able to do anything for us. We have to wet down the area ourselves."

"What about—everything? The house, the fields?" I felt dizzy. Things were moving too fast for me.

"Fred picked up his grapes. I've got the check in my purse," Meg yelled, squirting the side of the house with the hose on full blast. "And it looks like Peerless got theirs. We got the fruit in and distributed just in time!"

"This is crazy. It can't be all on us to save this place!"

"I'm sure the fire department's going to do all they can, but they have to worry about the more populated areas. Quit arguing with me and get moving, city boy!" Meg bellowed, clearly losing patience with my denial. "Hurry! Go turn on the other hose and wet down the barn!"

I was from the East Coast. I had only ever heard on the news about the fires in California that came on annually in fall, fueled by strong, hot winds just when the countryside was driest. Even with the smell of smoke thick in my nostrils and the flicker of orange to the north, it was hard to believe that we could be in imminent danger.

I ran to obey Meg, fighting a sense of unreality—*this couldn't be happening!* And yet the smell was stronger by the minute, and now I spotted bits of ash blowing past like foul snowflakes, lit briefly by our outdoor spotlights.

The hose by the barn had a high-pressure nozzle, and I cranked it on as hard as it would go and then aimed the stream at the side and roof of the barn. Meg was squirting the house, paying no mind to the open windows.

"Meg! We should close the windows so the air doesn't blow through!" I yelled. "It could help slow the fire!" She nodded and dropped her hose, running inside.

My mind finally clicked into analysis mode, mentally listing the things we should do and pack before we evacuated. I turned and wetted down the other side of the barn, squinting into the stinging wind.

The windows of the house slammed shut above me. Through the open door I heard Meg's footsteps as she ran from room to room gathering items.

And now I could see the leading edge of the fire, already on the foothills surrounding the flat area of the vineyard, a wall of dancing red and orange against the thick darkness of smoke.

Flea, plastered against my side, whined in distress.

I finished with wetting down the barn, and turned my hose onto the house Meg hadn't finished wetting down, just as she emerged, holding a cat carrier with a yowling Sir Henry Puddle-jump inside. She was also carrying a knapsack over her shoulders. "I got our laptops," she called. "We're taking your truck, right?"

"Right. Throw everything in back. You keep packing and I'll continue the hosing."

Meg gestured with the WeatherRadio she was still holding. "They're calling for our evacuation in this area immediately. But I don't want us to leave without . . ." Suddenly her face crumpled and her shoulders sagged. "Without anything."

"Meg, it's just stuff. Our lives are more important. The animals are important," I yelled across the yard. "Quit talking and get moving. We're going in five minutes, no matter what."

My strong direction seemed to get her moving again; it kind of felt good to give that back to her, after she'd verbally smacked me around when I needed it.

Meg opened the truck's passenger door and put Sir Henry in, along with the knapsack, and then ran back into the house.

The sight of Sir Henry reminded me of the kittens in the barn.

I pointed the hose at the ground around the house, propping it on a fallen branch, and ran into the barn.

Immediately the barn's familiar smells surrounded me, and my chest tightened—*I didn't want to lose this, not a bit of straw or broken shingle of it!* I hadn't had time to even explore this barn, let alone the wine cellar.

"No time, no time!" I didn't realize I was talking aloud until I felt the rasp of my throat. Even in the barn, the smoke stung my eyes and lungs as I ran to the old lawnmower where the kittens were curled in their cloth. A pretty orange tabby that must be the mama cat was there at last. She bounded up at the sight of me, hissing, but ran like a streak of light out through a broken hole in the wall.

"Shit!" Would the mama cat come back to her babies if the kittens went with us and we returned them later? Should I just leave them here, let all of them take their chances?

No. The babies deserved a chance to live, even if we couldn't save their mama. We could always turn them in to a foster place to be cared for and adopted, if the worst happened and we couldn't feed them.

I bent down and scooped up the old blanket with its precious burden, and ran out of the barn.

CHAPTER TWENTY-TWO

Meg

I clung to the sissy strap as Kane drove the truck out of the long driveway and onto Red Wine Lane, the aptly named country road that led past Villier. I couldn't resist a look back at the farmhouse: every light off, the barn a shadow against the even darker night.

I shut my eyes and said a quick goodbye to everything I'd ever loved. I opened them again and focused on Kane. "Where are we going?"

"We don't know where the fire is headed right now, so I think we'll be safest on the coast. The wind is blowing from that direction." The reflected light from the dash shone on Kane's tense, handsome face and his hands gripping the wheel.

I still clung to Grandpa's old WeatherRadio, but it had stopped burping out directives a while ago—the batteries hadn't been changed in forever. I set the thing down in the drink holder and glanced into the back seat, where the blanket containing the kittens rested in a cardboard box beside Sir Henry's carrier. Flea sat upright on the seat beside the box, his nose plastered against the window. The bed of the truck was filled with the belongings we'd triaged carrying out of the house, piled on top of Kane's travel bed.

The AC hummed, filtering the air somewhat, and I was able to breathe freely for the first time since I'd given Gabby a quick hug and run out of the taqueria.

"They have a shelter set up in Santa Rosa," I said, not that I wanted to go bed down in a gym smelling of sweaty socks with a hundred other anxious people.

Kane glanced at me. His eyes were red-rimmed from the smoke. "I don't want to go to one of those places. We don't have to. The truck's got everything we need, and we'll be a lot more comfortable and mobile. I hope you don't mind."

"I don't mind. I know you lived in this thing while on the road."

"Yeah, the mattress back there is pretty comfortable."

I stared out the window, feeling my neck heat up. We hadn't spoken a word about what had happened between us after the harvest . . . but in the scope of what was going on, sharing a bed was minor. "There's a vet clinic in Occidental, which is only fifteen minutes off of our route. That area isn't being evacuated. We should go by and pick up some formula and a couple of bottles for the kittens."

"Good idea." Kane hooked a right onto River Road, the main tributary to the coast and Highway One. I'd always loved the drive to the coast, meandering along the river, and lined with redwoods and stately pines—but today, our headlights were dimmed by the pall of smoke, and the country throughway was jammed with cars—most of them heading in the opposite direction than we were.

"Do you think they know something we don't?" I asked, pointing to the stream of cars going the opposite way.

"No idea." For the first time, Kane sounded stressed. "Why

don't you play with the car radio some, and see if you can find us any live news updates? Don't bother with your phone, though, there's hardly any signal out here."

"I know that." I sounded as testy as he did. I fiddled with the WeatherRadio, but it remained stubbornly silent, even when I took out the batteries and rubbed them on my shirt. Next, I scanned through the local FM stations, tuning in whenever I heard talking—but there was nothing available but general news, describing an out-of-control fire in the Santa Rosa area. "It's so frustrating that there's not more information."

"Maybe it's moving too fast for them to keep up with."

"Awful thought."

Kane glanced over at me. He must have seen my expression, because he took a hand off the wheel, and squeezed my leg. "We're going to be fine."

I wanted to believe him. I really did. I leaned my forehead on the cool glass and watched the trees flow by.

At the little village of Monte Rio, I pointed to a left turn leading over a bridge that spanned the river, a pleasant beach area in the summer. "Occidental is that way. I hope we can get there before the vet closes."

We pulled into the clinic's parking lot, and I jumped out of the truck and turned back to retrieve the box full of kittens.

The kits were awake, raising their wobbly heads and mewing pitifully. Kane had told me his dilemma in bringing them, and I agreed that he'd done the right thing. Catching the wild mama cat would have been impossible, and if the vineyard was okay, she'd likely come back to them when we returned.

I took the kittens inside, quickly explained our situation, and bought and paid for several cans of kitten formula and a couple of feeder bottles, getting a rough idea of the kittens' age and a quick set of shots, from the vet on call.

Fifteen minutes later, I stowed the box in the back seat. Sir

Henry yowled his displeasure from his carrier. "Yeah, buddy, I hear you. Got news—we're going to be all cozy like this for a while," I told him. "And you're officially a big brother, whether you like it or not."

Kane had been working his phone. "The news is behind and the phone lines are out, or just so crowded with calls they can't keep up. I was able to tap into wireless here at the vet's. They're still saying our entire area is under evacuation order." His jaw was tight when he turned to me, his eyes so dark a blue that they looked bruised. "We might lose it all."

"I'm sorry, Kane." I got into the passenger side. "I should call Maman while we have Wi-Fi signal. Did you get ahold of everyone you wanted to?"

Kane nodded, still staring down at his phone.

How much did I know about him? His background, his family?

Very little, it turned out, but then I hadn't been very forthcoming about my family either. We weren't a couple. We were employer and employee, and that was how it needed to stay.

Of course, Maman didn't pick up when I called, and it was just as well because I'd been giving her the silent treatment since she blew off coming to Gram's memorial. I left her a stilted message telling her I was safe and had evacuated, then I called my friend Gabriella.

"Oh my God, I was so worried! I've left three messages on your voicemail!" Gabriella exclaimed. "Are you okay? Is the vineyard okay?"

"We sure are," I chirped with fake cheer. "Kane, the animals and I are headed for the coast. How about you? Where are you going?" Gabriella lived in a suburb of Santa Rosa called Fountaingrove. "Have you guys had to evacuate?"

"Ha! Nothing left to burn over here," Gabriella said darkly. Fountaingrove had been hammered by fire the previous fall and was just beginning to rebuild. Gabby's house had been spared, but most of her neighborhood was still in the beginning of rebuilding. "We're fine. But wait a minute—you, Kane and the pets? That sounds awfully cozy. You haven't scooped me in on how it's going since your morning delight episode."

"Now's not the time, Gabriella, but I'll get to back to you on that," I said briskly. I slanted a guilty glance at Kane, who was still working his phone, apparently surfing the fire department maps if my glance at his screen was anything to go by.

"Oh, he's listening in. Gotcha. But you better follow through on what you guys started, okay? I'm rooting for you. Scoop me in as soon as you can."

"Of course. I'll call you ASAP." I ended the call. "We can go now."

Kane swiped to turn off his phone. "There's no signal on the coast. You only had two people to call?"

"Yep."

He didn't say anything more, just turned the key of the truck and pulled us out of the lot—but I was left with a hollow feeling in my gut.

I was so isolated.

Only two people to call—and only one of them actually cared, and she wasn't even a relative.

I could fall off the earth or die in a fire, and no one would notice.

CHAPTER TWENTY-THREE

Kane

I drove toward the coast, faster than the speed limit, but eager to get away from the tunnel of claustrophobic pines choked with smoke that surrounded the picturesque little town of Occidental.

The narrow, curvy road took both hands and all my concentration to drive as fast as I wanted to back to Monte Rio, across the bridge, hook a left, and on toward the ocean along River Road, following the mighty watercourse all the way out to the Pacific Ocean.

The river, low and calm in late summer, was only visible as flashes of translucent green through the trees bordering the road. If the situation hadn't been so dire, I'd have enjoyed the sights and sounds of the route—but I was intent on getting to the beach, where we could let Flea out to run on the sand, and hopefully breathe easier in the sea air.

I glanced over at Meg.

Her face was pale as she leaned on her car door, clinging to the handle, one cheek pressed to the glass. She looked wiped out, scared, and devastated.

I patted her blue-jeaned leg. "We're out of the danger zone with the animals. That's what matters at a time like this." The words sounded trite, but it was all I could think of to comfort her.

Yes, technically I owned Villier, but there was no doubt that in the time we'd been working together, I'd come to think of it as shared. *Ours.*

She had a claim of blood and birthright, while mine was that of money.

I turned the truck left again onto Pacific Coast Highway One. We headed over the bridge spanning the Russian River leading to the Sonoma State Beach Park. I turned my head to see the river as we spanned it, but a pair of turkey buzzards circling on an updraft gave me a chill.

I'd been working so hard to earn my place at the vineyard. To really feel like it belonged to me. I loved all of it: the old farmhouse, the tattered lawn it stood on, the decrepit wine cave with its treasured vintages, the cluttered, drafty barn, the fields, the oak tree on its knoll.

And all of it might be burning right now ...

I rolled down my window, gulping down nausea. Outside the vehicle, the stench of smoke was heavy, clogging my throat. I rolled the window back up again, feeling claustrophobic.

Meg glanced at me sharply. "Are you okay?"

"It's just sinking in that we might be losing the vineyard." I turned the truck into the coastal park, driving down a meandering, scenic road around windswept bluffs that overlooked a rugged beach. As I had hoped, the ocean breeze pushed the smoke inland, and visibility was better, though now sunset was approaching. "I don't know what I'll do if Villier burns."

Meg's hand patted my thigh, this time. Her eyes were green and swimming when I glanced at her—but she didn't speak.

She didn't take her hand away from my leg, either.

I was warmed by it. Anchored by it. I glanced down. Her nails were short, broken, dirty. A blood blister marred the nail of her pinkie.

She'd hurt herself trying to get us out of Villier, trying to set the place up to survive the fire, and helping with the harvest. I'd had to practically drag her to the truck to get her to leave when we did.

I took her hand, and it felt small and rough in mine. These were hands that had worked hard in every way there was, to help us and the vineyard survive.

The wave of nausea receded. *Whatever happened, Meg and I would figure it out. Together.*

I wouldn't want to have to do that without her.

I kissed her knuckles as I pulled into a parking spot overlooking the half-moon of beach, bluffs, and beautiful offshore atolls. One of these formed a picturesque open curve, giving the beach its name, Arched Rock. Pelicans flew by in a ragged arrow. Surf pounded on the beach below. If I half-shut my eyes, I could pretend the pall of smoke around us was the usual coastal fog. "I'm so glad we're together."

"Are we?" Meg's tone had gone flat. She tugged her hand away and opened her door. "Thank God the smoke is better down here."

She was asking if things had changed since our unacknowledged time together.

I could pick up the baton she'd thrown down, or I could ignore it for the moment, and leave her comment at face value.

Flea whined urgently from the back seat. I cracked the windows for the cats, and then got him on his leash and out of the truck.

No one else was in the parking lot or on the beach. The pall of smoke was dark inland, but the tide was low, and from where I stood, I could see all the way around the beach's curving bays. Once we reached the sand, I let Flea off his leash. He immediately bolted off to chase a seagull.

Meg walked beside me, her hands tucked in her sweatshirt pockets, her head down. That reddish-brown hair that seemed to have a mind of its own blew in the breeze, hiding her face.

Something swelled in my chest, a tight feeling. *I wanted to be with her*.

Facing challenges as a team. Making love as often as possible while we did so. *Together*. A couple.

I'd never felt like this before. Never.

But I had to go slow, say just the right things, because Meg was even more cautious than I.

Matching her speed as she walked along the silvery, pebble-strewn beach, I tunneled a hand into her sweatshirt pocket to take hers, knitting our fingers together. "I liked that. Earlier. Holding your hand."

She nodded, but didn't answer. Her hair looked like bright fall leaves against the silver-gray of the sand, the buff-colored cliffs, the slate-blue sea as the light dimmed. I liked its hanks and tufts, its messy coiling curls, but I didn't like it hiding her face. I squeezed her hand and brought us to a stop. "Meg."

She halted, but kept her head down. "What?" she sounded grumpy.

I kept hold of her hand and took it out of her pocket. I moved to stand in front of her. "Look at me."

"I don't want to." She let out a shuddering sigh. "You have so much. I have . . . nothing."

I totally got it. She had lost everything, including the people she loved most—and the economic and power differential between us was even bigger than she knew.

But I wanted to share everything with her. The suddenness of this realization was dizzying. She'd won my heart with her courage, hard work, passion and loyalty. I wanted to be the person she lavished those incredible gifts upon. Always.

"Meg. Please." I reached into her sweatshirt pocket and took out her other hand. Now I held them both. "Please look at me."

CHAPTER TWENTY-FOUR

Meg

I blew out a breath, looking down at Kane's hands holding mine. His were strong, clean, long-fingered—and raw on the palms and fingers with blisters earned during the harvest. Mine were rough, the nails broken.

Did these hands belong together?

Right now, they did. We'd become a team.

I finally looked up and met his gaze. The heat and intensity of his gaze made my eyes overflow. "I can't do this." I tried to pull my hands away.

Kane wouldn't let go. We struggled comically for a moment, tugging back and forth, until I gave up.

Once I did, Kane let go of one of my hands and reached out to smooth the tangled hair out of my face, his touch gentle. "I want to be with you, Meg. I can't say it more plainly than that."

I trembled from head to toe. *What was he saying?* "I guess you remember the blowjob, then. Must have been pretty good."

"I know you're scared." He tugged my hands, and I stumbled into his chest. He wrapped an arm around me, hauling me up against him. He pressed my hand against his left pectoral, covering it with his own. "Can you feel my heart, Meg? It's beating for you."

"Corny line, sir." But I could, indeed, feel the rapid thump of his heart. I could also feel a rigid hardness pressing against my belly. The evidence of his desire heated my core and loosened my knees.

This couldn't really be happening.

Not to me.

Incredible guys like Kane, who could have their pick of women, didn't declare themselves to an average-looking girl, with an average intellect, dubious prospects, and only two people to call in an emergency.

"I want us to be together, Meg. No matter what happens with Villier. I have—feelings." Kane's warm breath stirred the hair on my forehead. "It's okay that you're scared. I'm scared too."

I didn't know what to say or do. I leaned forward and rested my cheek on the smooth cotton cable of his excellent quality, summer-weight sweater. I shut my eyes so I could hear his thundering heartbeat, let it fill my terrified mind.

I rested against him until our pulses fell into sync.

He didn't move. Didn't push. Just held me there, waiting, as if he'd wait as long as it took.

Words seemed to float out of my mouth and hang above us in their own little conversation bubble. "I'd like to be with you, too."

Kane made a little muffled noise of satisfaction, and squeezed me hard. "Can I kiss you?"

I kept my eyes shut, but tipped my face up.

His lips met mine.

Oh. *This.*

This. Just like this.

So good, so delicious, so satisfying and yet hungry-making.

His lips, teeth, tongue were both feast and appetizer. A

conversation of feeling. A symphony of sensations. I'd entered a warm place swirling with wonder, and found myself not alone . . . for the first time ever.

The world could fall to ash all around us, and this would be enough.

Kane's hands wandered. Squeezed. Molded and stroked as he tasted and tormented.

My hands wandered too. I slid them under his sweater and explored his back, chest, abs, that tight butt.

"Mine," I murmured. "My Kane."

He felt so good: *warm, hard, strong, confident, gentle, urgent, rough but smooth* . . . Tastes and sensations were overwhelming me. "Meltdown alert," I muttered. "Mayday, mayday . . . I'm going up in flames."

"Burn me up, Scotty," he whispered back, and I could feel his smile against my neck.

"I love Star Trek, too, Kane. You're a nerd."

"Takes one to know one. And you're delicious." He was nipping at the base of my neck, sucking a spot just above my collarbone.

I was going to faint.

I clung to his shoulders for support, dropping my head back with a moan.

All of these clothes—they had to go.

Kane had found a way under my sweatshirt. "So good," he breathed, flicking my nipple with his thumb through my bra, making my whole body jerk in reaction. "We need to get naked."

"Yep, we're on the same page with that agenda." I was ready to find out what it was like to do it on a beach in broad daylight.

Flea barked nearby, and I came back to reality.

We were out in the open where anyone could see us making out like horny teenagers. Waves broke gently behind me. Light wind tugged at my hair. A fire raged somewhere in the hills near our vineyard. And right here, people were walking toward us on the dimly-lit beach.

I tried to pull away, but Kane held onto me too tightly.

"Dammit," he muttered. I turned in his arms to see a family coming toward us.

We removed our hands from under each other's clothes, and separated. I smoothed my hair; he tugged his sweater down over his hips.

The family waved, hurrying toward us. They looked frazzled and frantic—clearly, they'd fled the fire too. Flea barked at their dog, a fluffy white toy poodle, and romped toward them. "Maybe they know something about the fire."

"We'll have to find out. And then find a place to go." He turned back to me, and a cocky gleam brightened his storm-blue eyes. "Because this isn't over, and I want some privacy for what comes next."

CHAPTER TWENTY-FIVE

Kane

The family didn't know anything about the fire. Like us, they'd fled to the ocean, and were seeking any news they could find. But we'd come to the wrong place for that; there was no phone reception on the coast on a good day, let alone at a time when most of the cell towers in the area were down.

I was intent on getting us someplace quiet, safe, and private. I had things I wanted to do with Meg, many things, and they were making my jeans uncomfortably tight. And to judge by the way she clung to my hand, stroked my back through my shirt, and stayed glued to my side as we talked to the family, she was not averse to my nefarious plans.

We loaded Flea back into the truck and backtracked a bit to the little town of Jenner, but the few inns and bed and breakfast houses were already booked. So we headed the other direction, toward Bodega Bay, a little town to the south built around a boat harbor. Once again, everything rentable was already filled with other refugees. As night was falling, we ended up at Salmon Creek Dunes Campground, a state park outside of town.

Dark had rolled in fully, aided by the smoke, by the time we pulled into what seemed like the last empty spot in the whole maze of the camping area. Thankfully, the paved pullout was surrounded by its own shelter of arching, wind-sculptured cypresses. As I tucked the truck in under the trees, I felt an incongruous sense of coming home.

I *was* home. Anywhere on this wild, beautiful coast was part of my new life. *Our* new life, together.

I'd been so intent on getting established at the vineyard, knocking down one challenge after the next, that I hadn't let myself consciously form an attachment to anything but that bit of land—and yet it had happened anyway.

Meg and I cleared out the bed of the truck to expose the mattress that I'd spent so many nights on camping cross-country. As we did so, I realized that, even if the vineyard burned, I was ready to settle down out here. I was ready to embrace this stretch of rugged, stunning Northern California area, say goodbye to Boston and all its emotional connections, and call this wild coast home.

"I forgot to grab the electric lantern." Meg's eyes were just a gleam in the overhead light of the truck's interior cab. "I was so freaked out when I packed, just thinking about things that we wouldn't want to lose if the house burned. Not what we might need for camping."

"It's okay. Behind the seats in the extended cab, I still have most of my camping stuff. First aid kit, flashlight, a couple of pots and pans, emergency coffee. You know, the basics." I caught her eye and gave my best attempt at a sexy, panty-melting grin. "Including condoms."

I was taking a chance on that one, but Meg snorted a laugh. "You're a real Boy Scout, aren't you?"

"Always be prepared." I removed the last of the boxes that Meg had thrown into the back of the truck. "We can sort all this in the morning. I'm curious what you thought was worth saving."

Even without much illumination, I could tell she was blushing. "You're probably going to laugh. Mostly it's just sentimental junk. But I did grab some food for us and the animals, and I even threw in clean linens for us to sleep on."

"Why don't I get a fire going in the pit, and we can fix something to eat. Then I'm ready for bed." I wiggled my brows.

Meg pretended not to see, and turned away. "Okay."

Using the flashlight from my camping stash, I forged around the campsite in the trees, gathering enough wood to get the fire going.

The overhead light inside the truck shone on Meg's hair as she made up the bed.

The sight of her doing something so domestic for *us* did something to me, not only hardening my groin, but filling me with that same chord of homecoming I had been feeling about this entire place.

I finally got the fire going and a couple of cans of chili heating in a pan on the grill over the flames. I returned to the truck.

Meg was seated in the middle of the bed. She was holding one of the kittens, feeding it from one of the bottles we had picked up at the vet's. I could hear frantic mewing coming from the cardboard box.

"Whoa. Cuteness overload." Meg looked adorable with that little tabby tucked in the crook of her arm, its tiny paws wrapped around the nipple as it sucked like gangbusters.

"There's another bottle already to go. As you can tell, the little rug rats are hungry."

I took a moment to tie Flea up and climbed in with her. I picked up the black kitten with the white mittens and bib on his chest. I hugged him close against my side, though he wriggled and writhed, and offered the tiny rubber nipple. He didn't seem to get the idea, and I had to keep squeezing drops onto his nose until he licked them off. Finally, he caught on that he had to suck the nipple, and then there was no stopping him.

"The vet said we need to feed them every three hours." Meg set her satiated kitten back in the box, refilled her bottle from the open can of formula, and picked up the calico, who was mewing frantically. The poor little thing had to go through the same learning curve that Mittens had to, but it was so hungry that it caught on fast.

I got back out and dealt with the chili, serving it into a spare pot and leaving one portion in the one it'd cooked in. I reached behind the seat to pull out a bottle of Meg's grandpa's garage wine that I'd grabbed on the way out. No label on it but the year, 2012, was written on the side in Sharpie. I pulled the cork with my pocketknife corkscrew.

The fire smelled of the pine cones and manzanita branches I'd built it from, and the glint of stars through the trees overhead reminded me of all the days I'd spent on the road with Flea. "This is like old times, isn't it, boy?"

He whined and leaned against me. I sniffed the wine as the fumes rose from inside the bottle. *Nice and robust.* I took a sip from the bottle. Swirled it in my mouth. "Delicious pinot noir, Flea. We've got a good thing going, if that fire doesn't eat the whole place up."

Meg climbed out of the back of the truck and joined me to sit on a log in front of the fire. "I smell something good."

"Taste this." I handed her the wine bottle.

She looked at the date. "Oh, a nice one. This should be good. Everyone says 2012 was an excellent grape year."

"What makes a good grape year?" I cocked my head.

"The optimum balance of rain and sun hours to create maximum wine grape perfection." Meg sniffed the aroma rising from the deep green bottle. She took a sip. Shut her eyes, really tasting it. "Mmm. Delicious."

Her throaty purr hit me right where it hurt. I shifted uncomfortably. "Wish I'd had time to grab a whole lot more than one bottle."

She nodded, and sniffed again. Sipped. Swirled. Swallowed. I watched the muscles in her throat. The firelight on her skin was like gold dust on white silk. "That's very nice." She smacked her lips, smiling. "I love it. Mmm, yes."

Maybe I could get her to make that sound in bed . . .

I handed Meg her metal pot half-full of hot chili wrapped in a towel. She set it on her knees.

"Luckily I had some disposable spoons in the camping kit." I passed her one with a flourish. "Your dinner, milady."

"Looks fabulous, milord." She reached in with the spoon and took a bite. "*Tres* gourmet, sir. Your cooking skills are superb, not to mention your meal presentation."

I enjoyed the sight of her digging into the pot with every sign of enthusiasm. "One of the many things I like about you, Meg. You're the only girl I know who could eat canned chili out of a cookpot and call it gourmet."

Her smile slipped. "I'm that classy, huh?"

Clearly, I'd hit some sort of nerve, when I'd only meant to compliment her. I was so drawn to her lack of pretension, her willingness to make the best of every situation. I stared at her, unsure how to respond. Meg bent her head further, so that her long, tangled hair hid her face from me.

I set aside my chili, putting it on the log beside me. "Meg. Stop it."

"Stop what?" She was shoveling in the chili now, clearly barely tasting it.

"I meant what I said in a good way." I groped for words. "You're so different from the girls I knew at college. They were

157

fussy—always worrying about breaking a nail. The last girlfriend I had would have hated camping with me in my truck, eating canned food out of a pot. She would have wanted something fancy, like braised brussel sprouts with goat cheese. That's all I'm saying." I shook my head. "I was just trying to tell you that—I really like you, Meg. Everything about you. I'm sorry if I mucked it up somehow." I picked up the wine bottle and took a swig.

Meg set aside her saucepan. She looked around for a napkin, but there wasn't one—so she wiped her mouth on the back of her sleeve.

I smiled at that, too. "You're so pretty. Can I kiss you again?"

"I'm going to taste like chili," she whispered.

I handed her the wine bottle. "Palate cleanser. I'll kiss you after I eat, and then we can both taste like chili." I picked up my portion and took a bite. The stuff tasted like what it was—reheated canned beans *con carne*, and not a great brand. "Ugh. This is gross. You were nice to say it was good."

Meg moved closer and draped an arm over me. She pressed against my side. "I'm sorry I'm so sensitive. I know I can really be prickly about money stuff. It's a hard topic for me."

This was the first time she'd opened up about her past. "Tell me more." I kept eating so as not to spook her.

She sighed. "My mom had me in high school when she was seventeen. I don't even know who my dad is—she doesn't, either. She had several boyfriends she was sleeping with at the time. She wanted an abortion, but my grandparents pressured her to keep me. After I was born, Gram took care of me while Maman went to work as a cocktail waitress at the country club in town. She always had aspirations, and she was beautiful. Not like me."

I set my chili aside. "You're gorgeous." I reached over and tipped her chin up so I could look into her face, study her change-able eyes, strong cheekbones, that wide, supple mouth. "Unusual."

She shook her head. "Not like her. My mother is *beautiful*. Everyone says so. Petite, dark-haired, great skin, hourglass figure. She takes after my grandpa, who was also small with black hair. Gram was tall and big-boned, taller than him, actually. I look like Gram. Anyway, Maman studied hair, makeup, fashion, interiors —art history. She's smart and sophisticated in spite of being a teen mom. She met my stepfather at the country club. He fell for her, and she got the life she wanted."

I took a swig of wine, swirling it in my mouth, then handed her the bottle. Meg sipped as well, and went on. "Maman took me with her to San Francisco when they married. I was five, and I missed Gram, Grandpa and the vineyard so much. I don't know why she took me—she certainly didn't want the complication of a kid. I think she did it to hurt my grandparents—they said it broke their hearts." Meg stared into the fire, took another sip off the bottle. "The sad thing was, I was just farmed out to random babysitters until I was old enough to stay home alone."

"I'm sorry that happened. But you're not alone anymore." I gently took the bottle from her, set it aside, pulled her into my arms, and kissed her.

I gloried in the silky cave of her mouth, the tentative touch of her tongue, the taste of the wine on her lips. I threaded my fingers through her thick hair and tilted her head so I could nibble and lick the pulse beating in her pale, freckled neck.

And then I reached over and hauled her onto my legs, ignoring her squeak of protest. "I'm too heavy, Kane!"

I finally had her where I wanted her—asprawl across my lap, with my hands free to roam. I slid one hand up around her breast, palming it through her sweatshirt, flicking her nipple and watching her twitch.

"You're perfect." I kissed her again. "Your sexy mouth. Your long legs and great tits." I slid my hand down and around to grip her behind. "And this ass is sweet and solid. The perfect size. I can't wait to take a bite of it."

"You're so bad." She hid her face in my shoulder. "I'm not small."

"And I'm not either. Now shut up and let me make love to you."

Her eyes opened wide at that. "Oh." Her eyes went dark, a mossy color with amber and brown flecks. Her lashes were thick and blonde at the tips, her lips warm and pink. No makeup anywhere on her face. I loved that.

I chuckled as I got my legs under me and stood up with her in my arms. It was fun to make her squeak. She hid her face in my sweater, her arms looped around my neck. "You better not drop me. I can't believe this is happening." She giggled.

I could listen to that sound all day.

She felt just right in my arms. Once again, I had that "coming home" feeling, like a search I didn't know I'd been on was over. "Time for the love nest."

CHAPTER TWENTY-SIX

Meg

Kane carried me over to the truck. I'd left the tailgate down and the back of the camper shell open, so he set me on the tailgate and nudged my knees apart, stepping in to fill the space in front of me. He smelled of pine and smoke and man, and he took my face in his hands and kissed me some more.

And just when I thought we must be moving on to the main event, he moved away, but kissed me holding my face, my jaw, turning me this way and that by a handful of hair. Tasting and teasing, nipping and sucking, but not touching me anywhere else.

I couldn't stand it. I opened my legs further and pushed into him, rubbing my torso against his pelvis as I stroked his thighs and butt.

"Tell me you want me," Kane whispered harshly in my ear. "Tell me what you want me to do."

I didn't really know, couldn't put it into words. Sure, I knew the mechanics of sex, but John, my first and only lover, had been even more inexperienced than me—what they called a "minute man." I'd never had a single orgasm with him in our time together. I'd had a few drunken hookups after that, also barely noteworthy.

I didn't know what I wanted, but I knew it was *more*. More of these sensations. And for us to be naked while there was more.

"I want you, Kane." I fumbled with his belt buckle. "All of you. Clothes. Off. Inside," I panted. It was hard to form any sort of coherent thought when he was nipping and sucking on my neck like that, his hands stroking my jaw, tangling in my hair.

Kane raised his head to look around briefly. "I guess we are still out in the open at a public campground. Okay. Your wish is my command."

We got into the back of the truck. Pulled up the tailgate and shut the camper shell. The campfire flickered on the outside of the darkly tinted windows, a muted dance of patterned light that cast glimmering shadows over our bodies as we stripped, fumbling and laughing in our clumsy eagerness.

Was this really happening?

I must have spoken aloud, because Kane said, "Yes. Yes, it is, and I wanted it to from the first minute I saw you on the porch of the house in your frumpy black dress, dispensing wine."

"Impossible." I helped him tug off his jeans. "You were so out of my league. I looked terrible that day. I wanted to look terrible."

"But you couldn't. And you need to know your worth. Then, and now," he said mock-severely. He bore me to the mattress beneath him, sliding a leg between mine.

I rocked against it unabashedly. "You can keep showing me. Telling me how beautiful I am. I could learn to live with that."

He growled, moving down my body to cup my breasts. "Look at these glorious tits. So full and ripe and delicious. Like pick-your-own peaches." He sucked and nuzzled and swirled his tongue until I was bucking against his thigh between my legs, providing a hardness upon which to hurl myself.

And then his fingers slid down and started doing some magical things, and I felt a heat, a tightening, a sensation like a spring being wound and wound and wound until surely, surely it would fly into pieces. "Kane! I want you in me before . . . before . . ."

"Before you come," he said. "That would be nice for me too."

I smacked the chiseled globe of his tight ass. "Get that condom on, sir."

He rolled away for a second, groping in the pocket of his jeans to find the aforementioned item. "We'll take longer next time," he panted, finally seeming to lose his cool as I took the opportunity to lick his nipples and fondle him, interfering with the process. "But right now, I need to . . ."

"Get inside me. Fill me up, big boy." I started to laugh, enjoying my power—but he took it back a second later, lunging up over me to part my legs and kneel between them to put his mouth on me.

I arched up off the bed in shock, in bliss, and cried his name as the revelation of his tongue broke over me. I writhed, unable to deal with the intensity, with my shyness, with the atomic detonations going off in my nervous system.

And just when that tightly wound spring began to burst, he moved up over me and took my mouth with his, bracing his arms and sliding deep into me in one sure, hard stroke that made me scream into his mouth with the incredible, verging-on-painful, overwhelming sensation.

I began to come as his hardness nailed a spot deep inside of me, some interior bull's-eye that I'd never known existed until now. Skyrockets blew up behind my eyeballs in tiny explosions and my brain became a buzz of white light as my body disintegrated—but seconds later I was back, obliterated and reborn, with him pounding into me and chanting my name: "*Meg, Meg, Meg . . .*"

163

Shudder moan full overflowing goodness all over everywhere starbursts of wonder and then . . . *collapse.*

Harsh breathing. Pounding hearts plastered together. One body ended, another began, who knows where. Didn't matter.

One flesh.

And then slowing . . . deepening. Colors shifting.

New smells—sex and sweat and him and me.

Sniff, sniff. "Mmm." The scent of the warm place behind his ear.

A gradual separation.

I was here.

He was there.

But he was still in me.

Tears pooled in my eyes and rolled down my cheeks. No idea what I was feeling, but it was too intense to handle.

He was still kissing me—so soft, so sweet, so good.

I kissed him too. His pillowy but chiseled mouth. The edge of his jaw. That place at the base of his neck where his pulse beat its own pure song.

Oh wow . . . so amazing. The whole thing.

How sad we couldn't always fit together like this.

And now, he was leaving.

Kane withdrew and sat up. The sense of emptiness in his wake was alarming; fresh tears rolled down my cheeks. This was too much. Just too, too much.

I kept my eyes shut and threw an arm over them so he wouldn't see my tears.

I was being ridiculous.

He mustn't know that I'd cried.

"Gotta deal with this condom." Kane dug around at the side of the mattress. "Found the paper towels. All good."

The practicalities were intruding. *Ugh.*

Even in the tinted-window darkness, I was afraid to look at him.

To see his eyes.

To know if that moment of incredible union had only been one-sided.

I was afraid.

Scared out of my mind, truth be told.

It was like his cock was a spear, and instead of my vagina, it had nailed my heart.

I was in love with this guy.

He could destroy me with one laugh, one disparaging remark, one little put-down. How freakin' embarrassing and totally terrifying.

He was sure to leave me, just like my mother had. *Just like everyone I loved did.*

I had to stay casual. Detach.

Big deal. We shagged. So that's what good sex was like. "News to me! Ha, ha," I whispered. I made myself shrug, practicing casual, my forced smile a grimace in the dark.

"Hey." Kane tugged the comforter out from under me and tossed it over us. His body against mine felt incredible: *silky hard rough hot strong*—a collection of contradicting sensations, every one of them fascinating. He moved in close, spooning me from behind. He embraced me, sliding one arm under my head and neck, pillowing my head on his bicep. He took my limp fingers in his hand, lifting my sheltering arm off my face. His other hand explored my stomach and hip, trailing warmth and delicious shivers in the wake of his fingers. "You okay?"

I couldn't speak. I was still too choked up. I nodded. To distract him, I pushed my butt back into his groin, and gave a little wiggle.

That worked.

He grunted in satisfaction, and that wandering hand slid around my backside, bold and naughty as it explored my cheeks and cleft—and then over my hip to my front and into my lady garden, where he strummed, stroked, and teased until I forgot what my name was, let alone what I'd been worried about.

CHAPTER TWENTY-SEVEN

Kane

We slept eventually. I woke up later to feel her hands on me, and I slid into her from the side. We fit together perfectly—a completed puzzle.

The camper shell was too low to allow the full range of positions I had every intention of exploring, but we both fell asleep after that, Meg snuggling in my arms.

Flea shaking his collar loudly outside the truck, his way of waking me before he had to resort to something as crude as a bark or whine, got me up the next morning. Light sifted through the tinted windows of the camper shell, lacy with the shapes of trees.

The sun was up.

I lifted my head cautiously, not wanting to wake Meg. She'd migrated out of my embrace during the night and lay with her back to me. I took a minute to savor the look of her tumbled hair on the pillow, the triangle of her shoulder covered by the blankets, the inch or two of pale skin that I could see.

I knew how that skin tasted, smelled, reacted to me. The thought made me twitch—again. I'd never get enough of her.

I eased out from under the comforter and tucked it around her, sealing in the warmth. The temperature had definitely dropped here on the coast, and goosebumps rose all over my bare skin as I wrestled carefully into fresh clothes.

I eased the camper shell open and the tailgate down and got out, then closed it back up again.

Fog wrapped our campsite in a soft gray blanket, thinning overhead to show blue sky—whew. *Not smoke.* The California coast was often foggy in the mornings, but likely this would be gone by noon.

Flea whined as I laced on my running shoes. "I'll take you out to the dunes, buddy. Just hang on."

I wanted Meg to feel cared for before I left. Not to worry a bit about where I was, or what I was feeling about the new level of our relationship.

I eased the truck's door open and got into the camping stuff in the back seat, taking out the one-burner camp stove, a gallon of water, the coffee and French press. I got the hot water going and measured out the coffee. While the water was heating, I went back to the truck and dug in the glove box for my journal and a pen.

I'd written in that journal every day on my trip, sometimes just a log of weather conditions and mileage driven—but I hadn't touched it since I bought the vineyard. *What did that mean?* I wasn't sure, but it unsettled me.

I tore out a page and drew a big heart on it. Inside the heart I wrote:

"Meg. You are so beautiful. Never forget it! Hope you slept as badly as I did and feel as good as I do this morning. Took Flea for a run on the beach. Enjoy some coffee, I'll be back soon for more."
~xo, Kane

I almost wrote "I love you," on the note. There was actually a squiggle where I started to, and then turned it into *xo*.

I stared at the page for a moment.

There was already a heart on the note. I didn't want to over-whelm her, scare her off.

I hadn't seen her face last night, or this morning, to be able to tell if the incredible connection I felt with her while we were making love was mutual. I'd never even called the act that before . . . Sex was *getting laid, doing it, screwing, hooking up, the hori-zontal mambo*—but I'd never *made love* until last night.

It had *felt* mutual.

She'd trembled in my arms. I'd tasted the wet salt on her cheeks. She'd cried . . . but I'd been wrong about a woman's reac-tions before. Did she feel the same about me, or about what we'd done?

Maybe she'd cried because she was inexperienced, or missed her boyfriend . . .

I had to keep my cards close to the vest. Make sure of her.

I stared down at the note.

The heart was too much. The note was too much.

I crumpled it and stuffed it in the pocket of my sweats. I tore out another sheet from the journal.

"Took Flea for a run. Enjoy the coffee, I'll be back for more soon."

I drew a winky smile, and signed it *K*.

Better. Nice tone, a little teasing/sexy, not too sappy.

I put Flea on his leash and found a doggie bag for the inevitable. By the time I was done with that, the water was boil-ing. I poured it into the French press, gave it another five minutes while I located a couple of mugs in the camp stuff. I pushed down the plunger, poured myself a cup, and tucked the folded note under her empty one, a plain white china mug I'd bought at a garage sale on my cross-country trip.

I tweaked Flea's leash and said, "Let's go, boy. Clear the cobwebs out."

The dunes went on a while as we hiked through the park area, and I kept Flea leashed until we crested the last of them.

The beach was long, silver-gray and looked endless, veering away in a curve into the fog, the sand smooth with low tide below a surf line littered with washed-up kelp and driftwood from nearby Salmon Creek. A flock of seagulls rested near the glassy pool of the blocked-in creek area.

Flea strained toward them, whining eagerly. I let him go to have his fun, and he bounded away joyfully to ruin the seagulls' morning. I moved into a steady jog along the hard sand near the water.

The thudding of my feet near the ocean's edge reminded me of the hammering of my heart against Meg's, how perfectly right she felt in my arms, against me, under me, beside me, over me. *What was it about this girl?*

I wasn't just flattering when I told her she was beautiful. She really was, in a unique and natural way. But I liked so much more than her looks. She was brave, smart, hardworking, loyal and soft-hearted. She loved the grapes, the land, the house, even the oak tree . . . all of which I loved too.

I was in love with Meg.

The realization burst across me. I never felt this way before. *What a rush!* Excitement bubbled up inside, filling me with energy. I ran faster, breathing the salt air, an unbelievable natural high of exhilaration.

"I'm in love with Meg!" I shouted into the fog, over the breaking waves. "I'm in love with Meg!"

Flea, loping after me, barked in agreement—*he loved her too.*

We ran all out until I'd burned the burst of feel-good hormones off to a manageable level. I headed back to camp.

I couldn't tell her yet. But I could show her.

CHAPTER TWENTY-EIGHT

Meg

I woke up, feeling . . . *different.*

Something had seismically shifted inside of me—and my insides felt delightfully tender, wonderfully bruised. I smiled before I even opened my eyes.

Emptiness beside me told me that Kane was gone. We'd finally fallen asleep wrapped up in each other, so I had this moment alone to savor everything that had happened.

I wriggled deeper under the covers, keeping my eyes shut, stretching my arms and legs to feel the aches of a well-sexed body.

Because, oh yes, that's what I was living in this morning. A body that had been used and abused in ways the Captain hadn't even considered in *The Pirate's Savage Pleasure.*

Stormy Sea Guy was amazing in bed, as well as everything else he was good at.

But I wasn't.

Low Self-Esteem was back with her twin cousins, *Self-Doubt* and *I'm a Loser.*

I'd been such a klutz: overenthusiastic, my inexperience obvious as I clanked our teeth together when we kissed, bit him too hard on the nipple, and practically threw out my hip because I came so hard . . . but Kane had been great about it, praising me, encouraging me, taking over when I lost my way.

I finally opened my eyes and looked out the tinted window of the truck's camper shell. The shapes of branches and leaves made patterns on the glass, gray and black, moving like the design on a nature-themed ball gown, a dance of nature.

I imagined myself in a mist-gray silk gown with this pattern on it, dancing by the light of the moon in Kane's arms—and he'd be wearing a whole lot of . . . *nothing*.

"You're so bad, Meg." I clapped a hand over my mouth, glancing around, but of course, Kane was nowhere around. "You probably scared him off." My inner critic had shown up to the ball with a vengeance. "He's probably off wondering how the hell he can let you down gently and get things back to coworker status."

The kittens and Sir Henry mewed, hearing me, interrupting my bout of self-flagellation. "All right, me hearties. I'll get you guys and gals what you need."

I was naked and badly in need of a shower, but this was camping, so I made do with rubbing down relevant areas with a wet wipe and getting dressed in a fresh set of clothes.

I climbed out of the back of the truck and let Sir Henry out into the bushes to do his business. He sniffed around the area, commenting loudly about the circumstances of his removal from all that was beloved and familiar, but finally decamped to do the necessary.

The kittens, meanwhile, wailed a trifecta chorus of hunger. I fixed Mittens a bottle and carried him over to the picnic table to feed, where I found coffee already made and a sweet note from Kane.

"How cute. He'll be back for more. That could be taken a number of ways, couldn't it, buddy?" I asked the kitten as I sipped on the lukewarm but strong brew. "And he's thoughtful. Left me a note and a cup of coffee."

Yes, I could have wished for a declaration of undying love to match the one resonating in my own heart, but the flirty note was enough to calm the Inner Bitch Goddess who had been trying, in her dysfunctional way, to prepare me for the worst.

I put Mittens back in the box after his feeding and picked up Calico, inserting the nipple of the refilled bottle into her tiny, pink, yowling mouth. "I think he likes me, baby girl. Or at least, the sex was good enough for him to leave a note."

"The sex was fantastic." Kane's voice, warm with mirth, whirled me around.

"You're back." A stupid grin lit up my whole being.

"Had to come back for more. I told you I would." Kane took me in his arms for a kiss that went on awhile, squashing Calico between us until she squawked in protest.

Kane stepped back. "Oh geez. Poor baby."

"She doesn't mind, as long as the nipple's in her mouth." I reinserted it. "Tabby still needs feeding if you want to do one."

"Flee from a fire and go camping in my truck. Spend the night making love to a beautiful, amazing woman. Go for a run on the beach with my dog and come back to feed kittens and make more love. Someone pinch me, I must be dreaming." Kane's dark blue eyes were bright in a face flushed with exercise. "Right now, it's hard to even worry about the fire part."

"Now I know you're delusional." I was still idiotically grinning. The phrase "I got lost in his eyes" had new meaning as we gazed at each other.

The tabby kitten's shrill cries cut through our staring-and-smiling. Kane headed for the open door of the extended cab. "Your honorary papa cometh, bringing nourishment, Tiger."

I gazed down at the patchwork kitten I held. "All calicos are female, so I know you're a girl. Now that we have Mittens and Tiger, I think you deserve a name. And all of your color patterns remind me of art. I think I'll call you Frida, after my favorite artist, Frida Kahlo."

Kane came back to sit beside me at the picnic table, holding Tiger in the crook of his arm as the kitten enthusiastically tackled his bottle. "We should see if we can get any reception on the radio. Find out what's going on."

"Absolutely. If we can't pick up anything, we can walk back to the ranger booth and see what they know."

"That's my girl," Kane said to the kitten. "She's a smarty-pants, that Meg."

I felt my cheeks catch fire. *He called me "his girl!"*

I took Mittens back to the box and turned the key on the truck, getting power to the radio. Kane joined me, but we couldn't pick up any news. Neither of our phones had signal, either, so the internet was out.

"Guess it's the ranger station," I said, glancing up to meet Kane's eyes.

But he wasn't looking at my eyes. He was staring at my mouth. "What's another half hour from now? Or an hour or two? How about putting off reality for a whole lot longer?"

"Don't mind if I do," I said, and leaned in to kiss him.

Kissing Kane was a revelation. I'd never known a kiss to be more than a collection of actions that were a prelude to the main event: lips, tongue, thrust, thrust, hands going elsewhere, pants off, intercourse. That had been pleasant enough.

But our kisses were a whole language in themselves, as if our minds and hearts connected through the exquisite sensations and tastes of our mouths. I felt him asking if I liked this, or that, and I told him yes, and yes and again yes, more please and thank you . .
.

And it didn't have to lead to more.

Unless we wanted it to.

And we did.

So we tied up Flea with a bucket of water nearby. He promptly went to sleep, tuckered out from his beach run. We stowed the kittens back into their box. And then we, too, climbed into bed and took our time tasting, touching, and experiencing, and finally, catching up on sleep.

We were trapped for the time being in our love cocoon, and I was in no hurry for it to end—and neither, from what I could tell, was Kane.

CHAPTER TWENTY-NINE

Meg

We turned into the driveway of Villier Vineyard three days after we'd left. Though we'd finally been given the "all clear" to return by the fire department, I loosened a breath I'd been holding as the familiar old farmhouse, shingled silvery barn, and trees shading the patchy lawn came into view—all unscathed. Beyond the homestead, neat lines of picked-clean grapevines stretched into a distance punctuated by my beloved oak tree. "Oh, thank God."

"I know. I had to see the place with my own eyes, too." Kane pulled the truck into its usual parking spot beside the house. I glanced over at my car, realizing, for the first time, that it had never even occurred to me to take it. That sure said something— about what, I wasn't sure yet.

But I knew this: *I'd left in one emotional state, and returned in another.* I was in love, and ready to admit it—at least to myself. The last three days had been some of the best days of my entire life.

Not that I'd told Kane so. He hadn't talked about our relationship either, though I was starting to hope that the softness in his gaze when he looked at me had good possibilities.

Kane leaned over and planted a kiss on my lips. "I think we should clean out your grandparents' stuff and move into the front room." He wiggled his brows. "We need the space."

My cheeks warmed as I thought of all the hijinks we could get up to with more space—but sadness accompanied it, too, as I remembered Gram and Grandpa. "I'd like us to get a new bed, if you don't mind."

"Of course." Kane had his phone out as he opened the door of the truck. He scrolled to something on it and dialed. "I already shopped for one while we were camping and had some signal."

"Wow. I'm easy, I guess." It stung a little that he'd taken my consent for granted on something so personal, a whole new level of commitment.

Kane seemed to pick up on that and came back to me, standing so close I could feel the heat of his body. I kept my eyes down and my hands busy, bundling up the linens for washing. He took hold of my chin and tipped my face up. I finally met his eyes.

"I get what this means to you, and it's a big deal to me, too." His stormy-sea eyes were penetrating, seeing deep into my inse-curities. "We can take as long as you want, to really move in together. But I'm serving you notice here and now, that I want you and me in the same bed, at some point, every day. Being in one big one, officially together, just saves time and hassles."

I laid a hand over Kane's heart.

That gesture had begun to be "our thing," a way I could tap into something primitive that connected us. Under my palm I could feel his rock-steady pulse, elemental, a life force we shared. Within seconds of touching him, our bodies fell into the same rhythm.

I could shut my eyes and just be with him. In that darkness, with our hearts in sync, I could believe that he really wanted to be with me, too.

I had to take a chance. "Okay."

Kane drew me in for a tight hug and an exaggerated big wet kiss that made me laugh. "You'll see the wisdom of this choice in the days—and nights—to come."

"I'll look forward to your efforts to prove yourself." I winked.

Kane stopped me with a hand on my arm. "Hey. I don't want to seem like I don't understand what it means for you to move into your grandparents' room. But honestly—think about it. Wouldn't they be happy about this? About us?"

Tears prickled instantly, filling my eyes. "Yes," I whispered. Grandpa's wish for me to have someone had taken the form of little jabs about future generations and the vineyard; Gram had just wanted me to find love.

Kane drew me into his arms and kissed my forehead.

"We'll do a little ceremony to honor them." His ears were pink at the tops. "My parents taught me to honor those who went before. Dad would say it helps their ghosts rest easier. His parents died when he was around my age."

"Oh, I'm sorry." I covered my mouth with a hand. Kane hadn't talked of his family hardly at all. "That must have been so hard."

"That's how Dad understood that I needed to find my own way when Flea and I took the truck and left the East Coast. He took a walkabout, too. When they died. Only it was on a boat. He took a trip around the world, and that's how he met Mom in the Virgin Islands."

"What do they do? Your parents?" I picked up the box of kittens and followed him as he went up the steps of the porch to unlock the house.

"We have a family business." He didn't elaborate, so I just

took the pillowcase full of bric-a-brac he handed me, and carried it into the house along with the kittens.

Kane wrangled on the phone, ordering the bed he'd picked out, and negotiating for the old one to be taken away while I lugged the dirty clothes and linens to the laundry room.

The interior of the house still smelled like smoke, with an unpleasant tang from the garbage under the kitchen sink that we'd forgotten to remove. I opened all of the windows as Flea and Sir Henry, set free by Kane, romped through the house.

Putting away the sentimental items I'd gathered so hurriedly made me shake my head. Weird what you thought you'd miss if it was burned in a fire: a few framed old photos of the vineyard in its beginnings, Grandpa's dried up old fountain pen, two tattered photo albums, the logbook diary Grandpa had kept for years noting the things he'd done daily in the vineyard, my mother's cheerleading jacket, my own birth certificate and records, a couple of delicate teacups rumored to have been my great-grand-mother's that I'd thrown into a Tupperware container, along with the costume jewelry Gram had left me.

Nothing had any real value—no stocks, bonds, coin collections or diamonds.

But that's the kind of people we'd been—just regular folks, with our own idea of what mattered. Except for Maman. She owned all of those trappings with my stepfather, and none of them resided here.

I was lucky to still live in the family house at all, and to be able to put our things away on Kane's walls and in his desk and china cabinet. It took a lot longer to put things away than it had to gather them together, since it was such a reflective process.

I was catching up on the laundry with the kittens toddling around my feet and Sir Henry in the doorway keeping watch on them, when I heard the deep "Woof!" Flea gave for visitors.

Kane was out in the yard, working with Diego to deal with

the chores left undone by our evacuation, so I continued sorting the laundry. He could deal with whoever had stopped by—likely a neighbor, wanting to talk about the fire.

I liked this domestic stuff. *Was that wrong?* Was I betraying women's liberation that I enjoyed soaking the potholder we'd got steak sauce on while camping, and spraying the dirt on Kane's jeans with stain remover? I even liked sorting the colors and turning on the load, making sure the water was on warm wash and cold rinse.

We also used less energy by hanging up the laundry by hand. Until now, I'd never touched Kane's laundry, but it gave me a happy little zing to load our clean laundry, mixed together, into Gram's old wicker basket.

I went out through the back door and down into the sunlit yard. I shook out the sheets and draped them over the clothesline, anchoring them with a pin here and there, and then hung our jeans on another line.

I grinned, looking at the jeans. They looked nice side by side —like silhouettes of us together.

So silly. But dang, I liked the way that clothesline looked.

Male voices approached; Kane and someone else. I hung up the last of the load, picking up the basket and turning around with a smile to greet whoever had dropped by.

Kane came around the corner of the house, talking animatedly to a man about his age. "And this is the back yard—oh, hey. Here's Meg." Kane gestured to me. "Meg, this is my buddy Dan. We go back to grade school."

I took a step toward Dan, still holding the laundry basket on my hip. "Hi, Dan. Welcome to Villier."

The guy checked me out with a long slow stare and a wolfish grin. "Aren't you a long tall drink of tasty housekeeper."

My hair was down and messy, and I'd put my work apron on

over my jeans—but his assumption rankled. My smile faded. "I'm Meg *Villier*. Not a housekeeper."

"Isn't that nice." Dan didn't seem to get the association. Hands on his hips, he surveyed the land. "Good buy, Kane." His tone implied I'd been included in the purchase.

I narrowed my eyes, studying the guy. Dan wore a blue polo shirt with a designer logo, hipster chinos, white canvas sneakers for that casual touch. He reeked of country club, which was a look I was well aware of due to my stepfather's penchant for the style.

"Meg's my . . . vineyard manager." Kane stumbled over the title. "I hired her when I bought the land."

"Nice package deal, like I said. How enterprising of her to do the laundry, too," Dan smirked. "What else are you good at, Meg?"

My spine stiffened. I dropped the laundry basket. "Wow. Aren't you a prize asshole." I stomped past them, heading for the back stairs.

"Spitfire," Dan drawled. "Temper to go with that red hair."

I yanked the back door open and went inside. Sir Henry bolted, scared by the noise; the kittens mewed. I scooped the babies up from their crawling and put them back in the box.

Raised voices outside—Kane and Dan were yelling. Maybe Kane was sticking up for me now, but the damage was done as far as I was concerned.

He hadn't claimed me. He hadn't defended me. He'd let his jerk friend imply . . . I shook my head, too enraged to complete the thought.

I hurried upstairs to my bedroom and bath.

I had to get out of this house. Go somewhere to vent—and I only had one friend. *Gabriella.* I was way overdue to catch up with her.

I went into the bathroom and locked the door. While

shucking off my dirty clothes, I called her on my cell. "Gabriella? It's Meg. Got time for a cup of coffee?"

"Better than that! Come over to my place and have a margarita! You can tell me all about what you guys did during the evacuation. I hope it was fun!"

"See you in half an hour." I jumped in the shower and soaped up.

With every slippery touch of my hands, I remembered Kane's touch on my body.

I'd thought we had something. Something really special. But the very first time a friend of his comes by, the guy is a total jerk? What did that say about the man I'd fallen in love with?

The man I had opened my heart to had let his grade school "buddy" insult me. He had not made one move to claim or defend me in front of that creep.

And if Kane had friends like Dan, what did it say about *his* character?

How could I have been so wrong about him?

"Dammit!" I growled like an angry bear and pounded on the old tile wall—and one of the pieces came off and landed on my toe. "Ow! Crap."

That settled me down as I had to attend to the little bleeding wound. I dabbed it with a washcloth but it just bled more.

I was acting like a lunatic—that's how crazy this shit made me. I needed to be calm, cool, collected. I could not show how much this had hurt me. "I'm so bad at relationships," I muttered. "Dang it."

A knock on the door sounded as I was getting out of the shower. The cut on my toe was still bleeding. "Meg?"

"I have nothing to say to you."

"Meg, let me in. I want to talk about this."

"Too little, too late." The hurt of having Kane stand by and not defend me welled up, reminding me of all the times my mother or stepfather had talked over my head, disparaged me, dismissed me. And the sneaking suspicion that I *had* been a convenient package deal made my stomach hurt.

"Dan is a jerk. But you're overreacting." The reasonable tone of Kane's voice stoked my fire.

I yanked the door open and faced him, wearing nothing but wet skin and a towel.

"I don't think so. I know what I heard, and it was you, blowing me off. We were about to move in together, *and you didn't even tell him we were dating.*"

Kane's pupils dilated as his gaze swept over me. My almost naked state was affecting him—*good!* "You hurt your toe. It's bleeding."

"I know."

"You should put something on it." He frowned at my toe. "I can take care of it for you." He took a step closer.

I backed away, leaving a bloody footprint on the floor. "No, Kane. I will do my own first aid, thank you very much." I liked how frosty I sounded. "Did you have something to say to me? An apology, perhaps?"

"Dan is an asshole. You're right about that. Anything I would have said, would have just given him more ammo." He was still staring at my toe.

"Then why are you his friend?" I put my hands on my hips. *Who cared if my towel fell off?* It's not like he hadn't seen it all before.

"Our families are friends. I don't hang out with him anymore, but we've known each other a long time . . ." His gaze was bouncing between my toe, and the towel coming undone at my breasts.

"You know what? I don't care about your long-lost childhood buddy." I cocked a hip and the towel slipped further. "I don't care, except for the fact that it makes me wonder about *you.* I don't know anything about your family. Or their business. Or how you could have a friend like Dan, who would travel all the way from the East Coast to see you, and who would put down your girlfriend like that." I glared. "Assuming, of course, that I *am* your girlfriend and not just an employee with benefits. A nice 'package deal.'" I made air quotes with my fingers.

"Of course you're my girl. We're moving in together. With all that means." Kane pushed a hand into his hair, frowning. "I'll tell you everything you want to know." His eyes shifted to a spot to the left—still no eye contact. "But I don't want to have this conversation when you're angry. And bleeding. And almost naked."

The towel dropped into a puddle at my feet. "And I don't want to have this conversation at all, right now." I let him stare at my naked body and wish he could have it or cover me up, if his agonized expression was anything to go by. "I'm leaving to see a friend. It's probably a surprise to you that I have a friend—but hey, *your* friend was certainly a surprise to *me*. Gabriella is ready to drop everything and pour me as many drinks as it takes to feel better. I'll see you when I see you. I'm off to get hammered."

I gave Kane's chest a shove so he stepped backward, and I slammed the door, pleased with how the brittle old wood echoed as I banged it shut. Nothing quite so satisfying as a good door slam. I'd done several of those as a teen, trying to get Maman's attention.

Then I stood there, for just a moment, to see what he would do.

Would Kane turn the knob, come in to plead with me? Take me in his arms and kiss me? Soothe my hurt with his hands, his tongue, his magical love baton?

Part of me really hoped he would. If he opened the door, we'd make up. Maybe do it in the shower.

Okay, we'd *definitely* do it in the shower.

I was dying to do it with him in the shower, quite frankly, after three days of camping sex.

Then I'd go to Gabriella's, feeling a hell of a lot better than I did right now . . . but Kane didn't open the door.

He stood on the other side for a long moment. Maybe he was waiting for me to make the first move.

And as I stood there, naked and shivering, it came to me how much I really didn't know Kane McCallum at all.

He walked away—his footsteps heavy on the uncovered wooden floor. The squeaky stair creaked on his way downstairs. Flea gave a whimper as he reluctantly followed his master with a scrabble of toenails on wood. We really needed to put some carpet strips down for that boy.

I felt abandoned. Ugh. *My least favorite feeling.*

Even though I had sent Kane away.

Even though I claimed I wanted him to leave me alone.

I dried my bloody foot off with toilet paper, and stuck on a Band-Aid. I threw my clothes on, dragged a comb through my tangles, grabbed my purse, and headed down the stairs. My feet moved fast as I sped through the house, avoiding looking into Kane's office, and ran to my car.

I didn't want him to see me go. Didn't want him to witness my frantic flight, notice how I jumped into the car and shut the door too hard. How I turned the old Toyota on with a roar, sneezing at the musty smell, and then tore a gash in the dry grass as I pulled away.

I didn't want him to see me crying.

CHAPTER THIRTY

Kane

Meg's car roared out as I poked Dan in the chest with a fore-finger, so hard that he yelped and took a step backward. "Hey!"

"You have no idea what you just did."

"Got you in hot water with your 'package deal'?" Dan rolled his eyes.

Those were, in fact, the exact words Meg had just used. I grabbed Dan's shirt in my fist. "Meg's been through a lot, and you're being an asshole. She's pissed, and rightly so."

Dan slapped at my hand. "Ah. Well, if you don't tap that, I'd like a chance to."

"Shut up about her!" I shoved Dan again. "We're dating, okay? I didn't tell you because you're always such a prick to the women I go out with. I don't know what your problem is."

"What, I don't bend over and kiss your ass like the rest of the world?" Dan spat onto the grass. "By the way, I hooked up with your old girlfriend. Hayley and I are a thing now. Don't know why you didn't put a ring on that babe. I just might."

"Whatever! I don't care. Why the hell did you come here,

anyway?"

"Some friend. Don't even offer me hospitality for coming all this way to see how you were doing with the fire and all." Dan looked around at the disarray of the harvest tubs and the messy yard, covered with leaves and broken branches from the windstorm that had driven the fire. "Slumming it, is how you're doing. I'll be sure to let your parents and our friends in Boston know."

"You do that, Dan. And you can tell anybody you want to that I have no intention of returning. I love it here."

"Ingrate." Dan sauntered back toward his car. "Never deserved all the breaks you were given. Just had to throw it all away. Well, good luck to you with all of this." He gestured to the spoiled grapes that Diego was shoveling into a wheelbarrow for mulching. "Looks like it's a real success."

"Just get yourself gone, Dan."

Dan got into his Beamer and tore a big circle in the grass, overriding the one Meg had left as he pulled out.

"What a dick." I should have cut ties with Dan long ago.

Diego, never breaking his shoveling rhythm, nodded. "Glad to see his tailpipe, Kane."

"No shit." Diego and I had built a casual but positive working relationship, and I was glad he wasn't mad at me about Dan's behavior like Meg was. I shrugged off my shirt and tossed it over the porch railing. I needed to feel the air on my skin and sweat off the aftermath of the encounter with Dan and the fight with Meg.

I grabbed a shovel and went back to filling my own wheelbarrow with spoiled grapes. These were the ones that had been too far gone or fallen to the ground during the harvest, and in the days we'd been gone, they'd ripened far past their prime. Their sweet fruity smell swirled around me as I moved them out of the yellow plastic macro bin we'd thrown them in into the barrow. *If we had a forklift that worked . . .*

What had provoked Dan's visit? There was no way that vain,

lazy prick had driven all the way from the East Coast just to look up an 'old friend' and make fun of my new venture. He had some bigger ulterior motive.

And how was I going to patch things up with Meg? I could kick myself into next week for the paralysis that seemed to have taken over when Dan had said what he had. I'd been in shock at his behavior. I tried to remember if I'd heard judgmental slurs like that from Dan before—but I hadn't hung out with him in years, and I was glad of that now.

It was past time for me to find out what might be going on at home that had sent Dan all the way out here.

"Are you okay finishing up, Diego?" I swiped sweat off my forehead with my arm. "I've got to make a phone call."

"No problem."

I put away my shovel in the barn's toolshed and headed into the house.

The interior was neat and peaceful, but it felt empty without Meg. My belly hollowed at the memory of her hurt face and angry words.

I took a quick shower, changed, and went downstairs to my desk, where I took my phone off the charger and speed-dialed Mom.

I'd kept in touch with the family through monthly check-ins, Mom's minimum acceptable contact level.

"Kane, honey. It's been too long!"

"Hey, only a month since my last call. Happy to report that the fire passed us by and the house and vineyard are okay."

"Kane—wait—what?" Mom's voice cracked. "What fire?"

"Oh, sorry for scaring you, then. I thought it might've been in the news and had you worried. We were out of cell range while we were evacuated. We had to camp on the coast for three days."

"Oh, son of a beehive!" Ruby Michaels McCallum was the daughter of missionaries, and ever careful about taking the name of the Lord in vain. "I've been working on a major brief, and haven't had time for anything else. Your dad might have heard about it."

I heard the rumble of Dad's voice in the background.

Rafe McCallum was the head of our company, but Mom was the neck that turned the head, as the old saying goes. My parents were truly a team. They'd married when Mom was only nineteen, but she'd continued on with college to get her law degree. She had a private practice, of which McCallum Industries was the main client, but certainly not the only one.

As long as I could remember, Mom and Dad had both been working—but with six sons, they'd needed a lot of help. Mrs. McKnight, our housekeeper, had provided daily oversight and cooked meals, along with a string of overworked nannies. Both parents were home every night to problem-solve, read to us, supervise bedtime and generally get their hands dirty parenting-wise. Through all the ups and downs of a busy family and business life, we'd maintained a strong center that rotated around the powerful love between Mom and Dad.

Maybe that was why I had such a high standard for who I wanted to be with. Maybe I had unrealistic expectations for what marriage could be—because I'd seen what my parents had, and I wanted something like it.

"I miss you, Kane. Tell me everything." Mom's papers rustled. "I'm setting this aside so you can give us a full report. I'm going to put you on speaker so your dad can hear too." The phone crackled a bit as Mom set it down on the desk.

"Hey, Pete." Dad's warm baritone made me smile.

"Hey, Dad. Glad I caught you both. Let me bring you two up to speed." I filled them in up to current times. "We were lucky. The vineyard was fine in spite of the fire passing nearby. Diego, our worker, and I are almost done mulching down the mess left over from harvest."

"You mentioned that you hired the young woman who owned the vineyard as a manager. Is that the Meg that helped you find a buyer for the grapes? How is she working out?" Dad asked.

"It's going fantastic." I ran a hand into my hair. I wasn't ready to tell them about our relationship yet—not when we'd just had a fight and I wasn't sure how to proceed. "Meg is smart and hardworking. She's really earned her keep as a vineyard manager. But I'm going to have some fences to mend because Dan showed up out of the blue and insulted her."

"Oh, that boy. He's always had a chip on his shoulder about you," Mom said.

"Seems like it. He claims he was in this area for business, but why would he seek me out? He was just as much of a jerk as he used to be. I should have cut him off a while ago, but I thought you and his parents were friends."

"I wouldn't exactly call us friends." Mom's voice was definite. "Rex Williams is a politician, with all that entails. And Bethanie is the consummate political wife—she never does anything without a reason. Knowing their family has had its uses over the years. But I have a feeling Dan is a bit of a trial to his parents."

"Come to think of it, Rex did mention that Dan was going out to California, looking for some 'investment opportunities.' So maybe that's why he looked you up," Dad said.

"I would never go into business with someone like Dan," I said. "The guy's a snob and he's been trying to one-up me since we were kids."

"I thought he would've settled down by now," Mom mused. "All of you young people have such different paths."

"Well, if you hear anything more about Dan, give me a ring. I want to know exactly what he's cooking up." I forced a smile into my voice. "So. What're my useless brothers into?"

Mom laughed. "Funny you should ask. They were just asking

about you." She filled me in. "Colton is doing great managing the strip mall you handed over. David is loving having your room because the light is better for his painting, and he's preparing to submit some pieces for a show. Morgan is experimenting with something in the basement I don't even ask about. Ben is taking anatomy right now, and so he's working out and using his own muscle groups to study it better. Jesse is talking about coming out to visit you. He says he feels California calling to him, especially as winter comes on."

"That would be great—I'd love to see him. Any or all of you are welcome anytime. The house is plenty roomy." I crossed my ankles on my desk and leaned back in my new, ergonomic chair. "I love the thought of you all overrunning the place, and helping me sample all the homemade vintages they have stashed out in the wine cave."

"Meg wouldn't mind?" Dad's voice sounded curious. "It must be hard for her to have a new owner take over everything that belonged to her family."

"She's good." I rubbed the back of my neck. *I had to work things out with her, and fast.* "It's all good."

"Are you coming home for Christmas?"

The thought hadn't crossed my mind, but maybe I *should* go home for the holidays. Meg would be here to keep an eye on Flea and the vineyard.

But what if I took her back East to meet the family?

The thought hit me like a punch in the gut. "I'll have to play the holidays by ear."

We batted the conversation around a bit more, and I said goodbye.

I looked out the window. Dusk had fallen. I watched Diego's headlights cut through the thickening dark as he left for home.

When was Meg coming back? The place was awfully quiet without her.

192

CHAPTER THIRTY-ONE

Meg

Gabriella's presence was as reassuring as I remembered, as she opened the door to her Santa Rosa townhouse. Her brown skin gleamed and her masses of glossy black curls bounced as she hugged me to a copious bosom that smelled of Shalimar. She squinted without her glasses, checking me out at arm's length once she let me go.

"You look like shit. Come in, and I'll fix you something. You did right coming to see me, babe—and I can't wait to hear all about it."

"Sorry I never called—we were out of cell range on the coast."

Gabby turned and bustled into her unit's immaculate, cozily decorated kitchen. I trailed after her. "Scoop me in." She stirred a bright red enamel pot on the stove. "I've got some homemade chorizo stew going. It'll put some color in your cheeks." I sat on a tall stool at the counter, and she pushed a bowl of tortilla chips over. "I've already got the margaritas marinating."

"You're a lifesaver, Gabby." I sighed and nibbled on a chip. "There was nothing to tell until recently." I scooped up some salsa. "Kane and I were just working together. I thought he was attractive. I told you I called him Stormy Sea Guy, remember? But I didn't think anything could ever come of it, even after the harvest incident." I set the half-eaten chip down on the countertop and covered my face with my hands. "I think I've fallen in love with him."

"Whoa. Back up the bus." Gabriella turned, holding her spoon aloft. "Something happened, didn't it? You slept with him."

"After we fled the fire. Yeah." I made a circling motion with a finger. "Where's that margarita?"

"Coming right up. I need a drink to deal with all of this, and so do you." Gabriella pushed the blender button. I endured the howling screech of ice cubes being crushed until she poured two pale green, slushy drinks into tall glasses.

I took a huge sip of mine, and promptly grabbed my forehead in agony. "Ice cream headache. Ow!"

"You always do that." Gabriella sipped hers. "What led up to it? Tell me all the deets."

I filled her in on recent events. "For three days, we were perfectly happy in our love nest in the back of his truck." I sipped my margarita morosely.

Gabriella shuddered. "Camping sex and only washing up in a cold shower at the park or with baby wipes? Better you than me, girl. I like a nice hotel, running water and chilled champagne when I'm having a weekend love fest."

"That's just it—I loved camping with Kane. We're so in sync. We like so many of the same things. He's unpretentious. That's why I was so shocked when his friend Dan showed up with such a snobby attitude, and took me for the help."

"Well, you *are* the help." Gabriella stirred the stew and turned off the burner. "Need to let it rest for a few while we get these drinks down." She took another sip of her margarita. "It can't be a surprise that Kane has money somewhere. I mean, he got the cash to buy Villier. That cheese didn't come from outer space."

"He was living in his truck. Granted, it was a *nice* truck. I noticed that right off. At first I thought that he was one of those digital nomads, financing his travels with his followers or something. But he didn't take any pictures or make any posts, or spend time on social media except to create the website for Villier." I was already feeling the margarita, so I forced myself to eat another tortilla chip or three. "He said they have a family business. Sounds like it's a pizza joint or a plumbing outfit or something like that."

"I have the Internet right at my fingertips." Gabriella picked up her phone. "What did you say his last name was?"

I spelled it for her. Gabriella tapped something in with her fingertips. I took another swig of my margarita, smacking my lips. "Love that salt rim, Gabby." I set the drink down, feeling my heart hurt as I thought about Kane. I rubbed my left chest with my knuckles. "I can't believe I was so wrong about him."

"Always better to know sooner than later," Gabriella said. "That's how I like my assholes. Straight up, no deception."

I huffed a laugh. "I prefer no jerks at all, thank you."

Gabby didn't answer; she was too busy with her phone. Her round brown eyes popped open even wider. "Wow." She turned her phone around. "I just searched companies with the name McCallum in them. Look at this one, McCallum Industries. It's a top ten Fortune 500 company. Subsidiaries all over the world. Interests in real estate, manufacturing, alternative energy, and God knows what else."

I snatched the phone from Gabriella's hands. "It's a common last name. Look at all these companies listed! It doesn't have to be that one. Maybe their company doesn't even have their name in it."

Gabriella took the phone back and hit the *About Us* feature.

"McCallum Industries is not a publicly traded company. It's owned by Rafe and Ruby McCallum, 'and sons.'"

My fingers flew on my own phone as I searched those two names. "Whoa. The McCallum family has a Wikipedia page," I whispered. "Peter Kane Michaels McCallum is listed as the oldest son. Went to Andover prep school, then to Harvard. Major shareholder in the company, along with his five brothers." I looked up to meet Gabriella's eyes.

"This is like finding out you've been dating a Rockefeller," Gabriella crowed, holding her drink up for a toast. "Get in and get a ring on that boy, Meg!"

"Ew, gross!" I recoiled. "Don't even joke. You know that's the last thing I'd want!"

"And that's why it's so fun to tease you about it," Gabriella said. "Because you're positively phobic about class and money. You're a reverse snob."

"You didn't have a gold digger for a mother," I said. "I never want to be taken as someone who gives a shit about any of that. Because I don't."

"Methinks the lady doth protest too much," Gabriella said to her margarita. "It's easy to get an attitude until you need money. Just think how great it would have been if your stepdad's bacon had been able to bail you out of bankruptcy, and you'd been able to keep the vineyard for yourself."

"You have a point." I held out my empty glass. "Refill, please."

Gabriella got up to pour me more margarita from the blender. "It's going to be very interesting to find out why Kane's been hiding who he is." While she was up, she served the hot stew into a pair of brightly painted Mexican bowls. She topped the steaming concoction with cheese and chopped cilantro. "Bring your drink. Dinner is served in the dining room."

I followed my friend to the little round table under the

window, her playfully named 'dining room.' The geranium in the windowsill and the cheerful eyelet curtains seemed like the backdrop of a play to me in that moment as I tried to absorb this shock. "Kane has been hiding that he's the oldest son of one of the richest families in the United States. Why would he do that? Why has he been pretending he's broke? Why would he be camping in his truck?"

"You never asked him?" Gabriella blew on a spoonful of stew.

"Don't forget, the whole process with the way the vineyard was sold at auction was traumatic. I was so busy trying to deal with that, then decide if I wanted to work for Kane, then try to prove I was worth the wage he was paying me, then really getting into it. Liking him. Enjoying being a team. Starting to think of it as 'our' vineyard, because that's how he referred to it." I shook my head. "The fact that he wasn't volunteering anything about himself or his background—well, I hoped for the best." I set my spoon down. I hadn't taken a single bite. "For once in my life, I hoped I'd just been lucky. That I'd found a quality guy, or rather he'd found me. And that he was as into me as I was into him." My eyes welled up. "I'm never that lucky."

"Maybe he's had a falling-out with his family, and they cut him off?" Gabriella slid my drink over. "Don't say one more thing until you finish this."

We drank the margaritas as fast as we could, given their brain-freeze power. Gabriella poured another round and caught my gaze with hers. "The way I see it, you have a choice. You can wash your hands, take your fifty grand, and walk away from him and the vineyard. It's time to face the fact that the place is not yours; it's his now, and you're just the manager. Or, you can stay on as manager, and make sure your relationship is all business— but that's going to be hard now that you've done the nasty. What if he starts dating other people?"

"I dislike this topic intensely," I muttered into my drink.

"But here's the smart move: you go back to Kane and tell him exactly what he did that was so hurtful. Namely, that he did not stick up for you to his asshole buddy. He let the guy insult you and he didn't claim you as girlfriend. Take the incident at face value. See what he says. Don't read too much into it, and let him tell you about himself and his money when he's ready. Maybe he's as gun-shy as you are."

"Can we just drink until I'm blotto, and I'll figure it out in the morning?"

"We can. To procrastination," Gabriella said, and we clinked glasses.

CHAPTER THIRTY-TWO

Kane

I needed something to do. Something that made me feel connected to Meg. Something that made me feel a part of this historic place that I still didn't feel worthy of. I walked the fields with Flea after dark, wearing Meg's work apron tied on over my oldest pair of jeans. I pushed a wheelbarrow down the rows, a headlamp on my head, picking up discarded grapes and trimming vines that had come loose from the trellis. According to Diego, we had to wait a month or so to trim back the canopy for winter so that the plants could absorb as much nutrients and strength as they could into the roots—but a lot of cleanup was still needed.

The slowness of the work, the meditative quality of it, made me miss Meg more. She was everywhere out here, and everywhere inside the house. I eventually filled the barrow, and took it back to the mulch area. I looked down the road for her car for the hundredth time.

How was I going to fix things with her?

There was no way but to come clean, explain how I knew a guy like Dan—my quest, my family situation. I had to hope that she would understand I'd needed time to trust her with the truth about my part in McCallum Industries.

I'd had enough of dark and lonely thoughts. This time, when I went back out into the fields, I blasted German thrash metal. The intense music erased any thoughts I might've tried to have.

♡

Meg

I woke up in Gabriella's bed when she shook my shoulder. "Get up, sleepyhead. Some of us have to go to work, and I'm pretty sure you need a shower." She waved a hand in front of her face. "And I know you need to brush your teeth. You can use my guest toothbrush, because I'm thoughtful like that."

I swung my legs over to the side and my feet hit the floor, sending a reverberation through my whole body. "A good friend would have let me sleep in."

"That's not going to happen, because I don't want you moving in with me. Could see that all too clearly."

I flung an arm over my eyes to block out the irritating sunshine as I sat on the edge of the bed.

Kane and I had had a fight.

That was a bummer. It was unpleasant, but it wasn't the end of the world, or the end of our relationship. He had a friend who was a dick. And, there was a lot I didn't know about him.

But what I did know backed up what a good guy he was. And maybe he had his own reasons for not telling me he was the oldest son of one of the richest families in the United States.

Gabriella grabbed me by the elbow. "Up, up! I have to go to work, and you have to go to work too . . . Back to Villier. Or have you forgotten that your lover is also your boss?"

"I've just discovered that there is a downside to that. Okay, I'm moving!"

Fifteen minutes later, I drove back towards the vineyard, not entirely sure how Gabriella had gotten me on my feet, showered and dressed, and out the door so quickly. But turning up the driveway to the farmhouse, I sucked in a breath as surprise and dread tightened my stomach.

Parked beside Kane's truck was the shiny black Range Rover my stepfather drove.

CHAPTER THIRTY-THREE

Kane

I woke abruptly the next morning to the sound of pounding, accompanied by Flea barking an intruder alert. My eyes were gummy from lack of sleep, but the loudness of the knocking brought me to my feet quickly.

Maybe it was Meg, returned and on the warpath.

If so, I welcomed the battle. We'd work it out, and hopefully end up in bed for some epic make-up sex.

I pulled on a pair of sweatpants and shouldered into a battered Harvard tee. I clattered down the stairs. Flea followed, whining and anxious at the slippery treads, but right behind me.

I yanked open the front door.

A short, barrel-chested man with an olive complexion and heavy features stood on the porch, wearing the familiar uniform of wealthy people on vacation: designer jeans, a polo shirt with logo, and a white panama hat. A petite, dark-haired woman stood beside him in cream-colored pants, metallic bronze sandals, and a coral-pink silk blouse that set off beautiful skin and fine features.

"Who are you? And what are you doing in our daughter's house?" the man demanded.

"You must be Meg's parents." I extended a hand and deployed my best smile. "I'm Kane McCallum."

"Ray DeSylva and Nathalie Villier DeSylva." The man still looked nonplussed, but shook my hand.

Meg's mother's hand was soft. "Are you Meg's boyfriend?"

I wasn't ready to answer that, so I held the door wide. "Please pardon my casual outfit. I didn't expect company so early. Come in. There have been a few changes."

Nathalie DeSylva stepped into the foyer. "On the contrary. The place looks exactly the same as when my parents were alive, except you got rid of that awful furniture in here with all of the doilies. Where's Meg?"

"I'm not entirely sure at the moment." I squared my jaw. "I'm the new owner."

Ray's dark eyes flew wide and Nathalie took a step back. "Meg sold the place? How dare she!"

I was starting to be pissed off by the DeSylvas' high-handedness. "Why don't you come sit down at the table and I'll fill you in on what's been happening? I haven't even had a cup of coffee yet. Would you like some?"

Trailing me as I headed for the kitchen, Nathalie's voice had gone shrill. "Where is my daughter? What have you done with her?"

Ray's voice lowered into a soothing rumble. "Calm down, Nathalie. Let's hear the man out." I glanced over my shoulder to see him steering his wife by her elbow over to the dining room table.

I continued on into the kitchen. I fixed a pot of coffee and splashed water on my face at the sink, straightening my hair by combing it with my fingers. Flea sat like a giant furry dragon in the doorway of the dining room, eyeing the couple suspiciously.

Once the coffee was going, I carried a tray with creamer and sugar out to the table. "Those are my mother's things." Nathalie pointed to the coffee service. "Why are you using my mother's things? Did Meg just abandon everything in the house?"

Ray squeezed her shoulder. I schooled myself to reply calmly, trying to imagine what it was like for the couple to come upon this situation—*why hadn't Meg told her parents anything about the foreclosure?* "All of the furnishings were included in the estate when it went to auction."

"I think you'd better explain what the hell is going on." Ray drew himself up, his plump chest swelling.

"How about you tell me what you know, and I fill in the gaps, instead," I responded.

"First my father-in-law, then my mother-in-law passed within a month of each other. Meg was out here wasting time at the vineyard, when she should have been looking for a teaching job," Ray huffed.

"My mother informed me, via email before her sudden heart attack, that Meg was helping them out here and was their heir." Nathalie dabbed at her eyes with a paper napkin. "I was too devastated to pay much attention to specifics."

The coffee maker beeped as it ceased its gurgling. I returned to the kitchen and filled three cups, and carried them into the dining room. I flipped on the overhead chandelier with its dusty bulbs to chase the shadows from the room, and Nathalie DeSylva winced as if the sight of the vintage piece offended her eye.

I was beginning to dislike Meg's parents intensely, but that didn't explain why she hadn't told them anything about what was going on.

"Why don't we begin again." I smiled, hoping it looked hospitable. "So. You came to visit Meg?"

"Actually, we came to offer to buy the place from her,"

Nathalie said. "Imagine our surprise to find she had already sold it." Her voice dripped bitterness.

"My understanding is that the place was in foreclosure when Meg arrived to help her grandparents." I turned my cup restlessly in my hands. "Meg inherited it, with an auction scheduled. From what I understand, it was a complete surprise to her, too. She got nothing but a massive amount of debt from your parents' medical expenses, back taxes, and a mortgage she didn't know about."

Nathalie's eyes widened. Her tan seemed to leach away, leaving her skin sallow. For the first time she looked close to her real age. "My mother never said a thing about financial difficulties."

"But surely you spoke with them?" I groped for straws. *Why would Meg not tell her mother such important news?* "Or heard at the memorial?"

Nathalie looked down and fiddled with the large diamond rings encircling her fingers as if they hurt her. "I did not attend. My parents and I were estranged."

"You and Meg must've been estranged, as well. That explains the lack of information." The light finally dawned for me.

"My wife didn't agree with Meg's decision to throw her future away, to come back to nurse a couple whom Nathalie'd been in conflict with for most of her adult life." Ray squinted at me in an attempt to look intimidating. "Not that we owe *you* an explanation."

I shrugged. "No, you don't. I won the vineyard at the public auction. I felt sorry for Meg and her situation, and I hired her as my vineyard manager. She has been doing a great job. We brought in a bumper crop of grapes, sold them, and escaped damage from the recent fire in the area."

Nathalie looked around. "Then where is my daughter?"

"She is my employee. I'm not her keeper," I said stiffly. "But if you phone her, I'm sure she'll be eager to see you." This time, I didn't bother to smile.

Ray DeSylva spread his hands on the lovingly waxed surface of the dining room table. "Our daughter has some explaining to do. But in the meantime, my wife wants the vineyard to stay in the family. Regrettably, we weren't aware of the auction or we could have prevented this whole fiasco by buying the place then. But since Meg didn't see fit to tell us about it, we'd like to take it off your hands now. I'm sure an old farm like this isn't the kind of future a young man like you aspires to." He gestured to my worn tee. "Especially if that shirt really is from your *alma mater*."

I stood up carefully, easing my chair away from the table, giving no sign of the anger tightening my chest. "You must have misunderstood the situation. The vineyard is not for sale. At any price."

Ray DeSylva's brows rose in surprised arcs. He looked like a cartoon villain being denied a favorite toy. "Not at any price?" He named a significant number. "I did a little research before we came to see what comparable properties listed for, and that is a very generous figure."

My neck felt hot. "Fortunately, I have no need of money. I'm Kane McCallum, of McCallum Industries. As I said, this vineyard is not for sale. At any price."

"Glad to hear you're finally acknowledging who you are, Peter Kane McCallum." Meg's voice came from the doorway. I turned to meet her gaze, and it was as stark and furious as it had been on the day of the auction, when she stood in the gallery, radiating fury like a witch about to be burned at the stake. "You rich people always throw your weight around."

Ray DeSylva stood up, shoving his chair back so hard it scraped the floor. "Marguerite. We were just trying to convince this man to sell us Villier so we could keep it in the family!"

Meg put her hands on her hips. If her eyes had been hot

towards me, they seemed to shoot out flames to incinerate DeSylva. "If you wanted to keep it in the family, either or both of you could have reached out to Gram and Grandpa when they were dying in bankruptcy. Don't try to whitewash this into anything but an attempted land grab. I'd rather McCallum here keeps this place than you two hypocrites try to take it from him and pretend you give a shit about it."

"Meg, darling." Nathalie DeSylva extended a hand in appeal. "Imagine our shock coming here to see you, only to find this man owns our family home and the vineyard! Neither Mama nor you said a word about money troubles." Nathalie rolled her eyes skyward, clasping her fingers together as if in prayer. "My heart is broken by this whole situation!"

Ray nodded pompously. "We just want to bring the place back into the family. We could have helped you so much sooner if you'd reached out to us."

Meg held up a hand in a 'stop' gesture. "Save the performance for the community theater you're so fond of, Mother. And you heard the man, Ray. Kane's a McCallum, one of the top twenty richest families in America. And if he says the vineyard isn't for sale at any price, he means it. I believe I have some packing to do." She turned and headed for the stairs.

The same paralysis that seemed to have taken me over when Dan was insulting Meg froze me. I couldn't think of anything to say or do that would mitigate what had just happened.

Clearly, Meg had baggage.

I'd sensed that from the beginning and now the depth of it had been revealed.

Flea, however, did not care.

The faithless hound chased Meg up the wooden steps, whimpering with happiness to see her. Meg's voice, low and harsh, echoed down into the dining room: "Go back to your master, Flea. We're done here."

My mouth dried. My chest hurt. My hands clenched. But the paralysis finally lifted.

"Yes, we're done here." I leaned forward and splayed my hands on the table to stabilize myself as I stood up and made eye contact with Meg's parents. "Well, Mr. and Mrs. DeSylva, you heard your daughter. I believe our business is concluded. I'm sure you know the way out."

I straightened up and walked away, calling for Flea as I headed for the back door.

The kittens were mewing in their box; I grabbed the cardboard container up, along with the bottle and formula by the washing machine. Whatever drama Meg and her parents had to play out didn't need my attendance. Hopefully they'd all be out of my house by the time I returned.

I headed for the only place that could possibly make me feel any better: the big oak in the middle of the vineyard.

CHAPTER THIRTY-FOUR

Meg

It didn't take long at all to throw the things that I had just unpacked from our fire departure back into a couple of pillowcases and my suitcase, leaving behind anything that didn't fit in. After all, I had fifty grand to start a new life with. Maybe it was time to ditch a few pairs of my old granny panties and worn-out T-shirts.

Sir Henry, disturbed by all of the racket downstairs, arrived to hop up onto my bedspread. His fluffy tail snapped back and forth in annoyance as he yowled a complaint about the goings-on.

"Don't worry. I'll take the kittens, too," I told him. "They're going to need regular care until they're big enough to adopt out, and Mr. Fortune 500 McCallum's going to be very busy running the vineyard without a manager."

My mother appeared in the doorway. She plucked at her silk blouse with sparkly ringed hands, and her mouth trembled—she was a great actress. "I know you think I'm heartless for not coming to the memorial, Meg. It's complicated."

"They were both gone within a month. You, their only

daughter, left me to plan two memorials, which you didn't even have the decency to attend. I had planned to tell you about the auction then, but when you didn't show, I decided I didn't need to speak to you again. Ever." I picked up the pillow Gram had made me, folding my arms around it as if I could hold her close again. "Do you have any idea how hard it was for me to plan that, to do everything myself? And on top of that, to find out the vineyard was in foreclosure and then go through the sale to a complete stranger?" I could hardly make my lips form the words to speak. My face felt numb, my throat constricted. "They were your parents! What did they do to you that was so horrible?"

"They never understood me. I'd had enough of it." Mother's lovely skin reddened. "I don't expect you to understand. But trust me when I tell you, it had nothing to do with you."

"Time for honesty now, Maman. Did you think for one minute about *me*? About what it would be like for me to go through all of this, with no one to help?" Sir Henry chimed in with a loud mew, as if reminding me of his presence. I felt an incongruous smile tug my mouth. "Well, I guess I did have company of a sort. Sir Henry has been here for me through thick and thin."

Ray appeared in the doorway. He set a hand on my mother's shoulder. She shut her eyes and leaned into him. "This isn't over, Meg. We're going to get the vineyard back from that young upstart, don't you worry."

"Clearly you don't know who Kane McCallum is," I said. "Not only is he loaded, he's stubborn as a mule, seems to really love the place, and his mom's a lawyer. The McCallums could buy and sell this whole county without blinking, from what I can tell about their bottom line." I blew a frizzing lock of hair out of my eye. "Still, good luck with your attempted coup. Now, if you don't mind, I have more packing to do, and I believe Mr. Moneybags McCallum told you to get off his property." I turned my back, yanking open the drawers of the dresser and rummaging around. Maman wasn't the only one who could engage in a theatrical performance.

After a long moment I heard the *tap-tap* of my mother's heels on the wooden steps, the soft murmur of Ray's voice as he comforted her, and the squeak of his shoe hitting that tricky stair as they descended. The front door opened and shut.

I shut my eyes and leaned my hands on my suitcase as the subdued rumble of the Range Rover turned on and pulled away, fading into distance.

I might never see my mother and stepfather again, and that would be just fine.

I felt a big block of something cold and hard forming in my chest. I wanted to slam the door, throw myself down on the bed, bury my face in Gram's special pillow, and have a good cry. That was the way I'd always handled shit with my mother in the past.

But today I couldn't. Today, I was numb to it all.

I finished my packing, collecting the bare minimum of toiletries out of the bathroom and throwing them into my suitcase. I took a perverse pleasure in leaving my discarded belongings scattered around and a mess of makeup and tampons in the bathroom.

And every minute I fussed around and lingered, I was waiting to hear Kane's voice, his foot on the staircase, the clatter of Flea's toenails and his welcoming whine. I wanted Kane to come after me, to beg me to stay, to try to explain. "Please, Kane. Come back. Tell me you want me to stay," I whispered.

But the house was silent and empty. He was gone. He hadn't taken his truck so he was still here at the vineyard somewhere—but he didn't want to talk to me. Didn't want to work it out.

He was letting me walk away.

Flea was sad collateral damage in all of this. I was really going to miss that big, beautiful, galumphing dog. Thinking of Flea almost melted the ice around my heart enough so that I could cry.

I carried my stuff down to my car, then went back and looked for the box of kittens in the laundry room. They were missing—Kane had taken them somewhere.

"Guess that's how the custody agreement goes," I told Sir Henry, pushing him into his carrier. "He gets them and keeps Flea, I get you."

I wasn't worried about the kittens' welfare—if Kane had taken them, he would make sure they were okay.

He cared for what was his.

I'd almost been his, too.

I blinked and swallowed. I wouldn't cry, I wouldn't feel, I wouldn't drop everything and go looking for him.

Finally, there was nothing to do but go.

As I drove down the driveway, I flipped my rearview mirror up so I wouldn't look back at the vineyard even once.

CHAPTER THIRTY-FIVE

Kane

Sitting on the old picnic table with my back turned toward the house, I fed the kittens. Whatever was going on back there between Meg and her parents was none of my business. I was glad I had worn my sweats and thrown on my running shoes, because I sure needed a run.

Once the kits were full and sleeping, I pounded down the rows of the vineyard, soon leaving Flea behind. He was such a big dog that, though his legs were long and he was game, he couldn't keep up with me when I really got going.

I went up and down every single row in the entire place as fast as I could. My breath tore through my lungs, my heart thundered. Soon, the only thing I could feel was exhaustion that I'd fought hard for.

When I returned to the house, night had fallen. The back door was cracked open, and fall's evening chill had blown through the house, cooling everything off to a degree that was downright uncomfortable. The only light still on was the old chandelier over the dining room table. The place felt as echoing and empty as a shell washed up on some godforsaken beach.

I found a thermostat on the wall, but when I turned it up to 65, waiting for something to happen, I heard no answering rumble from the basement or even a sputter from the couple of wall-mounted radiators I spotted around the room.

"Dammit." Meg had never shown me what kind of heating system the house had, but I remembered seeing a furnace on the lowest level. I went to the door that descended from the kitchen area, pulled a string on a bare lightbulb, and illuminated a staircase badly in need of a guard rail descending into a basement ripe with the smell of must, dust, and mouse droppings.

Down in those dank bowels I eventually found the 'on' switch for the large metal furnace squatting in the corner in an octopus-like nest of ducting. Everything was covered with a layer of sticky dust. I flipped the 'on' switch anyway, heard a rumble and a gargle and a cough, and then nothing. A couple more flicks of the switch yielded an empty clicking sound.

Maybe Diego would have some idea how to get the damn thing running.

I thumped back upstairs. The house had never seemed so cold. The fireplace in the parlor had no wood. I didn't have so much as an electric blanket to keep warm.

I went out to the truck and retrieved the fluffy goose down duvet Meg and I had slept under while camping. Meg had taken in the sheets and washed them, but the blanket and duvet still smelled faintly of sex and her vanilla shampoo.

I cursed as I shook that comforter out over my narrow twin bed, feeling sick and empty. I loved her. Now she was gone. I didn't want to smell her on my comforter.

I wasn't much of a drinker, but if ever there was a time for that, it was now.

I trekked down to the wine cave, Flea at my heels, and looked for the oldest bottle put down on the shelves, discovering one from the nineteen-seventies. When I finally got the crumbling cork out, the stuff had gone to vinegar.

Several attempts later, I found a very mellow bottle of pinot that had gone sweet instead of sour. I carried it back up to the house.

I didn't feel like eating. I didn't feel like drinking, either, but trying to sleep under a blanket that still smelled like our love-making seemed masochistic in the extreme.

I called for a pizza, fired up an old RPG video game on my tablet. I went online and logged into a game me and my brothers had been playing together for years. I made myself play the game, eat the pizza, and drink the entire bottle of wine while pretending everything was fine with my brothers.

"Something happened," David said abruptly, his mellow voice distinctive in my headset. David was the 'sensitive one,' the artist who seemed to have an intuition about people.

I shook my head, and somehow that made my thumb slip and my character was abruptly eaten by the dragon. "Damn it!"

"Something happened. You haven't come online to play with us in months," David persisted. "Girl trouble?"

"Nah. Girls are more hassle than they're worth. Bros before hos!" I declared, feeling fake and ridiculous even as I said it. I took a swig of wine straight from the bottle.

"I can come out and keep you company," Jesse offered. Jesse, at seventeen, was the youngest of us and always looking for a reason to play, whether it was on a skateboard, snowboard, surf-board or paraglider.

"This is your senior year. You gotta buckle down," I said. "Besides, Mom would kick my ass if I let you come before winter break." I gave up and set aside my controller. "I suck at this game. I'll just watch you guys play."

"Good thing you gave up," Colton crowed. "Because I'm

going to ruin your score for all time!" The second down from me in age, Colton seemed to have been born trying to prove he was better than me—at everything.

"Whatever you need to tell yourself, Colt." I swigged from the bottle. "But I sure wish one of you could make it out here for a couple weeks or something—but not you, Jesse, so don't even ask, pipsqueak."

"I'm going into trials on my latest invention," Morgan said. "Can't get away right now, sorry." The quietest of us, Morgan was always working on some creation in his basement lab.

"I got into that show I was going for," David said. "Now I have to work my tail off and come up with six more paintings in three months. Can't get away."

"And I've got your strip mall to run. It's increased profits by forty-five percent since you left," Colton said. "You obviously didn't see its potential."

I rolled my eyes and bit my tongue—Colt was just trying to piss me off, as usual.

"And I'm in charge of the annual Harley Davidson Ride-A-Thon for muscular dystrophy," Ben said. Ben was a linebacker at his college, a huge guy who loved his motorbike, but a total marshmallow for animals and kids. I predicted he'd be married by the time he was twenty-one and starting on his own brood.

"Guess I'll have to hang with Flea until the holidays, but you can tell Mom I'll be coming back for some of Mrs. Knightly's pie," I said.

They all snorted and chuckled. Mrs. Knight was a superb housekeeper and a terrific cook, but one year she'd forgotten to put sugar in the holiday pies, and we'd been ribbing her about it ever since.

I said goodbye and left the game, taking off the wireless headset.

David and I were closest, and I wasn't surprised when my

phone rang a minute later. "I'm done with the game too. Want to watch a movie?"

"Sure." We settled in to watch the same movie on our tablets, so we could be connected across the miles. When it was over and we were both fairly sloshed (he was drinking beer at his end) David asked, "What's going on, bro? No word for months, and then you call us and want to get with the brothers. Must be a woman."

I snorted. "Hell no. I'm done with that crap."

"Ha! It's definitely a woman. You found someone, and she ditched your ass!"

I cussed David out. "You artist types are supposed to be all sensitive and shit," I grumbled. "Where'd that go wrong?"

David sobered. "I am sensitive. Deeply. Nothing like a broken heart to put me in touch with my creativity. Promise you'll come home at Christmas?"

"Will do. You'd like it out here. No snow, and a thriving art scene." We shot the shit for a little longer, and I hung up, feeling marginally better.

I had people who cared about me, even if they were thousands of miles away. I had dodged a bullet with Meg and her crazy parents. Maybe if I kept telling myself that, someday I'd believe it.

CHAPTER THIRTY-SIX

Meg

Gabriella would have put me up for another night, but she had made her long-term opinion about me couch surfing at her place apparent. Instead, I was going to treat myself to a fun getaway. Driving down the road, I called to find out if any openings were available at the kitschy Airstream "resort" on the Russian River. The Autocamp was a fun collection of eclectic, vintage Airstream recreation trailers parked around a central fire pit area, where guests could socialize if they felt so inclined.

I had no interest in socializing. The ice around my heart seemed to have frozen into something dark and solid. Maybe it had become a lump of coal, and someday it would turn into a diamond—but not anytime soon.

Only an hour or so after leaving the house, Sir Henry and I were ensconced in our very own tricked out silver trailer. Technically we weren't supposed to have pets in the Airstreams, so I'd smuggled Sir Henry inside under my coat. The space was cozily decorated like a gypsy wagon, with fringy red lace shawls pinned up over the lights, and a hand quilted down comforter on a big bed that filled one end of the trailer. Every modern luxury was available in the small, tidy space.

The manager, Amelie, had showed me around the secluded forest area adjacent, lined with paths through the forest and along the river. "You can use any of the kayaks, too," she said. "Just be sure to wear a life vest."

"Not in the mood for that just yet, but maybe in a couple of days." I bid her goodnight, and closed myself and Sir Henry in to our cozy getaway.

I had loaded several new pirate romances on my e-reader, the quilt on the Airstream's bed was snuggly and warm, and I had a couple of sleeping pills to make sure I wasted no time thinking about the scene at the house and how much I missed Kane.

Tomorrow I would spend in bed with Captain Bone.

On the next day in the Airstream, I would take a forest walk and soak in nature. And on my fourth day, I'd have a good look at my finances and visit my bank.

And the day after that?

No telling. I had no idea what to do with the rest of my life.

Kane

Diego was a fountain of information about the house when we met late the next day. Together we got the furnace serviced and refilled with oil, and I even figured out the baseboard heaters, which were enough to keep the living areas warm most of the time.

After that major project, I grabbed a fresh trash bag and handed it to him. "I know this isn't usually your area, Diego, but Meg moved out. She threw her stuff all around the room and just left a lot of it there." Torturing myself the night before, I hadn't been able to keep from taking a look in there, and the sight had almost been my undoing. My finger had hovered over her number on my phone way longer than I would admit to anyone but myself. "Would you mind bagging up her things? I think she's moved out, but she might want to come back and pick it up at some point."

Diego's dark brows went almost high enough to touch his hairline. "That's not like Meg. She's a tidy girl. Sentimental about her things, I would say."

I shrugged. "See for yourself. I'm too busy to deal with it."

Diego pushed the bag back at me. "No. Meg wouldn't like me touching her stuff. Besides, I am an agricultural specialist. Now, if you hire my aunt Marta, she can come clean for you, cook some food and stock your freezer. You need a woman to take care of you, now that Meg has left."

"I need a woman like a hole in the head, but someone to cook and clean sounds great. Call your aunt. I do need help with the house. You saw the state of that basement."

Between Diego and his aunt, I wasn't going to miss Meg at all in a week or two.

CHAPTER THIRTY-SEVEN

Meg

I enjoyed the Autocamp for the first week after my departure from Villier. It was great to just call for takeout food, take long rambling walks in the woods listening to audiobooks, and then spend the rest of the day and night tucked up in bed with Sir Henry and my romance novels, an open box of chocolates next to me.

Gabriella finally reached me when I turned my phone back on. "I called over to the house, when you weren't answering. Kane told me you left. Where the hell are you?"

"At an Airstream trailer park. You made it abundantly clear that you didn't want me moving in with you." I tried not to sound accusing.

"I didn't really mean that! Of course, you could've come to me. Silly brat. Tell me what you're up to."

"My current goals have been to drown my sorrows in chocolate and romance novels," I said. "And I've been performing admirably on them so far. I've gone to the bank and taken a look at my financial situation. I needed a week to just chilllax, read, and wash that man out of my hair. I think I'm about ready to consider my options—I need to get a plan."

"Ready to get back on the horse?" Gabriella said. "Good thing too, because I have a date with a new guy, and he's asking if I have anyone to double with."

"Not sure I'm ready for that—unless you are going somewhere with dancing, loud music, and lots of booze." I sniffed under my armpits. Yes, it was time for a shower.

"As a matter of fact, we're going to a line dancing place. They even have a bucking bull."

I felt the first flicker of something that wasn't misery for the first time since the fragile dream I was building had exploded. "Line dancing at a cowboy bar? I can saddle up for that."

But alas, even line dancing and a bucking bull couldn't glue together the pieces of my broken heart, and halfway through the evening I said goodbye to Gabby and our dates and went back to the trailer.

Kane

Diego's aunt Marta was a large woman with muscular arms and a no-nonsense manner. She arrived every morning at seven a.m., and left by one p.m. to get her kids from school. She never stopped moving the whole time she was at the house.

At seven thirty a.m. she'd yell to wherever I happened to be, "*La comida*, Kane! Pronto!" and whether I was hungry or not, a big plate of *huevos rancheros* awaited me at the head of the dining room table. She scolded me in Spanish if it got cold, so I yanked on my clothes and got down there to shovel it in—but I had no appetite. That breakfast was usually the only thing I ate all day.

The house got so clean and the floor so waxed that Flea kept spinning out. I finally got around to nailing down carpet on the stairs for him. And every day, Diego and I would work around the place, catching up on projects and doing improvements. I'd fall into bed at night too tired to think about much.

But having Marta there didn't stop me from missing Meg. Nothing did.

I ached with missing her, a constant nagging feeling of loss. I couldn't look anywhere around the vineyard without seeing her there—turning to tease me, passionate as she explained something, laughing at Flea, holding one of the kittens to bottle-feed it. And how she'd been in bed: warm, silky-soft, so freakin' responsive, eager and inventive and hungry.

She haunted me—an auburn-haired, long-legged ghost.

I tried to focus on the good things that were happening, but nothing seemed to matter: not the money in the bank from the harvest, not updating the website with our stats and photos, not the social media campaign Meg and I had come up with, not even beginning to trim back the canopy for winter, a chore I'd looked forward to. Even beginning to pay back my dad for the loan on the property, something I'd anticipated, seemed empty and stupid. Why bother? It was only money, and there would always be more of that whether or not I got the vineyard turned around.

I ached. Everything hurt like I'd been pummeled with little rubber hammers. My chest was tight and sore.

"I think I'm getting sick," I told Diego one day, sitting down abruptly in the middle of loading vine cuttings into his truck. I put my head into my hands and coughed, but my chest was clear. "I've got some weird kind of flu."

"You're heartsick. Lovesick," Diego said. "You miss Meg."

"Hell, no." I stood up as quickly as I'd sat down, and my jeans about fell off because I'd lost so much weight. I hoisted them up. "I'm just sick. No appetite. Maybe I'm anemic or something."

Diego cocked his head like a blackbird. He held out a hand and ticked off items: "You don't eat unless Marta makes you. You never smile or laugh. You work too long and hard. You don't want to see anyone, but you're lonely. You watch the driveway all the time, hoping she'll come back. Admit it. You miss the girl."

I looked down the driveway for the thousandth time. "I thought it would get better," I muttered. "But it seems to be getting worse."

"You should call her. Ask her to come back." Diego kept pitching cuttings into the truck. "Tell her how you feel."

"I can't take it if she says no, and I don't want to do this without her." I dropped the pitchfork I was holding, gesturing to the vineyard, the house. "But I don't want to go back to the way things were, either."

"What do you mean?" Diego frowned. The expression sat oddly on his good-natured face.

An idea took hold of my brain suddenly and completely, as if the solution to my misery had been waiting for just this moment to reveal itself in a decision that would fix everything, and set me free.

"I think I need to move on. Villier should have been hers all along." I felt energy flowing back into me for the first time since the DeSylvas had come up the driveway and ruined us.

I turned and walked away, leaving Diego staring after me, and went into the house.

I didn't want to own Villier without her, and I didn't want her obligated to me. I'd never know one way or the other if she'd ever really cared about me when I held all the cards, and I was afraid to find out. That was the simple truth.

My quest wasn't over.

I got on the phone and called my CPA. She referred me to an attorney, Lawrence Clark, Esquire. I told him my idea. Clark argued with me but eventually complied—after all, I was the customer.

Then I called my parents and told them that grape farming

wasn't the right business for me. I asked for more time to pay back the loan; they said they'd transfer some of my stock to their name, and call it good.

"Jesse still wants to come visit," Mom said. "Are you sure you want to leave now, right with winter coming on?"

"It's a great time to see the Grand Tetons and the Rockies. All that snowy mountain majesty and all," I said with false cheer. "I'll send him a ticket to come out and meet me snowboarding in Utah or something. Thanks for understanding, and I'll be home for Christmas."

I hung up the phone before I confessed that I'd had my heart broken by Meg Villier, that I wanted her to be happy and cared for—and that I just wanted to forget this particular chapter of my life as quickly as possible.

It still took three more days to tie up all the loose ends, but soon enough I said goodbye to Diego and Marta, prepaid for them to stay through the holidays, and got on the road in my freshly provisioned truck with Flea in the passenger seat.

The beautiful drive up Highway One was just the thing to kick off my new journey.

I flipped my rearview mirror up so I wouldn't look back at the vineyard even once, as I turned out of the long driveway and headed for the coast.

CHAPTER THIRTY-EIGHT

Meg

I was still at the Autocamp.

It was crazy that I was still there. I'd meant for my stay at the Airstream trailer park to be a fun little indulgence before I got on with 'the rest of my life,' whatever that was going to mean, but one day rolled into the next. I slept, read romances, ate takeaway and barbeque from a couple of nearby restaurants, and took long walks in the woods. I just didn't seem to have the wherewithal to figure out any next steps.

A knock came at my door one day. I rolled out of bed and tamed my wild hair into a twist skewered with a pencil, glad I was at least dressed, since someone had the temerity to actually knock on my door. I stuck my head out of my shiny aluminum shelter to see the manager, Amelie, and her partner Joy.

The couple owned and ran the Autocamp; I liked them as much as I was able to like anyone at a time when my emotions were muffled, and everything felt meaningless and existentially awful. My smile felt like a twitch. "Hey, Amelie. Joy. What's up?"

"We're worried about you." Amelie put her hands on her hips. She was a short, ample woman who wore burlaplike dresses with Birkenstocks and hand-knitted socks. "We think you're depressed."

"I'm fine. But if I'm behind on paying, I'm good for it." I yawned. "Let me get you a check." I withdrew inside, and Amelie took that opportunity to climb the steps and come in with Joy in her wake.

The two were a pairing of opposites—Joy was a tall, gaunt woman of sixty or so who wore mostly black leather and her hair in a long braid. She had to bend her head to stand inside the trailer. "We'd like to speak with you about your plans." She had a voice like a foghorn in a cave. "We have a proposal for you."

Amelie had already passed me and was picking up the pizza litter from the night before, shooing Sir Henry off the bed so she could tidy it. His existence had come to light early on in my stay, and after a discussion about cleaning the trailer professionally upon my departure in case of allergic guests, he'd been welcomed.

"We need a camp host. Someone to cover for us when we're gone. We've been completely tied to the place since we bought it two years ago, and we're dying to take a vacation together. What do you say?" Joy asked.

I sat down abruptly at the trailer's little dinette table. Sir Henry joined me, arching his back and rubbing his head against my side, purring like a chainsaw. I scratched him automatically, trying to muster my wits. "What's involved?"

"Well, for starters, you need to clean up the place," Joy rumbled. "And yourself. And be hospitable to our guests. You'd do the check-in and out when we're out of town. Even when we go to an event or something, you'd be the one available to answer questions."

Amelie picked up the thread. "In return, you'd get free rent. And a little stipend."

I scratched my scalp, trying to remember when I'd last had a shower. "Sounds good. What's the catch?"

"No catch," Joy said. "Except for the part about cleaning up the place. And yourself."

"You told us you were a local from around here, and we can tell you've been through some sort of loss or tragedy," Joy said, pinning me with her gray-blue gaze. "Did you lose your house in the fire?"

Tears suddenly filled my eyes. "In a way, I did. Our family's vineyard. But not to fire. It was foreclosed upon when my grand-parents died. And there was a man involved." The tears over-flowed but I didn't bother to wipe them. My chest felt as if my broken heart had shards that poked my lungs. "I'm done with men."

Amelie had found a trash bag and was bustling about. She already had the place mostly picked up. "There's always a man. Come to the other side." She winked.

I snuffled a laugh. "No, thanks. Sir Henry and I will be flying solo for the foreseeable future. But that said, I greatly appreciate your offer to be camp host. I accept."

Gone were the days of lying around in my shiny silver trailer, imagining myself a fair Sassenach maid chased by Highlanders, or a buxom captive being ravished by a pirate captain. Now that I was a camp host, Amelie and Joy found all sorts of extras for me to do: I raked the leaves in the entrance, created a seasonal gourd display around the communal fire pit, trimmed the overhanging redwood branches, and managed the place in their absence.

Keeping busy helped keep my mind off of Kane—and I badly needed the distraction.

Arranging a beautiful bank of crimson poinsettia at the entrance of the camp to mark the changing of the season was a satisfying little project. I wove silver and gold twinkle lights through the foliage for a classy holiday look. I was so grateful for this job—for somewhere to land after all the hard times.

I belonged to a little community, however peripherally. The guests at the Autocamp tended to be couples on some sort of romantic adventure, and I got the appeal of the Airstreams for a getaway. After all, three of the best days of my life had been spent camping with my lover in the back of a truck.

Tweaking the bright red leaves of the poinsettia, I blinked away tears. "I'm done crying over Kane."

"Glad to hear it." A male voice came from my elbow. I turned to see a small, dapper older man, dressed like a college professor in twill slacks, an Argyle sweater, and a blazer with patches on the elbows in that indeterminate color people call "camel."

I drew myself up and forced a smile. "Can I help you?"

"I'm looking for a young lady named Marguerite Villier," he said. "I have an important message for her."

I scanned the little gnome up and down. *He had the look of a lawyer*.

My stomach tightened with apprehension. "I am Meg Villier."

"And I am Lawrence Clark, Esquire." He placed a slender calfskin briefcase on the nearby picnic table. "I have papers to deliver to you. May I see an identification, please?"

"I suppose." This was more and more like I was being served.

I went back to my trailer. Sir Henry, trapped inside, slipped between my ankles as I opened the curving, shiny aluminum door. He was remarkably good at getting out, and though there was no great danger of him running away, I worried he might accidentally get hit by one of the cars coming and going from the camp.

This time, I let Sir Henry go, and he streaked into the nearby bushes. I fetched my purse and dug out my ID with trembling fingers. *What did this guy want?* Was this visitation part of my parents' threat to try to get back the vineyard? I had succeeded in putting that whole ugly debacle out of my mind.

I returned to Mr. Clark, and handed him my ID. "Here you go."

He made note of the numbers on it diligently on a form on a clipboard, even taking a photo of the ID. "Now, I can tell that you're feeling nervous, young lady. But this is good news." He picked up a sealed manila envelope with 'Meg' written on the outside in Kane's blocky hand; I recognized his writing from our time working together. I took the envelope with numb fingers.

"Do you need a moment alone to open it? I will remain to answer any questions you have," Clark said.

"Yes. Privacy please. And I would appreciate you waiting in case . . ." My voice trailed off. I had no idea what the heck Kane could be sending me via lawyer.

I hurried back to my trailer. Once inside, I tugged open the envelope, painstakingly careful in case I might need to reseal it and pretend I had never opened it. The mind is funny that way: it always tries to protect you, to delay the inevitable. As if any of that would make a difference.

I tugged out some official-looking documents on the kind of stiff, thick paper certificates and such are printed upon. Clipped onto the front of that was a short note in Kane's writing.

"*Meg:*

I have decided that Villier Vineyard is not my thing after all. I feel badly about how things went down, even more so now that I met your delightful parents. You should have it free and clear, so

I'm giving it to you and continuing on my road trip. What I'm looking for is still out there.

Best of luck, Kane."

No hearts and flowers.

No declarations of love.

Just giving me a property worth seven figures.

The pit of my stomach fell into my shoes as I began hyperventilating.

I moved aside the letter and scanned the documents. Sure enough, they were title transfers made out to Marguerite Villier, for the property known as Villier Vineyard, "and estate." Detailed sketches and tax maps documented the extent of the land and outbuildings at the back of the deed.

I whirled around, slamming the Airstream's door open in agitation, and hurried over to Mr. Clark. "What the hell is this?" I waved the papers. "What is going on here?"

The lawyer twined his fingers together over his little potbelly. "It seems rather self-explanatory, don't you think? Kane McCallum has deeded over the property known as Villier Vineyard to you. You own it."

"Yes, but . . ." I sputtered. "Why? Is there a loan out on it, any sort of mortgage?"

Clarke shook his head. "No. Mr. McCallum owned the property free and clear, and he has given it over to you in like state."

"Why?" I repeated.

"I believe he left a note as to why," the lawyer said. "Now, it took some doing to find you, and if you don't have any further questions, I would like to head back to my office in Santa Rosa." He handed me his card. "Call me if you need anything further. I believe the property is ready for you to return to. Mr. McCallum prepaid your staff's wages for three months to ease the transition. He also left your name on the bank account, so you will have funds to continue the vineyard's normal operations. Mr.

McCallum let me know that the property was in the black, after the profit brought in by this fall's harvest. Good day."

I stared after the little man, my mouth ajar, as he got into a vintage Volvo, fired up the engine, and pulled out of the central turnaround of the camp.

I didn't pack my things right away. I needed to see the vineyard again, check out what had happened there since I left, and try to make sense of all this. I told Amelie and Joy that I was going home to get a few things, I caught Sir Henry and put him back in the trailer, and I got on the road to Villier.

The weird thing was that the whole time I'd been gone, I had only been half an hour away from the vineyard—but driving there felt like traveling through time to another life, as I turned into the familiar driveway.

Villier Vineyard looked great, much better than it had when it had gone to auction. The grass was green, and neatly mowed. The overgrown trees in the yard had been trimmed. Bright pots of red geraniums marked the stairs leading up the porch to the house. There was even a string of Christmas lights, the elegant kind with the large clear bulbs, wrapped around the support beams of the porch and across the overhang.

The place looked loved, cared for, as good as it had in my grandparents' heyday. Kane had done all that.

I turned off my car and just stared at the house. *Could it really be mine?*

Diego came out of the barn, waving, a huge grin splitting his face. At the same time, a woman with a stern face and a long black braid came out onto the front porch. She wore jeans and a turtleneck with a bright, embroidered Mexican apron over her whole outfit.

Diego and I embraced as I got out of the car. "So good to see you, Meg," he said. "It took you long enough to come back."

"The strangest thing happened, Diego." I followed him up the steps toward the intimidating-looking woman who stood there. "A lawyer found me where I was staying, and brought me a deed of ownership of the vineyard. Kane McCallum appears to have given it to me." I stood in front of the woman. "The house looks wonderful," I said. "Are you the reason why?"

"I'm Diego's aunt Marta." She removed a hand from beneath her apron and extended it to me. I felt as if I were meeting a queen as I shook it. "Kane hired me to cook and care for the house."

"It looks beautiful," I enthused. I surveyed the festive appearance of the porch, and, when Marta opened the door, I smelled the fragrance of beeswax and elbow grease.

"Come inside. I'll fix us brunch." She bustled off.

Diego shook his head. "Might as well give in, Meg. She always gets her way."

"You'll get no argument from me. I'm starved." As we walked through the foyer, my gaze went to Kane's desk. Everything was the same, all the way down to the mug of pens and his shiny new monitor. His workspace gleamed, dust-free—and the sight of his empty chair made me feel like I'd swallowed a bag of lead.

"Did Kane say why he gave me the vineyard?" I asked Diego, as we headed for the dining room. The long table glowed, and the bulbs in the chandelier had been replaced and glittered brightly. "There was a note with the deed, but it just said that he found that Villier wasn't his thing."

Diego's expressive eyes were dark. "Do you really think that's it? That Kane just figured the vineyard 'wasn't his thing?'" he snorted.

"I don't know." A wave of color washed up my neck to heat my cheeks.

"Then let me fill you in. The guy was crazy about you. He tried really hard to move on and run the vineyard himself, but his heart wasn't in it without you."

I clapped my hands over my flaming face. "No way. That's not what the note he left said! There wasn't so much as a smiley face on it!"

Diego rolled his eyes. "After how you left, I don't think he felt in much of a position to declare himself. He seems more the type to let his actions speak louder than his words."

I literally had no response because what Diego said rang so true.

Marta returned, carrying three full plates skillfully balanced on her arms. She set down platters of eggs, chorizo sausage, refried beans, and tortillas. "Brunch. We eat together."

Diego helped his aunt by bringing plates, napkins and forks, and I took out the glass pitcher Gram had always used and filled it at the sink with the sparkling clear well water whose taste I'd missed. I poured us glasses of water, and the three of us sat down around the table.

"How long has Kane been gone?" I asked.

"Left last night." Diego had made little rolled up mini-tacos stuffed with beans and eggs, and he spoke around a mouthful. "I was in shock when he told us he was leaving, deeding the place over to you, and that our wages were paid for the next three months. Don't know what you did to the guy, but he lost so much weight in the time he was alone here that his pants were falling off."

I looked down at my sausage-tight thighs. "I guess I gained what he lost," I murmured.

"Kane wouldn't have eaten at all if I didn't make him eat his breakfast," Marta frowned fiercely. "That poor boy was wasting away."

"Well. He could have picked up the phone." I was feeling

guiltier by the minute, so I grabbed several tacos and stuffed them in my mouth to avoid having to say anything more.

"He's in love with you," Diego said. "He said the place should have been yours all along."

I made myself chew and swallow my too-big bite. "I love him too," I said miserably. "It just doesn't seem right to be here without him. I was just waiting for him to call me, make some move to show he wanted me to come back. But I never heard a word."

Marta waved the spoon, still covered with beans. "You go find Kane! And you tell him to come home!"

I shook my head. "If he's so in love with me, why didn't he come after me? Why didn't he try to stop me when I left? He never even called!"

"All I know is, he and that dog never stopped looking down the driveway, hoping you'd come back," Diego said. "Seems like you both had too much pride to reach out. Sad."

My appetite was gone. I couldn't even see the mound of food on my plate through the haze of tears. "Being here just doesn't feel right without him."

"On that we agree." Marta covered one of my hands with hers. Evidence of her hard work showed in roughened skin. "Life is too short for no love."

"I don't know about the love part. But I do want to make this situation right." I stood up from my barely touched plate. "I need to make a phone call."

CHAPTER THIRTY-NINE

Kane

There's just something about the open road; a sense of possibilities opens up with every turn of the highway. I glanced over at Flea, sitting upright on the passenger seat beside me, his eyes bright, his tongue hanging out, anticipation in every line of his big, furry body. "Yeah, buddy, we're on our way to somewhere new. Something else."

My plan was to go up Highway One on the coast, and just drive until I got tired and needed to stop. The great thing about the truck was that if we couldn't check in at a regular campsite, we could just pull over on the side of the road and hide behind a tree.

Meg. I shook my head to get her name and image out of my mind.

But it was hard not to imagine her face when that little lawyer handed her the envelope with the deed in it. I pictured her amazement, her jaw falling open—pictured her happiness as she drove back to the vineyard. Even though I wasn't going to be there to see it, thinking of that made me happy, too.

Giving away close to a million bucks never felt so good.

That's how I knew I'd done the right thing. There were no regrets, no strings attached. Maybe that would be my new plan. I would be a traveling philanthropist, driving across the country, giving away money and making dreams come true.

I was pretty sure Mom and Dad would actually be okay with that.

The Northern California coast was stunning. Steep cliffs with pounding surf surrounded jagged little atolls that were the remains of land that had been swallowed by the sea over time. The gleaming arcs of seabirds and hawks punctuated the sky; buzzards and crows glided on the updrafts. As we wound into deep, rugged canyons on narrow, two-lane Highway One, cypresses, sugar pines and redwoods towered over the road, creating tunnels pierced with light. Below us, creeks still low from summer sparkled over harsh gray rocks surrounded by variegated ferns.

From what I'd heard, Highway One was this scenic all the way up the coast through Washington and into the Pacific Northwest.

I didn't make it that far on my first night. Flea had to do his business around Russian Gulch State Park in Mendocino, and when I got out at the deserted beach beneath the soaring arched bridge over a mystical-looking canyon, I decided I didn't want to hurry this journey. I wanted to enjoy every minute of the drive, and stay distracted as much as possible.

And Flea wasn't used to being in the car for so long anymore. He went nuts on the beach, galloping to and fro and digging under rocks. "All right, boy. We'll stay here tonight."

With the shortening day glazing the ocean with gold, red, and bronze, it was already the sunset hour. I put on my windbreaker, sat on a rock, and sipped from a bottle of Villier pinot noir 1993.

A good vintage, a fine year, a nice sunset. Didn't get better than this.

I took a picture of the view from under the bridge, and posted it to my long defunct Instagram account. I didn't bother adding a caption. There was nothing to say to anyone who might still be following me, not that there ever had been many. I was simply resuming my quest, and the Instagram had been a fun project, a little visual map of my road trip.

Funny thing, though, I hadn't posted one picture of my time at Villier. Just as well. I didn't want to be reminded of my time there, or answer any questions about it.

I was moving on, and it was all good—or it soon would be, and that was almost the same thing.

Meg

I felt a little frantic by the time I got my errand in Santa Rosa done, and most of the day was gone.

Where was Kane? And how was I going to find him? I'd tried his phone and it immediately went to voicemail. But I was done waiting and hoping he'd reach out to me. I was going to have to go after him.

When I finally got back to the house, Diego came toward me from the porch, waving his phone. "I found Kane! He's at Russian Gulch State Park in Mendocino, and that's only a few hours away."

"Why would I want to know that?" I widened my eyes in pretend surprise.

"Meg, you're too smart to let this guy get away," Diego said. "I want you to do the right thing. You need to go after him."

"Whose side are you on, Diego? Never mind. Give me those directions." I grabbed his phone to see the location.

Marta, standing on the porch with her hands on her hips, growled fiercely. "Go get Kane, and treat him right. We want him back on the land."

"Good thing I want him back too, or I might have to fire both of you," I teased. "I figure I'll let him get his rest tonight, and I'll head out in the morning and catch up with him." I hurried up the steps. "Any chance that delicious smell is enchiladas?"

I set my alarm for three a.m. Now that the days were shortening, I knew it wouldn't be light until seven a.m., even at the ocean. I got into my old Toyota and went out to the main artery of 101 and over the 20 at Cloverdale, merging at last with Highway One along the coast. At first it was too dark to see anything, but the light was welling up behind the forest as I wound down the scenic connector road.

This countryside was beautiful even in the hilly areas. Grapes were taking over as the main agriculture crop, interspersing with velvety golden cattle pastures. I loved the way the buff color of the late fall dried grass contrasted with the deep olive green of the live oaks and conifers.

Turning into the park just past the picturesque village of Mendocino on the coastal side of Highway One, my heart sped up. I didn't know exactly what I was going to say, or even propose to Kane. I had an offer to make, and I couldn't accept his gift without making that offer.

He had seen the worst of me: my anger, fear and lack of trust, my fiasco of a family life. At least, now there were no more surprises or secrets between us—at least, I hoped not. I spotted his dark truck parked in a campsite along the creek just below the elegant arch of the bridge spanning the canyon.

Walking up to Kane's truck felt strangely like *déjà vu*.

I'd been here before, walking up to knock on the back of his window.

And I'd been with him inside, on that cozy mattress, under that soft, warm comforter. I wanted to be back there again, held close in his arms. I wanted Kane and me to be together, with Flea, and Sir Henry, and the kittens—our furry family . . . and for all of us to live together in the old farmhouse with Diego and Marta to help us.

I took a deep breath and knocked on the hatch.

Flea barked from inside, as I knew he would, and his deep-throated bellow sounded as intimidating as ever.

"Flea. It's Meg," I said softly, next to the glass.

The dog's barking changed instantly to slavish and frantic whining. Flea's claws scratched at the window, and Kane's muffled voice told Flea to be quiet.

He must be thinking I was a park ranger or something.

I stuck my hands in my sweatshirt pockets. I wasn't sure what to do with myself from this point forward. Should I try to act casual? Like I'd just happened to find them?

But how casual could it be that Diego had stalked Kane on Instagram? That I'd gotten up at three in the morning, and driven all this way to catch him before he could leave?

Nothing for it but to brazen it out.

I reached for the knob, and opened the camper shell.

CHAPTER FORTY

Kane

I sat up, reaching for my shirt. That knock on the back hatch had a definite, authoritative sound to it. Probably one of the Rangers wanting to check on my paperwork, or a cop telling me to move along.

Flea's barking suddenly changed to a high-pitched whine, the sound he made when he recognized someone he knew and liked.

The camper shell hatch cracked open, and the big dog wiggled out through the opening before I could stop him. I followed him, tugging up my loose pajama pants with a hand, as I fumbled to let the gate down so I could exit. *Diego had probably tracked me down, needing something . . .*

But Meg stood there, embracing Flea. My huge dog stood on his hind legs with his paws on her chest as he tried to lick her face and she hugged him, giggling. Her long auburn hair fell in a loose tumble around her shoulders, and caught the morning sun beginning to peek over the pines that surrounded us. Her eyes were greener than brown this morning, and she was wearing rose-tinted gloss on her wide, full mouth.

"Kane." She fended Flea off and held up a familiar manila envelope. "I need to talk to you about this."

I dragged a long-sleeved Henley shirt over my head, shrugging my arms into the sleeves. I tugged the shirt down over my stomach, lowering my gaze to hide the instant disappointment that had flared at her words. *She was refusing my gift.*

Meg was wearing a pair of unfamiliar running shoes. I tried to remember when I had last seen her wearing anything but her trusty rubber field boots.

"I thought the paperwork was pretty self-explanatory," I said stiffly. "Clark was supposed to hang around to see if you had any questions."

Meg jumped up and down and emitted a sound that sounded like "argh!" Her breasts bounced. That distracting motion brought my eyes up to her chest, then her face.

She chewed her lip, and the pink gloss got on her teeth. "I can't believe you did this." She flapped the envelope. "Kane. It's too much."

She had put lipstick on for me. There was no doubt about it. Meg was nervous. She cared.

"Well, you didn't need to track me down all the way out here and wake me up at the crack of dawn to refuse what I freely gave you." I didn't mean to sound surly, but that's how it came out.

"Please, Kane. I don't feel right about it." Meg flapped the envelope again. "I have an alternative idea."

My heart leapt.

Trite phrase—but that's exactly what it felt like . . . a fish jumping right out of the water with excitement. *She wanted to get back together!* I had to play it cool. Keep my pride. "Oh yeah?"

Meg walked over to the nearby picnic table, and gestured for me to join her. "I have a proposal to make."

I wanted to draw this out, this moment that I had dreamed of.

"I haven't even had any coffee yet. Can I get some coffee going? Maybe you need some too."

"Sure. Okay." Meg sat down on the picnic bench, crossing and uncrossing her legs, chewing the rest of her lipstick off.

I wasn't above making her squirm. In fact, I was kind of enjoying this.

I filled the metal teakettle with water and put it on the single-burner propane cooker. I took a moment to dig around behind my seat and extract our two mugs. Her eyes flashed with recognition as I set them down beside the kettle. Our time camping together had been so incredible—just the sight of the mugs took both of us right back there.

My hands itched to haul her into my arms. But I couldn't. Not yet. I had to see what this proposal was.

Hopefully, it was a proposal of marriage. I stifled a grin.

Once the water was going and the French press was full of coffee, I sat down beside her. I folded my arms on my chest, pumping up my biceps. "Okay. Lay it on me."

Meg cleared her throat, and pulled the papers out of the envelope. "I was deeply touched when I saw what you had done. But I don't feel right about it. You put too much into Villier. And even though I now know that you can afford it, I still don't feel good about taking the place free and clear. I would like to propose that we become fifty-fifty business partners." She pointed to a familiar deed. "Right here. I had Clark redo the title. We are equal owners. All you have to do is sign."

I was glad I was already sitting down, because the disappointment was so acute. I absorbed it like a punch to the gut.

Meg didn't want me.

She just wanted to be business partners and share ownership in the property.

I got up and went to check on the water, trying to work my

way through the pain roiling my stomach and tightening my chest. "Interesting."

Meg hurried on, clearly thinking she needed to talk me into it. "You don't have to stay at the vineyard if you don't want to. You can let me run it, and I will send your part of any profit we make to wherever you want me to. But I can't accept you gifting Villier to me. You put in a lot of sweat equity, not money, to get the place out of debt. You deserve fifty percent."

I stood over the teakettle and stared at her. Finally, reluctantly, she met my eyes. "Is that all?" My voice sounded like a rusty saw.

"What else would there be?" Her cheeks flamed crimson, and she looked away. Flea provided a distraction and she petted him.

The pot whistled. I poured boiling water into the French press. I sat back down, trying to think through my options.

Meg seemed to muster herself for another run at it convincing me. "We're going into the fallow season in the fields. You and Diego got so much done around the place, I'm sure it would be fine for you to continue on your road trip, if that's what you want to do. I won't stand in your way, or ask you for anything more." The blush had not faded from her face.

I could ask her if she wanted anything more from me, personally, if she wanted to work things out.

I could ask if she wanted to move into the front bedroom as we had talked about doing on a morning that seemed like forever ago.

I even could ask her to marry me.

But I couldn't take the risk of her pounding a nail in the coffin of my hopes.

Meg was making it clear that this was a business arrangement, nothing more.

But it was something. It kept me connected to her. And once

I was at the vineyard, I could work on winning her back. "Are you sure this is what you want to do?"

Meg bobbed her head like a marionette. "Yes. Yes, I'm sure. Yes, absolutely."

"Business partner. Huh." I drew the deed across the table, saw where I was supposed to sign the title marked with a little plastic tab and an arrow. "You didn't have to do this, Meg. As you say, I don't need it. Don't need the money, don't need the headache. But, since it's what you want . . ." I shrugged. "Okay, then."

Meg pushed a ballpoint pen over.

I picked it up, and signed.

Hurt emanated from Meg as she watched me. She bit her lip, this time to hide that it was trembling. *She was underwhelmed by my response.*

That was fine.

I was hurt too.

Had it never occurred to her that I might've wanted us to be more than business partners? Apparently not.

I got up. Pushed down the press. Poured the coffee into our mugs.

She picked hers up, took a sip. Then she set the mug down and stood up. "Well. If that's done, I guess I should get back. You guys got started with cutting back the canopy, but all of that needs to be completed. Diego and I are continuing the heavy trimming today."

"I thought that wasn't until after Christmas."

"We've been looking ahead at the forecast, and there's a frost predicted. I want to get the trimming done before the frost comes."

"That's a lot of work." My eyebrows rose. "Are you guys going to need any help?"

"Are you offering?" Meg smiled for the first time. "Because I wouldn't say no if you were. But I totally understand—you're on a road trip, and you barely got going."

"My brother Jesse and I are supposed to go snowboarding in Utah in another month. Pretty sure I can help out at the vineyard, and still get out to where we're scheduled to meet well before that." I kept my voice casual, but my heart rate had jumped and my palms were sweaty—I was *dying* to return to Villier, and though Meg'd given no indication she was interested in the romantic part of our relationship, she was opening a door for me—literally.

"That's excellent. I was going to try and find a couple of day laborers, but it's always risky to use untrained help." Meg picked up her mug and took another sip. "I guess, since I'm going to have my partner's help, I can finish this cup of coffee."

I picked up Flea's leash and clipped it on him. "Why don't you stretch your legs a bit, too, before we head back? The beach is right over there, and you've come all this way. I might as well follow you back to the vineyard in the truck, afterward."

Meg nodded but kept her eyes down. "Okay."

I locked the truck and pocketed my keys, picking up my mug. "After you, milady." It echoed some of our flirtatious banter from the past, and Meg peeked up at me through her lashes, startled.

I pretended not to notice and waited for her to precede me out of the campsite. I followed, keeping Flea at my side.

We walked along the road through the last of the fall leaves. There were still a few bright clumps of them on the trees here and there as we neared the entrance to the park. Flea walked between us, and Meg reached down to caress his head. "I missed you, boy."

I bit my tongue to keep from asking if there was anyone *else* she'd missed.

Or to keep from telling her how much I'd missed *her*.

No, I'd go slow.

I'd go back to the vineyard, work hard beside her, and wait for my chance to make a move. But it couldn't hurt to use Flea as my intermediary. I hung my hand down, and caressed his fur lightly. "Flea missed you, too."

Her hand swung lightly, her fingertips trailing in Flea's glossy black curls, occasionally brushing mine. "Sir Henry was so happy to see the kittens when I brought him back. I couldn't believe how much they'd grown." She nattered on about how great it had been to come back to the vineyard, how much she already loved Marta, what she'd been doing while she was away—managing an Airstream trailer park, apparently.

Our fingers brushed. I hooked my pinkie into hers, and our hands swung, touching Flea's back. "I'm glad," I said, at the end of her rush of words. "I'm glad you wanted me for a . . . business partner."

She nodded, but said nothing more. I let that be enough for the moment, and we walked the beach in silence, our pinkie fingers linked and Flea between us.

CHAPTER FORTY-ONE

Meg

"There's Kane! He said he'd be right behind me." A rush of joy brought energy to my voice as Kane's black Tacoma turned into the driveway and drove toward Diego and me, as we headed for the fields with our trimming tools. He'd ended up needing some time to pack up and organize his camp, and I'd left first, still uncertain if he was really coming back.

"Business partners, eh?" Diego cocked his head in his worn straw hat. "Chicken." He clucked mockingly under his breath as Kane parked the truck beside the house.

I poked Diego in the shoulder. "If Kane'd wanted something more he could have said something. I left the door wide open."

"He's chicken, too. You two are hopeless." Diego picked up the handles of the wheelbarrow. "Catch up with me when you can." He winked.

I took a deep breath for courage, and walked toward Kane as he got out of the truck. Flea surged out of the vehicle's open door and ran to me, thrusting his head into my crotch and lashing my legs with his tail as if we'd been parted for months instead of hours.

"Hey, buddy." I rubbed his silky head, looking over at my new business partner. "You made good time."

Kane put his hands on his hips and swiveled to and fro, surveying the grounds. "Seems like I was just here."

"That's because you were." My hands had landed on my hips too. How freakin' awkward was this? "You can have your old room back. If you want. Or the front room. Whatever." My tongue felt too thick for my mouth. *Oh God!* The last time we talked about bedrooms, I was going to move in with him! That unspoken fact lay between us like a stick of dynamite.

Kane turned away, opening the extended cab door. "My old room is fine."

"I'll be out in the field with Diego. Meet us out there when you get settled." I turned and fled.

Out in the rows, pushing my wheelbarrow and trimming the vines, my heart rate began to settle. The afternoon sun was warm on the top of my straw hat. I inhaled the slightly musty scent of the vines. A few spoiled grapes underfoot smelled ripe and fruity.

A row over from me and further down, I could hear Diego humming along to the Latin pop he liked to listen to while working. I had my phone and earbuds with me as well, but I was too keyed up to use them, listening for Kane—and finally I heard the crunch of his boots in the row beside mine. "I need a little refresher on where we make the cuts," he called.

"I'll be right there." I dumped my armload of trimmings into the barrow and hurried down the row toward him. It was hard to believe he really needed me to show him how to do the trimming again, but I'd take any excuse to be near him. Reaching where I spotted Kane's blue-jeaned legs, I ducked low and scraped beneath the lowest wire of the vine supports.

Flea took the opportunity to lick my cheek with a long, wet

tongue. "Gah! Stop it!" I pushed the dog away and straightened up, righting my hat from where the wire had knocked it off my head. "Got your pruners?"

Kane held them up.

"Watch me." I stood parallel to the central vine stock, and brushed aside the trailing branches with their crunchy dead leaves. "You make your cut right here in the notch where it comes out from the main stock." I clipped. "See?" I held up the dangling swath. "The new growth will come in at the notch."

"But how far back do we cut?"

"We trim each plant back to the main branches that are supported by the wire uprights." I took a few minutes to do a whole vine, shaping it into a T silhouette. "The extra length and branches sap the energy from the vine after the first frost. We're a little early, but like I said, with a frost predicted next week, I thought it best to begin now."

"Hmm." Kane tugged at his lower lip, storm-blue eyes guileless, a frown between his brows. "Maybe I should follow you for a while."

I flushed. "I guess. If you think you need to. Or you could follow Diego. He's the real expert."

An authoritative vehicular honking came from near the house. We both turned to investigate as Flea whirled with a bark and took off for the house.

"Oh, shit," I said. "It's my stepfather's car." My stomach plummeted. "Wonder what he wants this time."

"And the sheriff." Kane pointed to a green and white SUV with a light rack on top that had pulled up behind the black Range Rover.

"This can't be good." I hurried down the vine aisle toward the vehicles with Kane right behind me.

The sheriff was a big man, wearing a stiff-brimmed hat and a brown uniform. He stood beside his vehicle. My parents hadn't yet opened their doors, but as soon as we reached the cars, the sheriff approached and handed Kane a notice. "This property is being claimed through a legal proceeding contesting your ownership," he said. Kane scanned the document as he went on. "Mr. and Mrs. DeSylva have filed in Sonoma County Court to dispute the wrongful auction of this property. You both have twenty-four hours to vacate the premises, or I will have to return and remove you by force."

As if on cue, Ray and Maman got out of the Range Rover. They looked like something out of a movie set: Ray wore plaid golf clothes and that damn white panama hat, and Maman wore a pale linen suit and black and white spectator pumps.

Both Kane and I wore muddy rubber boots and work clothes, and somehow that made me angrier, as I became conscious of the contrast between us. "Maman. Ray. What the hell are you doing? Kane granted me half ownership of this property!" I was in no mood to put up with any more of their crap. "Stop this charade."

Maman's eyes widened at my exclamation, but Ray shook his head. "The vineyard never should have come to you in the first place, Meg. We're disputing the will that your grandparents left, as well as the auction. Your mother should have inherited this place, and if she had, we could have paid off the debts and avoided this whole mess with McCallum. You being part owner is irrelevant."

"What?" My eyes flew wide. My throat seemed to close so that my voice came out in a squeak as I turned to address my mother. "This can't be happening, Maman. You don't care about this land, you never did."

Maman turned away and got into the Range Rover. She rolled the window up, locked the door, and took out her phone, ignoring me.

"Maman! You can't do this!" I screamed. "No! This is wrong!"

Picking up on my anger, Flea's ruff rose. He moved to stand in front of me, barking his Intruder Alert bark as Kane's arms came around me from behind, both comforting and restraining.

"Shh, Meg. It's okay. Let them make their play. We will be fine," he said into my ear.

I shoved away, too furious to listen, turning my wrath on my stepfather. "How could you, Ray! Maman didn't even love Gramps and Gram enough to come when they were *dying*, and now you two swoop in like vultures to steal from us?"

The sheriff hoisted his belt, clearly uncomfortable. "Young lady. This is a matter for the courts to decide, and while owner-ship of the property is in debate, *no one* is to reside at this loca-tion." He walked over to the sparkling white, freshly painted roof support of the porch, and stapled a copy of the notice he'd handed Kane to the post. "The hearing is in thirty days. You're free to seek legal counsel on your own behalf."

I tensed to charge Ray where he lounged against the SUV, smiling that oily smirk I'd always hated, but Kane wrapped his steel-banded arms around me, clamping me against him. His voice was a sexy, gritty growl as he addressed my stepfather. "Mr. DeSylva. You and your wife are not welcome here. We have twenty-four hours to quit the premises, but *you* have no right to be here at all. You're upsetting my business partner. Get the hell off of our land."

Ray looked over at the sheriff.

The big man nodded. "Mr. McCallum is right, Mr. DeSylva. You'll have your day in court."

"I'll remember this when it's time for your reelection," Ray snarled at the sheriff. He stomped around the hood of the Range Rover and got in. My despicable relatives rolled out, tearing a new set of gouges in the grass.

My knees sagged and I turned into Kane's chest, clutching his shirt, trembling with the effort of restraining tears. His arms tightened around me, holding me up. He addressed the sheriff. "You'll be hearing from McCallum Industries' legal department shortly."

"I expect so. This was a bad business, McCallum. I'm sorry for your troubles." The sheriff walked over to his SUV. I heard the door slam, the engine rev, and the roar of it pulling away.

We were alone at last.

I let rip with the outraged weeping I'd been holding in. "How could they? How could they? How?" I wailed, balling my fists in his shirt.

I felt Kane's hands in my hair. On my back. Stroking, smoothing, petting. His voice was a gentle murmur, his lips on my forehead, at my ear. "It's okay. We're okay. We will win. Don't you worry. This place is ours, now and forever."

I gradually calmed into hiccupping silence.

Finally, all I could hear was the pounding of Kane's heart under my cheek. Smell his unique scent. Feel his powerful arms wrapped around me, and hear the echo of his words, protecting and defending me. I turned my face up for the kiss I knew would be there.

CHAPTER FORTY-TWO

Kane

Meg turned her tear-soaked face up to mine, her mouth tender and pink.

Finally. I'd stood up for Meg the way I should have all along.

Comforting her comforted me. Soothing her filled me with even more love. I'd hated my failures in the past—letting Dan insult her, allowing her parents to berate her.

That was never happening again. She was *mine.*

From here on out, no one could come at her except through me.

I took her beautiful, vulnerable, sweet lips.

No apologies.

No second-guessing.

No holding back.

I kissed her hard, delving into the silky cave of her mouth, tangling with the treasure of her tongue, a hand twined in her hair angling her head.

Meg gave as good as she got, her hands caressing me, one long leg sliding up to hook around my thighs as she pressed into me, our shared moans bringing us closer, deeper.

"Mine, mine, mine," I said, when we came up for air. I kissed her tears away, tunneling my hands into her hair, grinding against her. I wanted her—*now*. "No one can come between us. No one. Ever."

"Never. No one," Meg echoed, latching onto my neck with her lips and teeth, marking me with a delicious pain. "You're mine, Kane McCallum."

"I'm yours." I hefted her up against me by her solid buttocks. God, this woman felt good in my arms. Her legs wrapped around my waist. I turned to head for the house.

"Ahem."

Diego. We weren't alone, after all.

I held Meg in front of me to hide my raging hard-on. She slid down to stand, and I addressed him over my shoulder. "Diego. We've had some bad news." Meg hid her scarlet face in my shoulder, so I went on. "Meg's parents have challenged ownership of the vineyard. We all have to leave within twenty-four hours, until the estate is settled."

"Shit, that's terrible." Diego said. "Those bastards! Sorry, Meg."

She nodded without replying, still too embarrassed to show her face.

"Don't worry. I'll keep you and Marta on the payroll." Practicalities were cooling my jets enough to loosen my grip on Meg's ass, but I kept an arm clamped around her so she couldn't escape. "And as you can see, we're going all in on sharing the property."

"It's about time. Marta will be glad to hear it. I'll put the tools away and secure the grounds. Carry on." Diego's grin took up half his face. "Flea, come help me organize the barn."

I grabbed Meg's ass again and hoisted her up.

She squeaked and struggled. "Oh no, let me down!"

"We have Diego's blessing. Enough of your lip, woman."

Meg laughed and snuggled into my neck, wrapping her arms around my shoulders as I navigated the porch steps, kicked open the front door, and headed for the stairs. The effort to carry her up was well worth it when I took her into her grandparents' room, where I tossed her onto her back on the brand-new bed with its pretty blue duvet and a couple of her grandmother's crocheted pillows here and there for sentimental reasons. "This bed arrived a week after you left. I've been dying to get you into it ever since."

"Kane. Oh my God." Meg's hazel eyes were huge. She spread her arms as if making a snow angel, stroking the soft fabric and bouncing gently to test the springs. She looked sexy as hell. "I can't believe this."

"Believe it. I love you, Marguerite Villier." I spread her jeans-clad legs and knelt between them, grasping her waist and staring into her eyes. "You hear me? *I love you.*"

"And I love *you*, Peter Kane Michaels McCallum. More than ever, after you told my stepdad to get lost."

"Pompous asshole," I said. "Forget them. We have a bed to break in."

Meg's giggle was music. She patted the duvet beside her. "Come. Lie with me a minute."

What I wanted to do was bury myself in her, claim her in the most elemental way possible—but I could see trouble brewing in her hazel eyes.

"Okay." I lay on my side facing her, one arm propping up my chin. I reached over and played with a curl that hung over her breast, my fingers straying.

Meg turned on her side to face me, her hand caressing my cheek and jaw. "I want to be with you, Kane, but I want to have space to be private. Not to have to worry about Diego overhearing . . ." She bit her lip. "I'm not the quietest when you get me going, as you know. And we have to pack. Close the place up. Can we take a rain check? I want to have all the time in the world to be with you, to make this room really ours. A quickie doesn't feel right to me with the sheriff's order hanging over our heads." Her cheeks were bright red, her eyes suspiciously shiny.

"Rain check it is." I kissed her softly on the lips. "Let's get to it, then. The sooner we kick your stepdad's ass in court, the sooner we can come home and break in this bed properly."

Meg

I really hadn't had time to unpack my personal things from the Autocamp at all, so I threw my bags, the box of kittens, and Sir Henry back in my car and followed Kane out after we'd packed what we wanted to take and locked up the property.

We went to Gabriella's, and she got to meet Kane briefly. Her wink and raised brow were enough to let me know that he had her seal of approval. Once I'd waved goodbye to Gabriella, who was watching my car and the cats for us, I turned to Kane.

"Okay. What's the plan and where are we going?"

Kane had been preoccupied and working his phone pretty much every moment since we left the vineyard, so I knew something major was in the works. "I'll tell you when we're on the road."

"You really know how to help a girl relax."

He opened my door for me for the first time, grinning. "I really do, actually." That shut me up. Kane got in his side, and we pulled out, Flea poking his head between the seats to snuffle happily in my ear. "We're meeting Mom and Dad. They're flying the company jet out, and we'll be staying in San Francisco with them at a hotel. Mom's pulling together the West Coast legal team to deal with this land grab. Because that's what it is, no offense to your mother."

"None taken. It *is* a land grab." I stroked Flea's silky ears absently as I stared out through the windshield. The urban sprawl of the outskirts of Santa Rosa flashed by as we headed for San Francisco. It was about an hour and a half to the city, and as we drove, I had ample time to reflect.

That wasn't necessarily a good thing.

I rubbed my aching chest.

It was great that Kane and I were together again. That we'd spoken of our love and cemented the words with kisses—but the driving force that had united us was a terrible betrayal by my own parents.

I was heartsick.

It was one thing to have a mother and stepfather who'd never really loved me, and to be a victim of benign neglect. Quite another to have them come after us with a sheriff and an eviction order, challenging my grandparents' will, and stripping me of the evidence of their love, too.

And now, I was driving to meet Kane's billionaire parents as they came into town in their private jet to rescue us from my relatives' attack. "Just grand," I muttered aloud. "This is going to make a great impression."

"I heard that." Kane reached a hand over and took mine, squeezing it. "Don't worry about Mom and Dad. They're going to love you."

"Sure." I rolled my eyes. "What's not to love?"

"Exactly." Kane lifted my hand, kissed the knuckles. "I've told them a lot about you—made it clear you had nothing to do with any of this."

"Thanks." I couldn't think of any way to put my dread into words. "Can we get a hotel room so I can at least clean up before I meet them? I want to look my best."

"I already booked us one on the same floor as my parents."

Guilt and inadequacy squashed the breath out of me. "I really don't deserve you."

"Love is not about what anyone *deserves*." Kane frowned, weaving around another car, his expression severe, his words measured. His hand never left mine. His thumb traced a circle on the tender skin of my wrist. "All my life I've had a sense I was looking for something—that there was something essential missing. It turns out, I was looking for *someone*. You make me feel like —I'm really known and loved. Just for me. Nothing else." Kane glanced at me, his eyes the shadowed blue of a mountain lake. "And I feel that way about you. There's nothing you could do that would make me stop loving you."

"I'm glad." I pressed his hand against my cheek, then kissed the palm. "It's mutual."

"Plus, I want your body. All the time. Don't think that's going away anytime soon." Kane slid our clasped hands down into my lap. He rubbed them against my hot core, still sensitized from making out earlier. "Can't wait to get to that hotel room."

CHAPTER FORTY-THREE

Meg

Kane succeeded in distracting me from my angst in a titillating way until I could hardly wait to get to the hotel room either —but drawing up to the splendid turnaround of the famous Mark Hotel was a dash of cold water. "Of course. You and your family are staying at the Mark. I should have known."

"You mean, *we're* staying at the Mark." Kane flashed his dark blues at me. "When are you going to forgive me for being rich?"

"Don't know. I haven't had good experiences with rich people."

"Yes, you have. Multiple good ones, in fact—with more on the way." He leaned over to nip my ear as the valet came to my door.

My face was scarlet as the uniformed valet, resplendent in a crimson uniform trimmed in gold braid, opened the door of the truck. He offered a white-gloved hand to help me out. "Welcome to the Mark."

I hopped out. "Thank you." I kept hold of Flea's leash as the big dog followed me down out of the cab. I let Kane deal with the car, bags and staff as Flea dragged me over to nose around the giant brass urns containing seasonal displays in the hotel's gracious turnaround, while I took in the breathtaking view down the street into the heart of San Francisco. "What are we going to do with Flea?" I stage-whispered to Kane when he rejoined me.

"They've got a pet-sitting service." Kane handed a wad of cash to one of the bellboys. "Take good care of him, will you?"

"Absolutely, Mr. McCallum." Flea was led off with nary a protest.

Kane took my arm, tugging me up against his side. "Get used to it," he whispered in my ear. "This kind of accommodation is going to be a regular part of our lives."

I set my jaw mutinously, but allowed myself to be towed through the splendid, gilt-glittering, antiques-decorated lobby and over to a magnificent burlwood check-in desk.

"Welcome back to the Mark, Mr. McCallum," the clerk said. "Let's get you two settled in your suite."

I bit the inside of my cheek. *A suite?* Holy smokes! Probably cost more for a week here than my entire college tuition.

I was intimidated. And when I was intimidated, I got stubborn. "Mulish," Maman used to call it. Belligerence rose up. I caught the concierge's eye. "We've been evicted. He was living in a truck. And until recently, I lived in an Airstream at a trailer park."

"How lovely. Our guests enjoy all sorts of accommodations," the gentleman said, unflappable. His keyboard rattled. "Here are your room keys, Mr. McCallum. Ms. Villier." He handed each of us a little elegant check-in folder. "Enjoy your stay!"

Kane cocked his head. "What's the problem, Meg?"

"I don't know." I threw up my hands, and turned, and stomped toward the elevator.

What was I so freaked out about? People like the McCallums created jobs. Generated money for the rest of the world to earn by the sweat of their brows. Heck, the McCallums were the lifeblood of a capitalist society. What *was* my problem?

The answer was too tangled up in my head to explain.

But mostly, I was just terrified of meeting his parents.

Kane met me at the elevator. We stepped inside. "You're thinking too much." He pulled my stiff body into his arms for a kiss that lasted all the way to the twelfth floor.

"I see what you're doing," I said, when he finally let me up for air and the doors opened. "You can't keep me distracted forever."

"Just until you get used to dealing with my family and our lifestyle."

I jumped on that like a bird on a bug as he led me to our suite. "Aha! So you admit you're a part of the one percent."

Kane slid the key card into a resplendent door done in layered designs of gold leaf and cream enamel. "The point-oh-one percent, actually. But we have more so we can give more. I'll have Mom tell you about all of our charities and foundations."

"I just don't like it." I thrust out my chin.

"And now that I've met your mother and stepfather, I see why," Kane said evenly. He pushed the door open.

Our bags had somehow beaten us to the suite. I walked past them, and put my hands on my hips. I swiveled to take in the view, a triptych of windows showcasing the Bay Bridge. That spanking new edifice, a grand expanse of steel struts extending all the way to Oakland, twinkled with rhythmic patterns of light set off by the sea and the hills in the distance. "Wow. This is really pretty."

"High praise from my Meg." Kane pulled a bottle of champagne from a silver bucket standing beside a crackling gas fireplace. "I think a little something is in order."

An immense bouquet of yellow roses caught my eye on a side table. A card nestled among the foliage, and I plucked it out, removing the missive from a creamy envelope. *"Welcome to San*

Francisco, Meg and Kane!" I read aloud. *"Can't wait to see you. Cocktails in our suite at six, dinner at seven at the Top of the Mark. Love, Mom and Dad."*

"We have been summoned." Kane tweaked the card out of my hand and scanned it. "Thank God we've still got few hours to ourselves."

I gazed at the several dozen yellow roses. Each one was the size of my fist, perfectly formed, and the exact shade of a ripe Meyer lemon. I leaned forward and stuck my face into the colored mass, inhaling a big draft of sweet scent. "I could get used to this."

Kane chuckled and tangled a fist in my hair, arching my head back so that he could bite my exposed neck. "I'm counting on it."

The fire he had stoked in me through the long drive and up the elevator burst into flame. I turned and met his kiss with my own, arching against him, sliding my hands over his body. "We're not doing it until after dinner," I whispered, nipping his ear. "But consider this a preview of coming attractions." I slid down his body, kneeling and unzipping his jeans. "No sense we should go into the lions' den hungry."

He didn't last long with my mouth on him, and I didn't last long with his on me—but even after an orgasm, I was anxious about the upcoming cocktails and dinner. I wrapped myself in the hotel robe and grabbed my purse, opening my wallet to check out my credit card situation. "I need to go downstairs. I don't have anything nice enough for dinner with your parents, and I saw there was a women's clothing shop off the lobby."

Kane had ended up on the chaise in front of the fire, dressed in his birthday suit. He propped himself on his elbow, his eyes at half-mast, his hair rumpled from kissing me. "I don't want you to waste any time we could be spending in bed." He was an arresting sight, his muscles and tan standing out against the creamy backdrop of the lounge. "We can just call down and have dresses brought up for you to try on. We'll charge it to the room and what the hell, I'll get a suit too. Blow Mom and Dad's mind— I haven't worn a suit since college."

I sat down in a nearby slipper chair, frowning. "People do that?"

"All the time." Kane reached over for the phone beside the bed, dialed the concierge desk, and was soon connected to the women's clothing store. Within minutes, a variety of outfits and dresses were being sent up in my size, along with "appropriate underthings and coordinated footwear."

He then ordered a gray suit from the men's designer collection. He even knew his own measurements, and rattled them off into the phone. "I'll have ties sent up to coordinate with whatever dress you choose," he told me, and ended the call.

"I hate shopping so much that I think I could get used to this, too." I rewarded Kane by jumping back onto the chaise with him to pass the time until the clothing arrived.

The doorbell rang sooner than I wanted it to. I banished Kane to the shower and went to answer it, wrapped in my hotel bathrobe and wearing their slippers.

The next hour was unlike any other I'd ever spent. I'd never worked with a stylist before, but it changed everything. Bambi was compassionate and kind, and really seemed to get my worries about my curves, height, and generally large size. "Something women may not know is that size fourteen is the national average," she told me. "And at five-foot-ten, you look perfect as a size twelve. You're a goddess, Marguerite."

Bambi ruthlessly plucked my wayward brows into classy arches. Eyeliner enhanced my large hazel eyes, and brought out a tilt to them that I hadn't known was there. My mouth was barely emphasized by pale pink gloss with just a little sparkle to it, and the flavor of strawberries.

"He's going to be kissing that right off of you," she said. "So, there's no point in putting something on that we have to worry about maintaining."

Bambi also helped me choose five different outfits from all that were sent up. I charged them all to my card. I would pay it all back with my half of the profits from the Villier harvest, but now was not the time to skimp.

Kane's stunned expression made the whole thing worthwhile as I stepped out of the suite's large bathroom/dressing area. I spun for his inspection in a jade green, A-line satin slip dress that hugged the curves of my upper body and flared from my waist to skim my knees. Transparent black hose with old-fashioned seams at the back showcased my long legs, and my size ten feet had been coaxed into a pair of delicate heeled pumps. The hairstylist had blown out and curled my waist-length, thick auburn hair, trimming off an inch or two from the bottom to get rid of split ends and tucking it behind my ears with a green velvet band that matched the dress. She'd dusted my arms and décolletage with sparkling powder, and I wore Gram's good pearls.

I had never looked this good in my life.

"Can I kiss you?" Kane made a helpless gesture with his hands. "I know better than to try to touch anything, but I really want to kiss you."

I ran at him and planted a big one right on his mouth. His arms encircled me. He smoothed and explored, stroking the satin of the dress over curves made smooth by Spanx. "Are you sure we have to go meet my parents?" he murmured against my mouth.

"You're the one who said we've been summoned. And you still need to get dressed in that new suit. I'm looking forward to seeing you in it." I pulled back and gave Kane a peck on the jaw and a pat on the butt. "Get to it, mister. We're due in their suite in half an hour."

CHAPTER FORTY-FOUR

Kane

Half an hour later, we rang the bell at Mom and Dad's suite, looking so fancy we hardly recognized each other. I'd known Meg was beautiful, but she'd blown me away in her green dress, and from the way she kept petting my suit and stroking my tie, I got the feeling she wasn't disappointed in me, either.

Dad opened the door. "Peter! Good to see you, son." He looked good for an older guy, his silver-and-brown beard and shoulder-length hair neatly barbered. "You could have picked a different color." He pointed to his own suit.

I laughed. We were both wearing the same bluish-gray color, though our ties were different—mine was emerald green, to match Meg's smokin' dress, and his was a deep purple, likely to match Mom's outfit. Looking at Dad was always like looking in a mirror set to the future; I resembled him most, of all of my brothers.

Mom appeared at Dad's shoulder. "Come in, you two, and let us get a look at you." Sure enough, she wore a shimmery purple gown, and it set off her bright green eyes and wine-red hair done up in a twist. The McCallum emeralds that had been my grand-mother's gleamed at her neck, and the star ruby she always wore glowed like a drop of blood as she embraced Meg. "So glad to finally meet you, Meg. Kane has sung your praises ever since he hired you."

I grabbed Meg's hand. "She's not my employee anymore. We're partners now." I kissed her fingertips, meeting my mother's eyes. "In every sense of the word." I didn't want my parents to have any doubts about what Meg meant to me.

"Thanks so much for the warm welcome," Meg stuttered. "I'm nervous."

"Don't be, m'dear. Anyone our son cares for is a friend of ours." Dad took her elbow and led her over to their suite's seating area. "I'm sure Kane's told you our story."

Meg glanced at me. "No, he hasn't."

I smiled at Meg reassuringly as Dad sat beside her on the low couch. "I met his mother when I was a sailor and a handyman working for her parents; she thought I wouldn't amount to anything, and she married me anyway."

"Biggest surprise of my life," Mom said. "He hid who he was from me. For years." She punched Dad lightly on the shoulder as she headed for a gleaming champagne bucket. "Not sure I'm over it."

"That part sounds familiar." Meg grinned; I could see her relaxing by the minute.

"Want a bit of bubbly?" Mom held up the bottle.

I'd followed Mom to the champagne bucket. "Of course. But let me pour. You go sit with Meg. Get to know your new client."

I popped the bottle and poured four glasses of sparkling wine as Mom settled herself on the other side of Dad, leaving Meg at one end of the lounge. "Tell us about yourself, Meg."

"Not much to tell. I graduated from college with a teaching

degree, but I wasn't sure that profession was for me. I went home to Villier to visit my grandparents, and the rest is history."

"Not history we know," Dad rumbled. "Tell us what happened next."

"Give her a minute, Dad." I handed out the champagne. "Let's toast—to new beginnings."

Our glasses chimed. I took a seat in an armchair kitty-corner to Meg. She grabbed my hand in a death grip. "Thanks so much for the lovely champagne, Mr. and Mrs. McCallum."

"Please. Call me Ruby. I want to hear all about how this situation has developed." The light of battle gleamed in Mom's eyes as she sipped. "What I'm not understanding is the part about the shared title to the vineyard."

"Well then, let's clarify things, because there was a progression." I scooted my chair closer to the sofa, so that our knees were touching—and it was easier to hold Meg's hand. "Why don't you fill in the rest, Meg."

Meg cleared her throat. "I arrived at Villier more than a year ago. My grandparents were ailing—Grandpa was dying of cancer, and Gram had heart disease, though I didn't know it. They passed within a month of each other."

"I'm so sorry," Dad said, and Mom echoed it.

She went on. "I discovered the vineyard was already in foreclosure. I did my best to facelift the place before the auction, because I'd inherited so much debt. I was devastated by the sale, though. Kane came along and bought it. He felt sorry for me and hired me as vineyard manager." She glanced at me. "After a few bumps in the road, we started turning things around."

I squeezed her hand. "Meg and I fell in love. We were together, but broke up after her parents unexpectedly came to Villier, throwing around threats and accusations. Meg left the vineyard. I was miserable without her, and realized I didn't want to stay there without her. I deeded it over to her and left, to continue the road trip."

"Sounds familiar," Dad said, exchanging a secret smile with Mom.

Meg picked up the thread. "I was in shock at Kane's generous gesture. I was grateful, and glad to be home—but I didn't feel right about owning the place outright after all the work and care, not to mention money, Kane had put into it. So, I had the lawyer add Kane back on. And then I tracked him down and asked him to be business partners, fifty-fifty."

I gazed at Meg. She was so freakin' gorgeous in that green dress with her long curls spilling over her shoulders. "I was bummed you only wanted to be business partners."

"Well, of course I wanted more than that—but I was afraid."

"So was I. We were both idiots."

We stared at each other for a long minute.

Dad cleared his throat, reminding us we weren't alone. It was still hard to tear my gaze away from Meg's, even with that reminder. "We figured out we needed to be together. In every way."

"Everything clear now, Ruby?" Dad asked Mom.

"Crystal." Mom smiled back at him. When she turned back to face us, her eyes gleamed with tears. "My oldest boy has found his love. I'm so glad you followed your heart, son."

"Yes. I found what I was looking for." I lifted Meg's hand and laid it over my heart. I pressed it there with both of my hands. Her eyes were changeable magic. I could look into them all day. "I didn't plan to do this right now—but it feels right. I'd like to make our partnership official in every way." I paused, pulling in a deep breath, and pressed Meg's hand firmly over my heart to still the way my hands were shaking. "Marguerite Villier, will you marry me?"

CHAPTER FORTY-FIVE

Meg

My mouth fell open. *Kane was asking me to marry him!* In front of his parents!

I couldn't take it in. I ducked my head and shut my eyes, retreating inward. Everything seemed to slow down; in the warm reddish darkness behind my eyelids, I felt the pounding of my heart matched by Kane's hammering pulse beneath my palm.

He was scared, too.

But he was asking *me* to marry *him*—and that wasn't about his parents, or mine for that matter.

Marriage would mean being with this glorious man every day for the rest of our lives. We'd win the vineyard back and work in it, building a business and a life. And if we didn't, we'd drive away in his truck with our cats and our dog, and figure out the rest of the journey. Together.

One of his parents set down their glass, and at the slight noise my eyes flew open, and I yanked my hand away.

Kane cleared his throat. "You don't have to answer right away." His voice was raspy and deep, filled with emotion he was trying to hide. "I shouldn't have sprung it on you like that. I don't even have a ring."

"Yes, you do." Ruby McCallum tugged off the stunning star ruby I'd admired, and held it out to Kane. "You're the oldest of our boys. Your great-grandmother would want your bride to have it."

My mouth fell open and I covered it with my hand, but I couldn't seem to close it as I stared at the three of them.

Kane turned to me. The ring lay in his palm, glowing like a tiny fallen planet. He extended it to me hesitantly. "Will you be my wife, Meg?"

I gulped. I tried to scramble my thoughts together. *Yes,* my heart cried, *yes yes yes!* But my throat was too dry to make any sound but a squawk.

Kane frowned. "I get it. Not your style. No insult to Great-Grandma, but if you don't like this ring, we can pick you out another . . ."

I grabbed my champagne glass and swallowed a gulp, setting the goblet down with a bang that splashed bubbly all over my hand, my dress, and the table.

"I'd be honored to wear this incredible ring," I blurted. "Yes, Kane, yes. I'll marry you." I extended my hand. It was shaking like I had a fever. "If you'll have me."

Kane took my hand and slid the ring onto the fourth finger of it—a perfect fit. But I didn't have time to gawk at the gem, because he leaned over and scooped me into his arms and kissed me—*hard deep passionate perfect oh-so-right.*

"Ahem." A delicate tap on crystal. Rafe McCallum's deep voice. "I'd like to propose a toast to the happy couple."

Kane let go of me, but scooted his chair even closer so we were touching all along one side. God, it felt good to have him there. *My fiancé.* Peter Kane Michaels McCallum.

Rafe and Ruby lifted their glasses, and we lifted ours. "To a love that lasts a lifetime," Rafe said, and though he extended his glass to ours, his eyes were on his wife—and hers on him.

We toasted and drank.

I felt like I was floating and nothing was real except the feeling of Kane holding my hand. Somehow, we went to dinner. Somehow, we ordered, and ate. I remember nothing but the way Kane's eyes burned a hot, bright blue I'd never seen before.

The sense of unreality began to dissipate when the dessert course came around and Ruby once more broached the subject of the vineyard. "It sounds like you would have done anything you could to save the vineyard after your grandparents passed," she said. "Why do you think your parents challenged the will?"

"My mother and stepfather," I corrected. They might as well know all my dirty laundry; we were going to be family. "My real father is unknown. I was born while my mother was in high school." I squashed my chocolate mousse to and fro, avoiding eye contact. "From what I can gather, my stepfather took it for granted that my mother would inherit Villier—and neither of them knew about the debts, the foreclosure. Nor did I, as I'm sure Kane told you." I raised my eyes to meet Ruby McCallum's assessing gaze. "Honestly? I think they thought we'd be keeping it as a family, and they did this to get it back from Kane. I could tell that finding out I was a half owner, thanks to Kane's generosity, was a surprise to them. I hoped they would back off, cancel the case—but it seems they really want the place, if just to spite us."

"Maybe there's more than you know going on," Rafe McCallum said in his rumbly, gentle voice. "We can understand why they'd have wanted to get it back from Kane. Perhaps this all just got out of hand and became too hard to back out of. Lawyers can do that to people."

"Hey! Whose side are you on?" Ruby smacked his arm playfully, then addressed me with seriousness. "Should I ask for a formal mediation? That might save us some hassle and the ordeal of court."

I glanced at Kane, finding his storm-blue gaze on me. "I have to ask my partner. But for me, it's a yes."

Kane squeezed my hand. "A yes for me, too."

Rafe caught the eye of our waiter and ordered another bottle of champagne. When it was opened and poured, he held up the slender bubbling flute. "Let's toast to a speedy resolution of all of this, and to our son's engagement to a lovely young woman. Welcome to the family, Meg Villier."

"We are so delighted," Ruby echoed.

"To my future wife." Kane's eyes burned, promising passion.

My throat had closed, but tears of happiness spilled out of my eyes as my elegant glass clinked against theirs. This was my future—my new almost-family.

CHAPTER FORTY-SIX

Kane

At last we were alone. My skin felt tight, hot and itchy with need, my whole being wired with electricity as if I'd picked up static walking through the dining room, my hand lightly touching Meg's satin-covered back.

I could already feel what it was going to be like to be inside her, a hot ache at the base of my spine.

Meg was *mine.*

My fiancée. Soon to be my wife.

"As soon as possible," I muttered under my breath as I inserted the keycard into the door of our suite.

"What's that?" Meg tilted her head to look at me. She'd been silent on the way up in the elevator, though her hand caressed mine.

"You're going to be my wife as soon as possible." I followed her into the room, but turned to hang a 'Do Not Disturb' sign on the door and put the bar on. "We don't want to be interrupted."

"Oh." Meg's cheeks flamed. I stalked toward her, pulling my

dress shirt out of my pants, tugging my belt through its loops, tearing off my shoes.

Meg seemed shy all of a sudden, retreating from my bold advance in her pretty dress and high heels until the edge of the king-size bed hit the back of her thighs. She sat down abruptly. "Don't you think we should talk that over with your family?"

"Talk what over?" Her position was just right for what I had in mind. I dropped my pants and boxers and ripped off my shirt, sending buttons and cufflinks flying.

"Our wedding date."

"None of their business." I reached for her.

"Wait, please. I want to go slow." She held up a hand, though her eyes roved over my naked, heavily ready body. "I want to savor this."

"Oh, don't worry." I lifted her skirt, sucked in a breath. "Savoring is definitely on the menu."

She wasn't wearing panties.

And those long, long legs wore black stockings, a garter belt, and heels.

Also—she'd waxed.

I pushed Meg gently back so that she reclined on her elbows. "Marguerite Villier. Who knew you were so naughty? No panties at dinner with my parents. *Tsk, tsk.*" I managed to click my tongue chidingly, though it was thick in my mouth.

"It was Bambi the stylist's idea," Meg murmured, as I kissed my way up her inner thighs, stroking my hands up and down the silk stockings, making her twitch and wriggle. "I've never been waxed before and I probably won't ever again. Painful doesn't describe it."

"I'll kiss it and make it better." That sweet peach was so ripe, pretty and plump. I held her down with both of my spread hands, and delved in for an experimental nibble or two. "Oh, so tasty."

Meg covered her face with her arms, clearly still embarrassed —but that would be over soon.

She moaned and writhed and bucked as I licked.

I sucked and bit. Nibbled some more, then lashed her with my tongue. "You taste like summer. Sweet, juicy, delicious. *All mine*. Now and forever."

She tossed to and fro. "Kane, Kane, oh . . . Kane!" she cried. "I want you. Now, now, I want you!"

"What happened to taking it slow?" I teased, nuzzling her tender inner thighs, teasing her with my fingers, zapping her with my tongue. "I want to undress you. Really take my time."

"Screw that," she snarled. "Do me now!"

I smiled. I rewarded her with the pressure she craved, an assault with my tongue and three fingers.

Meg clamped her thighs around my head, rode my face, and screamed my name as she came. "Yes, Kane, yes. *Yes yes yes*!"

Summer was her flavor, and I drank her down to the last drop.

Meg

Kane was as generous in bed as he was everywhere else. How was I so lucky?

I fought the lassitude brought on by orgasms and sat up. Kane's eyes sparkled with satisfaction and his teeth gleamed in a feral grin. "I think I heard you say yes, future Mrs. McCallum. A few times, in fact."

"You heard right." I tugged his hair. "Get this dress off me, Mr. McCallum, so I can practice being your wife."

"Gladly."

We peeled the delicate garment off, but when I tried to roll down the garter belt, Kane laid a hand over mine. "No. I like it just where it is. The shoes, too."

I smiled. Somehow, in all the ripping-off of his clothes, Kane's tie remained loosely knotted at his neck. I grasped it, tugging. "Get on the bed then, cowboy, and let me take you for a ride."

I got Kane right where I wanted him, on his back—and then I kissed my way over his body, flicking my tongue over his flat brown nipples until he twitched, nipping my way down those marble-hard abs all the way to the main event.

Kane moaned and tossed, clenching his hands in the fine cotton of the coverlet as I teased and tormented him—and just when I felt that telltale tightening and surge, I rose swiftly and guided him into me.

Bare.

We both groaned at the sweet, incredible sensation as I sank onto him and locked my thighs around his hips—but Kane's brows quirked in concern. "No condom?"

I laid a finger over his lips. "I'm on something. And I trust you."

He grasped me by the hips, clearly reaching the end of his self-control. "And I trust *you.*"

No sweeter words were ever spoken by two guarded people who'd finally found each other.

And then, nothing filled us but aching, urgent need. I reached over to grasp the ornate filigreed steel headboard, holding myself upright, as he surged up into me and I rode down on him, over and over

A burst of overwhelming sensation overtook me; my back bowed as his pelvis thrust, lifting me right off the bed. My ears rang with our cries. And then we quivered, boneless and spent, collapsing onto each other.

I lay over him for a long moment, not sure where he ended and I began.

There were no words.

He rolled with me onto his side. We didn't part, a first for me, and I suspected, for him. We fell asleep that way—wrapped in each other's arms, connected and trusting.

CHAPTER FORTY-SEVEN

Kane

We spent the next month prepping for court with Mom, spending the holidays with the family in Boston, and working on plans for the vineyard. Now, the big day had finally come.

Meg's parents had refused mediation, and the hearing to decide the ownership of Villier Vineyard was a strictly lawyers-only affair in closed court. I sat with Meg and waited on a hard bench in the anteroom outside, as my mother and the DeSylva lawyer duked it out in front of the judge. My father and brothers had come out on the company jet to support me, and they formed an intimidating row along one wall. Diego and Marta had also come, and stood chatting in the doorway.

I looked around, but not one person had showed up from the DeSylva side.

I glanced over at Meg's tense, pale face. The few freckles she had stood out like flecks of paint on her nose; her thick lashes threw shadows on her pale cheekbones. Was it better, or worse, that her parents didn't even care enough about the outcome of the hearing to attend?

I squeezed Meg's hand, and she leaned her head against my shoulder. "I'm sorry," she whispered.

"What for?"

"My parents are putting us through this."

"It's not your fault. And we're fine, no matter what." I let go of her hand to put my arm around her, and draw her even closer. "As long as we're together."

The glass exterior door of the anteroom opened. All heads turned to look at Nathalie DeSylva, Meg's pretty mother, as she entered. Mrs. DeSylva was done up in a blush-pink silk dress and heels, with a strand of big baroque pearls at her neck. A little hat with a net veil was perched on her head, like she was on her way to the Kentucky Derby.

She walked quickly forward and stopped in front of Meg. "I need to speak with you."

Meg glared. "I don't know what we have to say to each other."

"It's important."

"We're engaged, Mrs. DeSylva. Anything you have to say to Meg, you can say to me, too." I stood up slowly, uncoiling to my full height, with Meg still tucked against my side. The need to protect swelled my chest, pumped my muscles—though my rational mind knew there was no way to mitigate pain coming my beloved's way from this petite woman who'd given her life.

"It's okay, Kane." Meg gently detached from me, giving my hand a final squeeze. "Maman. We can talk over there." She gestured to a corner of the room, the only one that didn't contain a large, intimidating McCallum or two.

I watched the two of them go, frowning. My father's hand landed on one shoulder, and my brother David's on the other.

"She's going to be fine," Dad said. "She's a fighter, your Meg, and she's had a lifetime of dealing with her mother."

"I know."

"Sure has to hurt, though, having her own parents try to rook her out of her inheritance," David said.

"It kills me that I can't help her with this." I balled my hands into fists.

"But you can't. Just be there for her to cry on later," Ben said. I glanced quickly at my other brother to make sure he wasn't making fun of me. Ben's bright blue eyes were clear and kind under ruddy brows—he was the only one among us that had inherited Mom's red hair, and he wore it in a lionlike mane around his shoulders, a total chick magnet Tarzan look.

"Good advice." David looped an arm around my shoulders. "You'd think Ben knew a thing or two about women."

"You'd be wrong about that," Colton chimed in with a wink. "But I sure do. And I can tell you, that's trouble right there in that pink dress."

"Thanks for the backup," I said to my brothers. But I wasn't the one who needed it.

Meg

I faced my mother, but kept both of our backs to the room because I could feel Kane's hot, protective gaze between my shoulder blades, not to mention those of his dad and five burly brothers. "Have you come to gloat, Maman?"

"Far from it." Now that we were close to each other, I saw that her eyes were puffy, her skin pale, and her jaw tight with strain. "I left him, Meg. I left Ray."

"What?" I reared back a bit at this. Of all the words to come out of her perfectly lipsticked mouth . . . She'd always made Ray and his desires a priority from the moment she set her sights on him.

"Ray's taken this bid for the vineyard too far. It should never have come to this; we should have dropped it once we found out you and the McCallum boy were equal owners. I told Ray so, but he wouldn't listen—and I realized that he's always wanted the vineyard. Since the beginning." Maman drew a shuddering breath, reached into her little clutch bag and dabbed at her eyes with a tissue. "He thinks owning it will give him—legitimacy. A history. He's a first-generation immigrant, you know."

"No, I didn't know."

"His family is from Mexico. But he calls himself Spanish. And he hides everything about it." My mother's dark eyes flashed with temper. "Class is not something you *buy*. It's something you *are*. I wish Ray realized he is fine as he is, but nothing seems to satisfy him, and I'm tired of it." She reached out a hand to cup my cheek. "You, my dear Meg, have class."

"Yeah, me and my overalls and rubber boots. Real classy." But I drew myself up a little taller, warmth tingling through me at her compliment. "I don't know what to say, Maman. I always felt—like you didn't want me."

"I know you thought that." Tears slid from my mother's eyes —and they weren't her usual dramatic performance, because she just let them flow, sniffling wetly. "I was trying to break away from my parents, and build a better future. For both of us. And somehow, along the way, I lost myself—and you. I am so sorry, Meg." Maman tossed her head back, meeting my eyes. "I told Ray I wouldn't stand for this, and he actually tried to restrain me." She held up a bruised wrist for me to see. "That was the last straw."

"What do you mean?"

Maman dabbed her eyes, blew her nose, tucked the purse under her arm. "I'm going into that courtroom right now and ending this farce." She grabbed my hand. "Come with me."

I flung a helpless glance over my shoulder toward Kane, as Maman tugged me across the room to the closed courtroom door, and opened it.

CHAPTER FORTY-EIGHT

Meg

We stepped inside the courtroom and shut the door.

All heads turned toward us. The judge, a white-haired man in the standard black robes, frowned. The lawyers, Ruby McCallum in a red power suit on one side, and a lean dark-haired man in gray on the other, also frowned. The bailiff, a portly, uniformed gentleman, advanced toward us. "This is a closed courtroom!"

My mother, still clutching my hand, advanced toward the lawyer in the gray suit. My addled brain finally supplied his name: *Jesus Garcia*. "I'm pulling the plug on this, Garcia. We no longer want to pursue this matter."

The bailiff caught hold of Maman. "Do not approach the bench, ma'am."

"I want to revoke this challenge to my parents' will and the whole thing!" Maman's voice rose. "Stop this proceeding at once!"

The judge banged down his gavel. "Order!"

Garcia held up a hand toward Maman, palm out. "A moment to confer with my client, Your Honor?"

The gavel banged down again. "Please. Control your client. Five-minute recess." With a flourish of robes, the judge rose and left.

The bailiff let go of Maman. She continued her approach toward the lawyer, with me still in tow. "Mr. Garcia, please reverse this motion."

"I can't do that without Ray's say-so. He's the one that hired me." Garcia peered over my mother's head. "Where is he?"

"Ray's not here, but I am. And I'm telling you to pull the plug." My mother set her jaw.

"Now, Nathalie, it's not that simple. We're in the middle of a hearing. There are procedures . . ."

Ruby McCallum tugged me by the elbow over to her table. "What's happening?"

"My mother appears to have had a difference of opinion with my stepfather about the case. She's changed her mind about bringing suit," I said.

"What brought that on?"

"I don't know." I shrugged helplessly, glancing over to where Maman was still arguing with the lawyer, who was now calling someone on his cell phone—presumably Ray. "She says she never wanted to go ahead with it once she found out we were sharing ownership. As I suspected, my stepfather was behind the whole thing—apparently he's always wanted to get his hands on the property."

We watched as the lawyer reached whoever he was calling; they talked. Garcia handed the phone to Maman; she yelled into it. "Let it go, Ray! This isn't happening. You aren't getting our vineyard, and that's final!" With the flair she was known for, she chucked the lawyer's cell phone. The device flew across the courtroom and bounced off the stenographer's desk; the woman jumped, and yelped.

Garcia cursed and went after his phone.

The bailiff grabbed Maman. "You're under arrest, lady!" He put handcuffs on her and hustled her toward a side door.

"Make Ray drop the case, Meg! Get him to give it up!" Maman yelled, and then was shoved through the door and out of sight.

"My. Isn't this an interesting development?" Ruby's eyes were alight with triumph. "Looks like only your stepfather is in the fight now, and without your mother's support, he has a very thin claim."

The judge returned. We were all still standing, so there was no need to rise. He banged his gavel. "Court is in session." He sat down, fluffing his robes grumpily.

I sat down directly behind Ruby, hoping my presence would be overlooked as proceedings resumed.

"Permission to approach the bench," Ruby said.

"Granted."

Both lawyers approached, leaning in for a heated exchange with the judge. Five or so minutes later, they returned. Ruby squeezed my shoulder with a wink, and seated herself.

The judge cleared his throat. "In light of the lack of consensus on the part of the plaintiffs bringing suit, I hereby dismiss this matter. Ownership of the vineyard will revert to the current owners listed on title, until and unless such time as the plaintiffs choose to bring suit again." He paused to glare at Garcia. "Mrs. DeSylva is remanded to jail on a charge of contempt of court for disturbing the proceedings. Forty-eight-hours, without bail." He banged down his gavel with an attitude of disgust.

He got up and left, as Ruby stood and turned to me. We

embraced as Garcia gathered the pieces of his broken phone and briefcase, and exited, scowling.

"We won," Ruby clarified. "The door is open for your parents to bring suit again, but your mother seems pretty adamant that won't happen."

The double doors of the courtroom burst open. McCallums poured in, with my fiancé at the forefront. Kane reached me and swept me up for a bone-cracking hug and a hard, hot, claiming kiss.

All around us a babble of voices, a whirl of color and motion —but all I saw was the one I loved, and all I knew was that we were going home.

Kane—five days later

The dining room that had always seemed too big, was full.

The long, beeswax-polished table groaned with food: Mrs. Knightly had flown out to help Marta prepare a welcome-to-the-vineyard feast for the whole family, and they'd been at it in the kitchen ever since we got the go-ahead from the sheriff to reoccupy the property.

Most of our family were already around the table, and several bottles of Villier pinot noir were greasing the wheels of conversation. Meg's friend Gabriella was flirting with Colton on one side and David on the other, as if she didn't know whom she liked better. Jesse was carrying dishes to-and-fro from the kitchen; Mom and Dad were scrunched together at one end of the table, canoodling like teenagers. Diego was deep in conversation with Morgan, who had an interest in agriculture, along with inventions. Ben, who had a thing for animals, sat on the floor covered with kittens and laughing his ass off as they crawled all over him.

The only person missing was my fiancée—and Flea.

Was Meg okay? She'd said she was happy about the outcome, and excited to show the family the vineyard—but maybe she really wasn't.

I hurried up the stairs, relieved that the creaky one was finally silenced by a good oiling and the padded bit of carpet that helped with Flea's difficulty on the slippery wood.

"Meg?"

"In here."

I stepped into our sanctuary—the big front bedroom. We'd finally moved into it together after we returned to the house, and I still wasn't over a slight feeling of trespassing when I stepped inside.

Flea looked up from where he was draped like a bear rug over the end of the king bed. Meg sat cross-legged, propped on the pillows against the headboard. Her arms were wrapped around the needlepoint pillow her grandmother had made, and her face was hidden in it.

"Hey, sweetie. What's going on?" I approached and sat next to her cautiously, reaching over to caress her shoulder.

"I'm just sad. About my grandparents. And my mom, being in jail." She didn't take her face out of the pillow, so I pulled her over into my arms.

"I'm sorry." I gently pried the pillow away from her face. She shut her eyes and turned away, but I kissed her forehead. "Your mom would have been released a few nights ago. Why don't we call her, and invite her to dinner?"

Meg's brown-green-fascinating eyes opened and met mine. "Really? You'd do that?"

"Of course. She's family. And even proved it by going to jail so we could win the case." I fumbled around in the fluffy skirt of Meg's new dress, copping a feel here and there. "Where's your phone? We can call her now."

Meg reached into a hidden pocket and pulled it out. "Are you sure?"

"Yes, I'm sure. Let me call her." I wanted Meg and her mom to reconcile. I genuinely wanted Nathalie DeSylva to come to the family dinner; I wanted the wound in Meg's heart to heal. Meg unlocked the phone, looked up her mom's number, and handed it to me.

Her eyes were huge and got bigger as the device was answered with a tentative greeting. "Meg?"

"Hello, Nathalie? This is Kane McCallum, your daughter's fiancé. Are you busy? Any chance you could hop in your car and come on over to Villier for a dinner to celebrate our engagement and return to the vineyard, and to meet my family?"

Whatever happened later between Meg and her mother, I knew I'd done the right thing in making that call—because when I ended it, Meg sprang out of bed, almost knocking me over with hugs and kisses, grabbed me by the hand, and towed me toward the stairs to join the party—though she still kept the pillow tucked under her arm.

Nathalie arrived half an hour later, just as Mrs. Knightly, still spry even though in her seventies, carried in the soup course. Meg jumped up from beside me at one end of the table and ran to embrace her mother. "Maman! How was jail?"

"Just the line I want to hear when I meet my future in-laws," Nathalie deadpanned, and everyone laughed. The ice was broken and the room erupted into conversation again. Meg towed her mother down to where we'd made a place for her at our end of the table. I pulled out my future mother-in-law's chair and leaned down to kiss her cheek. "Welcome home to Villier, Nathalie. Would you care for a glass of your father's 1997 garage wine? My dad says it's awesome."

Dad held up his glass. "Best pinot I've had in years," he

hollered over the noise my brothers made. "Got some good grapes here, obviously."

"And it couldn't have worked out better." Nathalie reached over to take one of my hands and one of Meg's. "Congratulations, you two. May we all have many fine, noisy dinners in this dining room in the years to come."

We held hands in a private moment—but when I looked up, every McCallum at the table, including Mrs. Knightly and the Lopezes, raised their glasses. "Hear, hear!"

The feeling I had, gazing into Meg's eyes, was of coming home.

My quest was over.

Turn the page for a sneak peek of book 2,
Somewhere in Montana.

SNEAK PEEK

SOMEWHERE IN MONTANA, A SOMEWHERE SERIES SECRET BILLIONAIRE ROMANCE, BOOK 2

Colton

I opened the door of my cedar-lined walk-in closet and stepped inside. Usually the sight of my neat rows of tailored suits in a range of hues brought a feeling of calm satisfaction. Of all of my brothers, I most knew and appreciated what a good suit could do for a billionaire.

But not today.

Today, I'd had the proverbial rug ripped out from under me.

I advanced into the closet to a cabinet at the back and opened it. Inside, a garment bag hung from a rod, placed over a pair of pristinely cleaned cowboy boots. I yanked out the garment bag, picked up the boots, and then grabbed a fistful of button-down shirts and a stack of jeans from the shelves. I pulled down my travel bag, one of those deluxe duffels that doubled as a backpack, and jammed the clothing inside. Boxers, socks, a couple of belts, some running clothes and shoes, and I was done.

A knock came from the door. "Colton? Are you in there?" Mom's voice sounded anxious and sad. "You don't have to do this, son."

I yanked the door open. "I would've done this a long time ago if I'd known you were going to do *this* to me."

"It's for your own good." Dad stood behind her, his dark blue eyes flashing with temper, his silver-streaked hair flowing to his shoulders like some old-time patriarch. "You're throwing a tantrum. This is your chance to prove yourself, and I thought you wanted that."

My own eyes felt hot as I stared down the mighty Rafe McCallum. "I've spent my life proving myself to you and Mom. Showing I was worthy of being a McCallum, with all that means. But you only saw the grand gesture of what Kane did in walking away, and as usual, you think one size fits all of us brothers. Since he threw away his future and went out on his own, all of the rest of us should, too." I sucked in an angry breath. "You're making a big mistake. Some of us would have been happy to work at your side all of our lives, sharing everything and being close—forever." My eyes were stinging, but I couldn't let that show. "That's your loss. So long, Mom and Dad. Hope you have better luck with my brothers."

I stomped past them, shouldering Dad out of the way, surprised he let me go, and a little bit heartbroken when neither of them tried to stop me as I slung my backpack duffel onto my shoulder and headed toward the long staircase that ended at the black-and-white, marble-flagged grand entrance to the foyer.

I was blinking hard because I had a bug in my eye or something—but I stopped short at the top. "Oh, dammit."

All of my brothers were ranged around the bottom of the stairs with Mrs. Knightly, our housekeeper, who was sobbing into her apron.

I walked down the stairs, my dress shoes thumping on the luxe carpet that lined the treads. This was the last time I'd hear that sound, and the suit I currently wore was the only one I'd take with me.

David smacked my shoulder as I passed him, crystal-blue eyes filled with compassion. "This sucks for you, Colt," he said. "You don't have to stomp off to prove anything to us, you know."

"Screw you, Dave," I said without heat. I wanted to hate him for taking the news so well, but I wasn't surprised. David was wired differently than me. All he cared about was his art.

Big Ben tackled me in a bear hug. "Don't go, bro," he said into my shirtfront.

I ruffled his red mane, though my little brother was bigger than me. "Just wait. You'll understand someday," I growled. "You guys can all come visit when I get settled. Not Mom and Dad, though. I'm done with them."

"Don't say that," Jesse pleaded, adding to Ben's hug. The youngest of us, he was still in high school. This break in our close-knit family was freaking him out.

I finally dropped my bag so I could hug my brothers fully. All four of them piled on me, squeezing me and pounding with their fists like we'd done a hundred, maybe a thousand times. I could barely breathe, and I soaked in the love with my eyes shut. "I'm going to miss you guys so damn much."

They finally let me go. "Kane. This is all his fault," I said. "And if you've got a problem with the new family policy, let him know for me that I don't appreciate it. As the oldest, he set a bad precedent that now, we all have to follow."

"You'll be fine," Ben said. He was the animal lover among us, and a kinder soul you'd never meet, even though he was built like a grizzly and twice as mean on the football field. "You'd be fine if Mom and Dad kicked you out without a nickel. Instead, we each get a college education and a hundred grand. That's more than most people get to start out in life."

I snorted. I'd been playing the stock market with millions since I was thirteen, and I didn't plan to stop now. I had a shit-ton of stocks already that Mom and Dad didn't know about. Their pitiful cashier's check was just a down payment to me. "A hundred grand is chump change. But never mind. I'm going do great, because that's what I always do."

"Where are you going?" Morgan finally spoke, combing his long black hair out of his eyes. The quietest of us, his purple-brown gaze was laser-sharp for once—the family drama had pulled him up out of the basement where he was working on his latest Elon Musk-style invention.

"Somewhere that I feel free." I wasn't about to tell any of them what my crazy-ass plan was until it succeeded. "I'll see you when I see you."

I hugged Mrs. Knightly last. "You still have four of us to chase around and feed," I told her, with a kiss on the top of her head. "You'll be okay, Mrs. K."

"I never wanted any of you to grow up," that dear lady said tearfully, and pressed a bag of my favorite kind of cookies—peanut butter chocolate chip—into my hand. "Take these with you in case you get hungry."

I took the cookies. "Love you, Mrs. K."

As I was stepping outside onto the front stoop of the brownstone, my hands on the heads of the stone lions fronting the door, I made the mistake of looking back.

Mom and Dad were at the top of the stairs, holding onto each other as if they'd tip over, and all four of my remaining brothers and Mrs. Knightly waved goodbye.

"Come home soon, Colt," Mom called from the top of the stairs. "We love you!" She was definitely crying. *Good!*

But my eyes were stinging, too, when I threw my duffel into the back of my Viper, and peeled away to join the traffic flowing down Massachusetts Avenue out of Boston, heading west.

Jess

I set the old-fashioned handset of the landline phone down carefully in its cradle, as if it might explode if I were careless. Because that's what that phone call had done—*blown me up inside.*

As if I wasn't already torn apart by Brad's death.

I stood up, a hand on the back of one of the ladderback kitchen chairs my dad had made.

Brad had been gone a year. I'd been about to go put flowers on his grave, then head into town to have a drink with Siena at the Only Restaurant and Bar. I'd decided it was finally time to get on with living, maybe say yes to one of the townie dudes bugging me for a date.

But now I didn't know what to do. The whirling sensation, the utter disbelief, the sense of my feet being so far away that my head had floated off like a balloon—all of it reminded me of the day Sheriff Jones had pulled up in his green and white SUV to tell me that Brad had died in an ATV accident.

Only this was worse, in a way. I'd just found out from my best friend that my loving husband had been having an affair, and that his illegitimate child was born.

A child. A baby boy named Bradley William Croeses, Junior.

That should have been our baby's name, and that name was ruined for me now.

I was thirty-four years old, and we'd been trying to have a child since I was twenty-eight. I'd thought we'd both suffered over the miscarriages, the lost ones, but he'd apparently found comfort elsewhere, with someone fertile.

"Not fair," I said aloud. Bella raised her head, her intelligent brown eyes on mine. She jumped up and trotted across the polished wooden floor, toenails clicking, and leaned her head on my thigh, fitting under my dangling hand so that my fingers stroked her ears instinctively.

Bella was an Australian cattle dog, and one of the most intuitive and intelligent animals I'd ever had the privilege of knowing. She could always tell when I was upset. Now she leaned some weight on my leg, gently herding me toward the front door.

"I'm not going to his grave," I told Bella. "Not ever again. *She* can go there. With flowers. And her baby."

And then tears came. Great big fat oily tears, that seemed to squirt out of my eyes to hit the ground without touching my cheeks. I hadn't cried for Brad since the first month he was gone; apparently the water had stored up inside me, and now it came gushing out of my eyes, my nose, even my mouth, as I gasped and sobbed.

Bella was still pushing me, and she herded me through the screen door—but that was as far as I went before collapsing onto the old leather couch that we'd retired out on the porch. "This is the best view in the house," Brad used to say, as he toasted the sweep of land that swooped out in front of the ranch, a long cascade of blowing grass dotted by the whimsical shapes of the alpacas as they grazed in the front meadow, and ringed in the far blue distance by mountains capped with snow even in late summer.

I sobbed into the handwoven pillows made from antique wool trading blankets that Siena had given me.

Bella jumped up beside me, snuggling. Over in the paddock on the right, Ramses bugled. The sound of his ringing stallion's neigh, so distinctive, reminded me that I was supposed to have had him gelded soon—but I hadn't been able to bring myself to do it as my long-legged, gentle Appaloosa colt matured into a gorgeous, easygoing Appaloosa stud.

Thinking about Ramses and how much I loved him made me feel marginally better. I turned my head on the pillows to address him. "Ramses, you love me too, don't you?"

Ramses, like Bella, was tuned in to my moods. He trotted

back and forth at the fence, tossing his mane at the sounds of my crying. He snorted loudly and nodded, pawing.

Yes, Ramses loved me.

I had lovers.

A dog, and a horse. Oh, and *alpacas*.

The alpacas, drawn by the kerfuffle, trotted in from where they were grazing to clump up in a multicolored, milling herd against the side fence. Their curly, pompon heads and bright eyes reminded me of affectionate, curious poodles. They snorted and commented in their soft voices at the unusual sight of me, flopped facedown on the couch.

"Jess?" I heard Penny's voice echo inside the house. "The animals are making a ruckus. Is everything okay?"

I didn't want to talk to Penny right now, and I'd have to if she saw my tear-streaked face. Penny was more than a housekeeper. She was a friend, and things would grind to a halt around here without her many talents constantly helping to keep the ranch going. But she was not good at hiding her feelings, and I had my hands full right now, just dealing with my own.

"Everything's fine," I hollered with false cheer. "Taking a ride into town on Ramses. See you later!"

"Okay, I'll leave you something on the stove!" she called back. "Don't stay out too late, ya hear?"

"When do I ever?" I yelled back, sitting up at last.

Bella whined, looking toward the barn. I dragged myself upright and stumbled my way down the wide stone steps and across the flagged area in front of the house. Brad had quarried and hauled that stone himself to fill in the muddy ground where we used to park the trucks when I first inherited Faraway Ranch. "He used to care," I muttered. "What happened? How did I miss it?"

The ripe smells of horse manure, alpaca, and sweet hay inside the barn immediately soothed my frazzled emotions. I opened Ramses's stall. He trotted in to meet me through the swinging gate that led into the paddock, coming forward to press his blazed white forehead into my midsection, nosing at my pockets for a treat.

I dug a carrot stub out of my pocket and fed it to him, then cross tied his halter. He didn't really need any restraint, but it was best practice to use the ties. I tacked him up, my hands moving on autopilot, and in a few minutes, led him out of the stall to the mounting block at the front of the house.

I stood on the mounting block, a square of gold-veined stone from the same quarry as the flagstones, and looked over at my home for a long moment.

The ranch house was long and low, painted a soft warm terra-cotta that contrasted with its slate-rock shingled roof. Two wings wrapped forward to embrace the courtyard and a covered porch ran the length of the main building. Hanging pots of geraniums, leggy at the end of the season, bracketed stone steps leading to the wide front door with its handles made of torch-worked horse-shoes. On the front porch a couple of hickory rockers and the leather couch, bright with patterned cushions, invited a rest at the end of a hard day.

To the left, the alpacas. To the right, the horse paddock, empty but for Ramses now that it was the end of the season and all the trail horses were turned out onto the range. Beyond the paddocks, snuggled against a row of bright sugar maples and conifers, stood the row of "tiny houses" in bright jewel colors that were accommodations for dude ranch guests who were already gone for the year.

We'd made Faraway successful by being creative and working hard from a number of angles. I'd inherited a funky old cattle ranch about to die, and Brad and I had made it into some-thing beautiful. I was proud of what we'd built, and Brad's betrayal couldn't steal that from me.

"Faraway Ranch is mine," I murmured as I swung up onto Ramses's back. "I'm glad you died, Brad. This way, I don't have to go to jail for killing you."

I clapped my heels to Ramses's sides, and we galloped down the road to Nearby, Montana, and the Only Restaurant and Bar. Siena would know what to do. She always seemed to. And if she didn't, maybe I'd find a cowboy who did.

We hope you enjoyed this snippet of Jess and Colton's story in Somewhere in Montana! Keep an eye on this link for upcoming information about the next release, *Somewhere in Montana:* tobyneal.net/Mnwb

ACKNOWLEDGMENTS

Dear Readers!

Oh my goodness. What a lovely "quest" this has been for me to write!

After I completed the stories of the Michaels sisters and their trilogy, *Somewhere on St. Thomas, Somewhere in the City,* and *Somewhere in California*—I wasn't sure where to go with the family I had created. And then I remembered the precocious, adorable dark-haired boy born to Rafe and Ruby of *Somewhere on St. Thomas.*

I was inspired to write about Sonoma's gorgeous wine country and the beautiful Russian River area by an unexpected move to Northern California to care for my mother-in-law. I have come to love the rugged, wild coast, and have enjoyed visiting the many beautiful wineries in the area and learning about viniculture from my niece Paige, who is a wine educator. Paige served as an early consultant for the art of grape growing, and the concept of "terroir," and I thank her wholeheartedly.

Once I got into Kane and Meg's story, I realized I wanted to spend a lot more time with the philanthropic, lovely McCallum family—and eventually, create a whole world with the Michaels' sisters' grown children.

If you haven't yet read the first three books, you can get Somewhere on St. Thomas as a free welcome gift by signing up for my Romance Lovers Newsletter and read the tumultuous love story of Rafe and Ruby firsthand: tobyneal.net/TNNews.

Thanks so much for joining me in the lush world of wine country. Let's go to Montana with Kane's brother Colton, next!

So much love,

Toby Jane

FREE BOOK

Read Rafe and Ruby's story FREE when you join my newsletter list and receive *Somewhere on St. Thomas,* Somewhere Series Book 1 as a welcome gift.

tobyneal.net/TNNews

TOBY'S BOOKSHELF

ROMANCES
Toby Jane

Somewhere on Maui

Co-Authored Romance Thrillers
The Scorch Series

Scorch Road

Cinder Road

Smoke Road

Burnt Road

Flame Road

Smolder Road

PARADISE CRIME SERIES
Toby Neal

Paradise Crime Mysteries

Blood Orchids

Torch Ginger

Black Jasmine

Broken Ferns

Twisted Vine

Shattered Palms

Dark Lava

Fire Beach

Rip Tides

Bone Hook

Red Rain

Bitter Feast

Razor Rocks

Paradise Crime Mysteries Novella

Clipped Wings

Paradise Crime Mystery
Special Agent Marcella Scott
Stolen in Paradise

Paradies Crime Suspense Mysteries
Unsound

Paradise Crime Thrillers
Wired In
Wired Rogue
Wired Hard
Wired Dark
Wired Dawn
Wired Justice
Wired Secret
Wired Fear
Wired Courage
Wired Truth
Wired Ghost

YOUNG ADULT

Standalone
Island Fire

NONFICTION
TW Neal Pen Name

Memoir
Freckled

ABOUT THE AUTHOR

Toby Jane is the romance pen name for author Toby Neal, a mystery author who can't stop putting romance into all of her books! Toby Jane is the place where she gets to indulge her passion for happy endings, big families, and loving pets..

Toby also writes memoir/nonfiction under TW Neal.

Visit tobyjane.com for more ways to stay in touch!

or

Join my Facebook readers group, *Toby Jane's Romance Readers,* for special giveaways and perks.

www.ingramcontent.com/pod-product-compliance
Lightning Source LLC
Chambersburg PA
CBHW051957240626
47153CB00005B/1798